ACCRETION

THE QUESTRISON SAGA: BOOK THREE

J. DIANNE DOTSON

Tom,
Enjoy the ride!
Ad astra,
J. Dianne Dotson
6/4/20

J. DIANNE DOTSON

CONTENTS

ACCRETION: THE QUESTRISON SAGA®: BOOK THREE

Copyright © 2020 by J. Dianne Dotson

All rights reserved.

ISBN 978-0-9994082-6-1

ISBN 978-0-9994082-7-8 (EBook)

Published by J. Dianne Dotson 2020

San Diego, California, USA

*Cover Graphic Design by **Dash Creative Group, LLC***

*Cover Art from **Leon Tukker***

www.jdiannedotson.com

❀ Created with Vellum

DEDICATION

For Anne Norris Sturgill. Through light and through shadow, you always lifted me up. I love you.

ACKNOWLEDGMENTS

Without the encouragement of friends and family, I could not complete my work. I therefore want to thank a number of people for their support, friendship, and love, which buoyed me during the writing of this book. I thank my family: James, Daniel, and Allen, who remained steadfast through a turbulent year, always believing in me. I want to thank my editor, Lisa Wolff. For the glorious cover, I thank Leon Tukker for the art, and Dash Creative Group, LLC, for book layout and design. I want to thank my dream team of beta readers, James Dotson, Pam Magnus, Chris Schera, Anne Sturgill, and Bradley Nordell. And I want to thank my wonderful friends, and really there are too many to name, but I will start: Mya Duong, Jonathan Maberry, Rusty Trimble, Noah Kinsey, Aaron Cohen (the best person to search for cherry pie with at 3 AM in Los Angeles), Avrohom Gottheil, Tone Milazzo (whose considerable stature is only surpassed by his kindness), Melissa Milazzo, Jessica Springer, and Diane Duane.

1

QUESTRI

A lonely black and silver ship hung in a void between stars, waiting. It bore the ornate silver markings of its original owner, the mage Governor Aeriod. Yet the ship and its crew no longer followed him, and they owed him no allegiance. Its captain, in many ways, still commanded a part of him, however. Her name was Galla-Deia, and she was a Questri.

Galla looked like a human, except for a few telltale features. Her coiled hair grew in different colors, full of fire and sunlight and violet shadows, and it moved and shifted according to her mood. She looked at the Universe through clear, copper-colored eyes, and she wore a long purple crystal around her neck: her diamethyst.

While she was ageless, in some ways she seemed quite young still, due to a long, sheltered time raised by androids on the star-city of Demetraan. The galaxy's governing body, the Associates, had tasked Galla as one of its Representatives to aid in mitigating the Event, a cataclysm that split open the very fabric of space and tore systems apart. She had trained first with Aeriod on his world Rikiloi, and then she became his lover. She spent decades of cruel tutelage on Bitikk, which she struggled to remember, or tried to forget.

She helmed her former lover's ship alongside humans, human

hybrids, and a great insect. They were all Questri: part of a new era of beings that stood against the two greatest threats to the galaxy. There seemed no way to defeat the malevolent force Paosh Tohon, which spread rapidly, as did its minions, called Valemog. But she had found a new way forward to try to stop it, and she could only hope that it would work.

Galla had learned from a being on the planet Perpetua that the huge underground Devices on twenty-one worlds could be used to stop the Event. The Device systems were arranged in a strange, horseshoe pattern, hinting that their original designers had some sort of alignment in mind for their purpose. They would each require a telepath to work, and for Galla to activate them with her diamethysts. As for the method of activating the Devices, and where she would find that many telepaths, Galla needed more information. It was the only solution she knew of, for she felt she could not trust the Associates to help.

The Associates barely kept control of the galaxy, between the chaotic situations of the Event and Paosh Tohon. The twofold crises strained their leadership and resources. As for Galla, she and her team stood apart, rejecting all that came before.

Their mission was interrupted, however, by a broken signal that burst out of a nearby junction. She had commanded a full stop to wait and see if anything else would follow it.

The *Fithich* sat shielded and silent, with the distant tendrils of a pale blue nebula for its backdrop. If anything came out of the nearest junction between star systems, it would not see this birdlike ship. Galla felt on edge waiting, just the same. She was not fond of sitting still for long in any scenario.

She drummed her fingers on the arms of her captain's chair. She swiveled her chair back and forth, and her strange hair drifted upward.

"Anything on long-range scans, Rob?" she asked.

The pilot, a red-haired young man named Rob Idin, swung around in his chair to look at her. He detested Aeriod and took Galla's offer of naming the ship with impish delight. A full human, he bore no special abilities, but he was a good pilot, and rapid-fire with quips. He considered her with bright blue eyes...eyes that she had finally noticed held green starbursts in them, making them look turquoise from a distance, and mesmerizing close up. And she avoided getting that close again.

"Nothing yet," he replied. His thoughts danced. Much as he had danced with her, though it seemed long ago now. He sometimes wondered if he had dreamed it: bossa nova thrumming in their ears; her eyes bright, her smile broad, her cares for the moment gone. After their crewmate Trent had died, she had closed herself off from Rob. Not for the first time, he mused, *Let me see another smile, another shocked face, another wild laugh. Let me feel your hair in my face, and your...*

"Time for a dance?" he dared.

Galla clicked her tongue, but she smirked, and then so did he, triumphant.

As for her opinion of him, it seemed to change by the hour.

Meredith Brant, nearly eighty, was the matriarch of the crew, a human woman who had served alongside Rob on the space station Mandira. That was before a man named Forster and her own daughter, Ariel, had moved Mandira across the galaxy after Paosh Tohon attacked it. Everyone loved Meredith. Galla watched her closely these days, as a tremor had set into her hands, which she clasped tightly.

Ariel Brant looked twenty years younger than she was, due to her time frozen in space as part of a failed experiment with telepaths. A telepath herself, she was dark-haired, pale, and bore the green eyes of her mother, and as did her infant son, Paul. His father, Dagovaby Ambrono, was a half-human empath with brown skin and dark eyes, with a golden ring around their pupils. To Ariel alone, he smelled like cinnamon.

Jana Okoro was the multitasking technical whiz of the crew. She was human, dark-skinned, and often wore her hair in a Mohawk. Usually her only other adornment was a series of green gems that trailed down both her ears. She often buried herself in her work, which grew more difficult as she navigated alien worlds and coded data.

The last crew member was the most peculiar. They called it Beetle, for it was a huge, beetle-like, sentient creature that came aboard after they lost their crew member Trent. Beetle had proven useful, weaving materials from its silk, and was able to communicate telepathically with Ariel. Beetle had lately grown listless, however, due to the lack of fresh leaves in its diet.

Jana had decoded the message as best she could, and she read out: "*World gone—disrupted—chased—need assistance,*" and that was it. The Event continued to disrupt all communications, and it had amazed the crew that Jana could decipher anything at all.

Galla said over her comms, "There's something coming, and we just need to know if it's friend or foe. So we'll wait. Dagovaby, are you ready?"

"Yes, Captain," answered the empath. He kissed Paul's little head and gave him to Ariel.

"Ariel," said Galla to the telepath, "see if you can pick up anyone's thoughts."

"Will do," she said.

At last the junction opened, startling all of them with the bright light, and then it immediately closed. One ship came through, a battered-looking hulk of a thing, built for interstellar cargo and not atmospheres. Bulky and golden brown, with pipe-like appendages snaking around it, the ship appeared damaged but operational. It drifted forward slowly, cautious or compromised; Galla was unsure which.

Rob glanced up at her. She looked down at him, and they held each other's gaze for a moment, copper eyes meeting blue ones. She broke the moment and nodded.

"All crew, stand by," she announced. "Rob, unshield us."

He wheeled back around, grinning, excited.

The *Fithich* shimmered into view well ahead of the incoming ship.

"Hail them," commanded Galla.

"Yes, Captain," said Rob, and he sent a signal. "Ready for you."

She spoke clearly and hoped the ship's translation signals would take care of the rest: "Unknown vessel, I am Captain Galla-Deia of the vessel *Fithich*. I acknowledge your request for assistance. I request an audience with your commander."

Jana and Dagovaby walked to the cockpit. Galla stood to offer Jana her seat.

"See what you can decipher," she said to Jana. "Broken translations are better than none." Jana nodded and set to work. "Dagovaby, can you pick up anything?"

The powerful man pushed his twisted hair behind his neck and looked out at the view of the other ship. The gold rings around his pupils glowed as he put all his focus on it.

"Suspicion, a bit...fear. Exhaustion, weariness, hopelessness," he said in his deep voice. "The passengers are tired and depressed, basically."

Galla bit her lip. "We need more than that," she said with a sigh. "Jana?"

Jana motioned to her. She showed the tuning of a feeble incoming signal. "The ship is translating, and...here we go."

An image formed on their viewscreen, of an alien with deep folds in its large ochre face, and two drooping eyes. It wore elaborately draped, yellow-orange attire. It seemed not to have much in the way of shoulders.

"Captain Galla-Deia," it said, "I am Udramoth Dur-Mithtoth, leader of the Shorudan contingent. I submit to you."

Galla scrunched up her forehead and glanced around at her crew, but remained erect.

"No submission necessary," she answered. "We come in peace, and to your aid, if it is possible. Tell me, Udramoth Dur-Mithtoth, what is your situation? Where did you come from? We received your signal, but it was broken from Event disruption."

The Shorudan leader lifted its yellow garment to reveal appendages, not quite hands, which joined together into an oval. Galla was not sure how to interpret this, so she waited.

"Thank you, Captain Galla-Deia. We fled our system just in time, for the Event splintered through it and consumed the outer worlds first. Most of my world is now gone. The escaping ships fled, and encountered a fleet whose leader we at first did not know. They bore a red mark on their sides."

And this knowledge settled over the crew like a cloak of ash.

"Valemog," said Galla in a cold voice.

"We were given a choice, to submit or be killed. They told us they would make us better. But then they said we must submit to Paosh Tohon, so that it could feast and grow on our pain. We tried to flee, but their ships were stronger."

And at this point the creature let out a high-pitched, looping sort of yell, and Galla's crew covered their ears.

Dagovaby said in a whisper, "This guy is in complete anguish. Just devastated."

No wonder! thought Galla. She fought a full-body shudder, for the creeping dread that cast a net over her crew grew more evident by the second.

She said to the Shorudan, "Take your time." A few minutes passed, and the being collected itself.

"I apologize," it said, seeming to shrink in size on the screen, sucking in the folds of its face. "This...Valemog, you say, they were much too powerful. They took advantage of our panic, and surrounded our ships so we could not escape. I don't know if anyone else got out, or if this is the last ship of my world."

The disaster grows, and the galaxy shrinks, Galla thought.

She said, "I am saddened to hear of this terrible news. How can we help?"

The Shorudan captain inflated its neck folds.

"You are but one small ship; I do not know how you could help us."

"We have powerful tools," said Galla. "We can help you find a way out of here, and safe passage elsewhere."

The Shorudan leader sat in silence for a moment. Several figures emerged behind it, and they communicated with each other. The captain then said, "We accept your offer, and would like to give you something in return."

"There is nothing that we need," said Galla, but Dagovaby lifted his purple stone from his chest, so she added swiftly, "but we do seek information. We need telepaths for a mission. Do you know of any?"

The captain balked visibly, shrinking back from his screen. "We Shorudan do not have telepaths," it said. "We do not work with them, either."

Galla sighed. "Very well."

"But," the captain said, slowly, as if remembering something, "there is a world where you might be able to find one. They are scarce these days: rumor has it Paosh Tohon seeks telepaths as well."

Galla shuddered, thinking of Ariel, Dagovaby, and little Paul. "Go on."

"I can give you the coordinates. I should warn you, be on your guard on this world. It is a labyrinth of trickery!"

Galla took a deep breath. "I'm grateful for your help. Should you need anything else from us, you have our information. We'll do what we can to assist."

The Shorudan captain told her, "Many more ships are trying to escape both the Event *and* Paosh Tohon. Beware of this!"

"Thank you, Udramoth Dur-Mithtoth. We will keep a watch. We will send the junction coordinates to you. May your journey be safe."

"Thank you, Captain Galla-Deia," said the Shorudan captain.

Galla turned to Dagovaby, who observed, "Great relief."

She nodded in satisfaction. "Thank you."

The screen went dark, and Rob and Jana both turned to stare up at her.

"Where are we sending them?" asked Rob.

Galla arched her eyebrow and smirked down at him.

"We don't have the exact coordinates, since Aeriod has hidden them from us. Jana, send the nearest coordinates for Rikiloi to the Shorudans," she said silkily.

Jana snorted and Rob burst out laughing. Dagovaby shook his head at Galla, but he smiled.

"Smooth," he said. "Is that going to be your backup? Send everyone to Aeriod?"

"Maybe it should be," she said furiously. "He has the means to help, and so he should."

The Shorudans then cruised away from them and shot off toward the nearest junction.

"Deal with it, mage," she said under her breath.

2

CONTENTION

Galla sat in her chair and stared out at the blackness. Soon they would pass through another junction, to another Device world. She took advantage of everyone else on the ship being asleep, curled her legs up in her captain's chair, and wrapped her arms around them.

She thought back to her days on Demetraan long ago, the great star-city that carried the last of the technology and culture of the ancient Seltrason era. Its shepherd, Oni-Odi, had found her inside a large stone in space, and brought the stone aboard, and there she was born. She knew a peaceful life, growing up among androids. There was never any drama, except from her. She had been volatile, and truth be told, untamed.

Oni-Odi had been a patient steward with her, eventually loving her as a sort of daughter in his android way. But he had not known that he had shielded her overmuch. When Aeriod took her to train to be a Representative for the Associates, everything had cascaded from there. She felt more at home among the humans she represented, and she took her position as captain of the *Fithich* seriously. But she did feel a creeping isolation.

So much to think about. And not much of it to like.

They had helped the refugee ship, and listened keenly to everything its Shorudan captain had said. The galaxy seemed to unravel before their eyes, with entire solar systems consumed by the Event. The cataclysm showed no signs of stopping; rather, it grew and disrupted everything as a fissure in space-time. What other effects it had on the cosmos, she was not sure. And she did not want to get close enough to find out. But she had to do something: that was her duty, she felt sure of it.

And something else out there threatened everything: the entity Paosh Tohon. It would feast on suffering, and make every being bend to its will and suffer to feed it. Where the Event tore worlds apart and sundered beings from their home worlds, Paosh Tohon lurked. It subsisted on continued pain, pain that it polished and preserved, and in which it kept its owner imprisoned. With the Event, that meant an endless buffet all along the fissure. Even worse, part of it still could break off in isolated patches and appear elsewhere in the galaxy, threatening everyone.

Galla considered what the Shorudan had said, that there likely were many more fleeing the Event. They would encounter more, and every time, they had to be cautious. Aeriod had warned her that the Event would continue to unfold. One thing she felt quite sure of, however, was her desire to help. It overrode everything and permeated every scale.

Rob entered then, and her legs shot down.

"Good evening," she said to him, staring straight ahead.

"My turn," he said. "Get some sleep."

"I'm not sure I can," she replied. "I'm thinking too much."

"Do you...need another dance lesson?" he asked eagerly. He had relaxed her once by dancing with her, and was at every moment ready to hold her again.

She rolled her eyes at his expectant face.

"Not right now," she said crisply. "I'm thinking of refugees. We have to be ready for more, and we have to help them."

"They're not our problem!" said Rob.

Galla stood up, and her coils of bronze, gold, auburn, and purple-

tinged hair rose and danced around her shoulders. Her coppery eyes
bored into him.

"They need help," she said with a sharp edge to her voice, "and
we'll do whatever we can to help them."

"What's your plan, then?" Rob countered. "What if we come
across whole fleets of them? What if there are enemies among
them?"

"We probably *will* come across fleets of escaping ships," she said,
"and as I've said, we'll try to help. I'm not sure why Valemog would
choose to infiltrate them, rather than round them up for their master.
But I'm not going to let your fear-mongering get in the way of responsibility for those in need."

"We—don't—have—the—resources," Rob said, his face growing
red, making his hair look orange. "You're not the galaxy's savior!"

"No, I'm not! But I have a responsibility," said Galla. "It feels like
I'm the only one out here doing it. Where are the Associates? Who
else is helping? I feel very much alone."

"Well, you've got me, anyway," said Rob with a sigh and a lopsided
grin.

She scowled and said, "Yes, and you're telling me we shouldn't
help. Maybe the Associates *are* helping. We have little access to any
updated info right now, thanks to the very Event that's causing all
this." She squeezed her hands together under her chin. "Maybe if we
can set up a relay for them, we can send refugees their way."

"We can't get to them all," Rob protested. "I don't think we should
play that role. Just get to the Device worlds, and get everything in
place, and boom! Good to go."

"It won't be that easy," said Galla, taking hold of her stone and
watching the light bounce off the violet facets. "Paosh Tohon would
never let it be, even if we had all the resources at our disposal. That
doesn't mean we shouldn't try to do *something*."

"I think it does," said Rob, turning away.

Galla said, "Look, we helped the Shorudans, and they helped us.
We know things are happening fast out there. If we had turned them
aside, we wouldn't have as clear an idea. Not with the Event

disrupting communications everywhere. And now we have a lead for telepaths!"

And so Rob sat between the oscillation of her coldness and her blaze, not agreeing with her, but still on some level knowing she was right. *This time*, he thought. *But at some point this is not going to go well.*

"You're setting aside an awful lot of energy for strangers, rather than our mission," he said.

Galla got right into his face. "We're going ahead with our mission. And we have considerable advantage in this ship. Maybe if you did *your* job, you'd realize its potential more."

Rob stood then too.

"Is this how it's going to be between us?" he said suddenly. "You also put a lot of energy into everything but *us*."

"What?" said Galla, flustered, for Rob stood very close to her, close enough for her to see his gold-red eyelashes and the spokes of color in his blue-green eyes.

Rob lowered his voice and took hold of her hands, and said, "Every day we pass each other by, and you don't *ever* stop."

"I can't stop," she said, looking at his ear to avoid his eyes. "I'm the captain, and there's too much going on. I don't know what you want me to say."

"I know you're the captain, and I'm your first mate; I *know* these things," Rob muttered. "Just...think of alternatives."

"I can't really avoid them, because you're so insistent I know them," snapped Galla. Then she sighed. "And I do appreciate your opinions. Which are aggravatingly strong, by the way. Can't you ever tone *those* down?"

Rob shrugged. "No," he answered.

"Then I guess it's business as usual," said Galla, pulling her hands from his. "Good night, Rob."

And she turned and walked out, feeling his eyes on her as she left. She walked along the hall to the room she shared with Meredith, but she slowed down, and her steps felt leaden.

He irritates me to no end, she thought, shaking her head. And yet she was still attracted to him, and felt herself wanting to take his offered hands and pull him along to some closet or something to work out their frustrations and... "Ugh!" she groaned, and she squeezed herself and leaned against the hallway, making sure she was far out of sight of him. *It couldn't work. Captain and first mate. No. No, right?* And not knowing what else to do, she entered her room and collapsed on her bed.

ARIEL, being a telepath, picked up on many of Rob's thoughts. Dagovaby could sense the young man's feelings. The couple complained to each other in their room at night about Rob.

"He's *exhausting*," groaned Ariel. "The back-and-forth of his thoughts about Galla drive me insane. Everyone on this ship—hell, maybe even Paul and Beetle—knows he's wild about her."

"It's too much," agreed Dagovaby, as he spooned with his wife. "I'm glad we don't have *his* problem. I kind of feel sorry for the guy."

"Well, you would," snorted Ariel. "You're an empath, after all!"

"He needs to settle down," said Dagovaby, "or he's going to cause problems for himself. And maybe for us."

She sighed. "What can we do? Galla's not interested in him."

"Are you sure about that? We can't read her thoughts or feelings. But her body language..."

Ariel squirmed. "I kind of hope she's *not*. To go from an asshole like Aeriod to an idiot like Rob—"

Dagovaby laughed. "That's a bit harsh. He's just young and in love."

She grumbled. "She deserves better than either of them."

"True. But...well, it's Galla. She's going to do what she wants."

Ariel rolled onto her back and kissed Dagovaby. "That's why I love her."

3

TURBULENCE

They woke to violent shaking. Galla flew from her covers, wide-eyed, and dodged a plant of Meredith's that flew past her head. She swept over to where Meredith lay in her own bed, and found the elderly woman shaking.

"What—what's happening?" Meredith asked, confused and groggy.

Galla held onto her and said, "We must be going through some sort of strange medium, or particle flow. I'm going to check it out. Will you be all right here?"

"Fine, fine," said Meredith, but her voice quavered and her hands would not stop shaking. Galla had noticed that every day they seemed to tremble a little more. Meredith would grip her fingers together, as if trying to hide it.

Their room comms squawked, startling them both.

"Boss lady!" called Rob's voice. "I need you."

"I'll be right there," she called back.

Galla sighed. She squeezed Meredith's shoulders. "Hang tight," she said.

She slipped into the dim hall and its lights brightened as she walked quickly to the cockpit. She heard a loud retching sound, and slowed on her way past Ariel and Dagovaby's room. Paul was wailing, Dagovaby was soothing, and Ariel was vomiting. Galla pursed her lips and kept walking.

I would rather just comfort my friends than deal with whatever this is. But I'm the captain, so that's how I'll help.

"What is it?" she asked, holding onto anything she could as she made her way into the cockpit. Jana and Rob turned briefly to look at her from their seats.

"Something's happening with the junction," said Jana, whose voice sounded a little higher than usual. "We entered the coordinates for the next Device world, and entered the junction fine, but there are little gravity wells forming everywhere. There's no record of this being a thing."

The ship shuddered and bounced along.

"Bumpy ride," said Rob curtly.

"This is awful," Galla groaned, clinging to some tubing. "I sure hope no refugees are having to deal with this! Can we get out of it?"

"Not sure," Rob replied. "I've never had anything like this happen before. Where would it put us? We have to get to that planet. Maybe we just sit tight."

"Jana? Any ideas?" Galla questioned.

Jana gripped her seat as they hit a nasty spot, which spun the ship over and over. She and Rob were sweating, and he looked as though he might be sick.

"No ideas," she finally answered, and she closed her eyes for a second and took deep breaths.

"Head to your quarters, Jana," said Galla quickly, "and hold on tight!"

Rob turned long enough to stare at her.

"I'm taking the wheel," she said. "Go back to your quarters. That's not a suggestion. It's an order. Go!"

Rob staggered out, and was immediately slammed into the wall. Galla winced as he stumbled. She heard distant retching again, and was not sure whose it was. She turned and took control of the *Fithich* and let the ship's movements flow through her body.

It can't be any worse than flying a sky bike into a screaming storm or through some laser blasts, can it? she wondered anxiously.

She righted the ship and let her eyes slip out of focus a bit. *It's not air, so it won't behave like air. But it's not simple space either.*

The junction was a conduit with occasional bright light pulsations, and the *Fithich* shielded the worst of them from the eyes of its passengers. But Galla needed to see the fluid more clearly.

She called out over the comms, "Hi...Don't look out any windows until we're out of this, okay? I'm going to fly us through this mess, and you're going to be fine. Hold on."

Ariel, hearing this, turned to retch again. "Oh God, she's at the helm," she said miserably to Dagovaby. "She never backs down when she drives, and she scares the shit out of me!"

And little Paul lifted his face and howled lustily, as if broadcasting to the entire crew just how his mother's anxiety made him feel.

Galla, meanwhile, sat staring into the fluid junction pulses. She kept the shielding down just a bit, for even she could not bear too much brightness. It reminded her of her time on Bitikk, where she had been "trained"—essentially tortured, put through brutal tests of her abilities and endurance. And while she could not remember much of the fifty-two years they kept her there, she did remember bright light. It wasn't her forced exposure to it that bothered her, it was her tormenters. And the fractured memory of it all made her clench her teeth.

She was so absorbed in piloting the ship through the swirls of light and dark, she did not see Beetle creep into the cockpit. Beetle, being essentially a giant insect, put its several legs through any crevice it could, and in so doing, made easier progress through the turbulence than the other crew members. So Beetle eased in silently at first, and then perched on all its legs on the floor and let out a long trill.

Galla shrieked, and for a moment broke concentration, and the ship bounded around like a toy.

"Beetle!" she gasped. "What the *hell*, Beetle!"

Beetle clicked and trilled again, then said calmly, "This is a strange place to be in a storm."

She cast a wild look at Beetle and said, laughing nervously, "A *storm*? That's what you think this is?"

"It is very like being on my planet during a storm," Beetle responded simply, with a few clicks of its mouth. "I found it best to stop and hold onto something if I was not flying."

"Well, I can't *do* that, Beetle," snapped Galla. "I can't stop flying until we're out of this."

Beetle continued, unconcerned, "In the times I was caught in a storm while flying, which was very rare, because it was natural to avoid such things—"

Galla let out a small growl.

Beetle went on, "I found that moving along through the air currents, rather than against them, helped me to get where I needed to go."

Galla could feel her hair twisting above her head, mirroring her feelings. Her face had gone scarlet.

"In case you didn't notice, Beetle," she said through closed teeth, making a valiant effort not to scream her words as they hit more eddies and tumbled again, "that's not air out there."

Beetle lifted its antennae.

"It is very bright and strange, and I cannot look at it much," said Beetle, "but it has many swirls and dips in it, and that is very like air. I think flowing with it would work."

She turned and stared at the great insect.

"Flowing with it," she repeated. "Do you mean, just let go?"

"That would not be wise, for you still have to fly," answered Beetle. "But you would flow to work with the currents instead of avoiding them."

"So it's *not* all that different from air," said Galla quietly. "And I know about dropping and flowing through the air. I'm sure Ariel remembers that too," and she was rewarded with another distant retching sound. "Fine. Here we go."

And she eased off the propulsion and let the ship fall, and slide, and turn, and spin, but only until she found steady paths, and then she accelerated again. The *Fithich* responded well to the pattern, and soon they worked together as a unit. One final slide, and light bloomed all around them, and then she stared at regular space, pierced by a blue-white star.

She exhaled, and wondered how long she had been holding her breath.

"Thank you, Beetle," she said with a long sigh, and she unstrapped and stood up and wobbled.

She called out on the comms, "We're out of it!"

Jana whooped, and Rob skidded back down the hall and shouted, "Thank *fuck*!"

Galla stood and met Rob, and they hugged each other. She said into his neck, "No, thank Beetle!"

4

THE LAST APPEAL

Aeriod tossed his long white braid over his shoulder and settled into his seat. His ship hurtled him away from his sky palace. Its towers shone black and red on the floating asteroid he had suspended over the surface of his planet, Rikiloi. He tipped the ship for a moment to look with his silver eyes below to the surface, where he had shielded a Device. It had been years since Galla lived there, decades in fact since she first entered a Device. She had been his student, by his own choosing, and later, his lover, by her choosing as well as his.

He was also ageless, but far older than she. He was not human, being taller and having pointed ears, in addition to those strange silver eyes. He had witnessed many things, and had been in other relationships over the long arc of his unusual life. But the moment he had laid eyes on Galla, on android Oni-Odi's star-city Demetraan, his life had shifted irrevocably. A cold mage-governor of many worlds, she had made him feel alive in a way he had not felt before. She was a searing fire, and he could not resist getting closer. He could not budge from his orbit of her; only she could keep him away.

So he respected her boundaries, and he focused on his own duties. He hosted refugees, for there were always refugees, and he

had a soft spot for rescuing others in need, to a point. He knew immediately, of course, that Galla had sent the Shorudan ship to him. He
had sighed, and then laughed. His other duties, as an aide to the
Associates, and shepherd to other planets, he tended like a garden.
There was one thing other than Galla that maddened him, however.

Humans. Forever the thorn. This one especially.

His ship burst out of the junction and swept toward a chilly,
forested world its human transplants had named Perpetua. He and
Ariel and a man named Forster had worked with one of Galla's small
diamethysts, and had moved an entire space station across the galaxy.
Aeriod knew Forster would never have gone farther without his love,
Auna Kein, and so Aeriod arranged for them to live on Perpetua. This
planet was far across the galaxy from Ika Nui, around which Mandira
Research Station now orbited. The time dilation meant that Forster
had aged and given rise to generations of offspring, while Ariel had
passed only three years of her life away from him.

Forster's final descendent, a man named Kein, was a latent
telepath, but reluctant to open himself to his powers. And so Aeriod
was at an impasse. He needed Kein's mental ability, combined with
Ariel's, to help Galla defeat Paosh Tohon and stop the Event. The
Summoners of the Associates had foreseen that they should play a
role in all of this before they were even born. But Kein had a
husband, and a good life on his world, and did not want to leave.

So here Aeriod was again, likely for the last time, for Kein was
growing older. Now in his late fifties, his hair was greyer than when
Aeriod had seen him last. His eyes, hazel and crinkly as ever, bore
new wrinkles.

Aeriod met him in the rain, for it always seemed to be raining
where Kein lived, and their meeting was not joyful.

"You know why I'm here," said Aeriod briskly, as Kein led him to
his cabin. Rez opened the door for him. His giant red beard and his
red hair had faded with the addition of grey, but his eyes still shone in
a warm grey. Despite his general disdain of humans, Aeriod had
always liked Rez. That was a rare emotion for the mage, and he
welcomed the change.

"Have you gone into the woods yet?" asked Aeriod, hulking over a bowl of hot soup and a large beer in his black cape. The warm light of the sconces and candles shone off the elaborate silver threading of his dark raiment. He could not have looked any more out of place in this rustic home than he did then.

Kein and Rez had exchanged amused glances over this, but they sobered quickly.

"No," said Kein simply.

"You must!" hissed Aeriod. "Don't you understand? You've lived in peace here for your entire life. The galaxy, meanwhile, is a shambles! A rash of zealotry and madness has taken over, in succor to Paosh Tohon. Perpetua will fall as well."

"What about your protections?" Kein said, frowning.

"I am strained to my absolute limit," Aeriod warned them. "Not only for providing security for the worlds I govern, but to help in other...ah, ways and means. You are the only person left in this puzzle. And you need to be in place!"

Rez released a deep sigh. Startling Kein, he said, "Kein, it's time."

Kein went pale. "No," he said vigorously. "No. I'm not leaving you."

"It gives me no joy to encourage you to leave," Aeriod said with a sigh. "It never has, when clearly you've got the best example of a marriage I have seen in my many years. And I have some experience in the matter."

Kein and Rez gaped at him.

"Not Galla?" Kein said, a little too loudly.

Aeriod took a long, deep breath, and slowly exhaled.

"Regrettably, no, not Galla," he answered. "It was...long before I met her." And a small shiver ran through his cheek, though he tried to stop it.

Kein noticed it, however, and wondered.

"Can't he come with you?" asked Aeriod sincerely.

"The Curator passed away," Rez told him. "I've taken over the role, and I'm acting mayor now as well. If I left, there might be no town. There would be no history of it. Kein, your parents settled here. We can't let all this be torn down. I have to stay, and you have to go."

A quiet devastation fell upon the men. Aeriod recognized the need to exit.

"There will be a transport," he said to Kein. He bowed his silvery head. "There's nothing more I can do to convince you. But go to the woods, my old friend. That is all that is left."

Kein's eyes were raw and his spirit crushed. He did not say goodbye to Aeriod, who climbed into his great black bird of a ship and ascended into the dark grey clouds above.

5

A PALACE IN THE DESERT

G alla and her crew had just long enough to ponder the hot blue star in the distance, when dozens of small ships appeared all around the *Fithich*. They gleamed metallic gold, and the reflection from the star on their hulls dazzled her and Rob through the cockpit window.

Galla took a deep breath and twisted her hair into a bun. It promptly sprung loose, and she sighed. The communication channel opened.

Multiple voices announced simultaneously, "You are ordered to identify yourselves, by the command of the High Prince of the Twelve Planets of Mehelkian."

"Drone ships," muttered Rob.

"Yes," Galla whispered back. She said aloud, "We acknowledge the *request*," and Rob raised an eyebrow at her. "And we have a request of our own. We seek a recruit for our cause, and offer protection in return."

"Identify yourselves," repeated the several brassy voices. Beams of light now shone out of each gilded ship onto the dark, iridescent surface of the *Fithich*.

"Anything, Ariel? Dagovaby?" asked Galla quietly.

She turned to see her crewmates behind her. Ariel squinted at the ships.

"Nothing," Ariel said, pushing her dark hair behind her ears.

Dagovaby shook his head. "Completely automated response." The gold rings around his pupils shone as he opened up to any emotional signatures.

Galla straightened and put her hands behind her back.

She said in an assured tone, "Tell your High Prince I am Captain Galla-Deia, Representative of the humans, and Questri."

A few minutes passed.

The voices returned, saying in robotic unison, "Your ship will be scanned. Await further instructions."

Galla twisted her mouth and shrugged.

"Very well," she agreed, noting Rob's look of alarm and head-shaking.

The beams of light on all the surrounding drone ships changed to broad sprays, and the ships rotated as the ball-shaped swarm of them scanned the *Fithich*. This took over twenty minutes. Then the beams switched off, and the ships hung motionless, glinting only from stellar reflection, and otherwise dark.

Galla and the crew stood looking at each other in silence.

If they don't let us in, we have to move on, thought Galla.

After several more minutes, the ships suddenly opened up into an oblong shape, like a stretched football.

Their drone voices intoned, "You will be escorted to the Fourth Planet of Mehelkian. You will be guided to a landing spot."

Galla folded her arms. "Is this typical?" she asked, her tone skeptical.

"This is an order by the High Prince himself," came the multi-voiced reply.

Galla looked at Rob's cautious expression, Jana's lifted eyebrow, and Ariel's narrowed eyes. As she considered the situation, she rubbed her diamethyst.

She said quietly to them all, "I don't know what to expect. All we have to go on is the fact that this planet has no Representative, and is not under governance by the Associates. I don't think we all need to leave the ship. You may stay behind. That's your choice."

Meredith spoke up, blinking her bright green eyes and smoothing her grey hair. "I could use some fresh air."

Galla noticed her clasping her hands together tightly.

"I'm definitely going," said Rob, sitting upright and winking.

"Who's watching the ship, then?" Galla asked sternly, a crease forming above her nose.

"The ship is watching itself," Rob replied, stretching his hands out over the console. "We'll be parked on the surface, and we'll know if anyone tries anything. I'll give your ex-mage-governor this credit: he makes good space planes."

Galla rolled her eyes.

"Fine," she said. "We'll all go. Ariel and Dagovaby, I will need you to be extremely careful. We don't know who might be lurking here. Everyone, make sure you have your stones." She patted the large diamethyst on her chest, and it sent little rays of pale purple light out as if in response.

They all clutched their little pieces of diamethyst, and even Beetle twitched its own into place. Paul's was tied in a soft band around his chubby little ankle.

"Are you taking any extra?" Ariel asked with a grin.

"Of course," said Galla, with a wink. She slipped her hand into her left pants pocket and opened her palm to reveal three of the diamethysts, each about the size of a robin's egg and a paler purple than her great hexagonal stone. She tucked them into a makeshift pouch of webbing that Beetle had spun.

Rob piloted their ship among all the drones, which upon entering the atmosphere spread out on either side of the *Fithich* like a fan. From above, this fourth planet looked mostly barren, with only small patches of water ringed by green vegetation. Its ice caps were small and receded. The drones escorted their ship to a patch of flat desert, an immense basin that was pale gold and white, and almost blinding in the Mehelkian sunlight. Rob landed easily, and the ship's final updraft cast a cloud of sand and dust high around them.

Jana rubbed the space between her eyebrows and announced, "The air is thin, like a high mountain, but it's breathable. A lot of dust, though."

Galla nodded. "Everyone will need to bring something to wrap your face with."

"I'll get Paul's sling for you, Mama," Ariel said to Meredith. "You can cover him a bit with it." And she hurried off to her and Dagovaby's quarters.

Before anyone else could go to their quarters to look for fabric, however, Beetle spread out several little masklike cowls onto on the floor.

"These might be useful for the air," said the creature.

Galla beamed and patted Beetle's head.

"You craft master!" she exclaimed. "Thank you for spinning these for us, and so quickly!" She donned one of the cowls around her neck and found it lifted nicely above her mouth and nose. "Perfect!"

A ripple of appreciation made its way to Beetle from everyone else. Rob even attempted a handshake with one of Beetle's claws. Beetle clicked in satisfaction, and its antennae swayed.

Galla stood before the door of the *Fithich*, with Ariel and Dagovaby on one side of her, Jana and Rob on another. Meredith, carrying Paul in a sling, followed behind with Beetle.

"Open," said Galla, and the ramp door opened, swirling dust in all directions, and the scene of piercing bright light made them blink. They adjusted their sunglasses and walked down the ramp. It was intensely hot, but extraordinarily dry. The arid air made some of them cough, and so they all adjusted their cowls.

They found a long, ornate green rug on the ground at the bottom of the ramp. A line of golden beings stood on either side of the rug. Most, but not all, of them were bipedal. Their helmets (or heads; she was unsure which) were overly large, and they bore formidable, spiked staffs with tips that looked as if they were made of fire. They flashed in the sun, burnished to a high gloss, dazzling the crew of the ship. Galla could not tell if the beings were androids, but sensed there was something strange about them.

I know a thing or two about androids, after all.

A billowing of dust and sand arrived at the end of the rug, dissipating to reveal a rolling, gilded vehicle with rounded edges. It in turn opened automatically. The golden beings all turned in step and pointed their fiery staffs at the vehicle.

"A royal welcome indeed," said Galla, and she stepped forward onto the rug and walked toward the vehicle. The crew followed suit, with the *Fithich* closing and sealing up behind them.

They entered the vehicle, but the golden guard did not follow them in. Its interior revealed deep emerald-green seating, all in a circle, and ornate gold surfaces in between and around the windows. The air inside was fresh and much cooler than outside. After everyone sat, the vehicle began rolling along at a high speed, kicking up gales of dust into the fierce blue sky. Distant stony mountains shot up from the flat landscape.

Galla leaned forward to see where the vehicle was driving, and she could just make out a long line of structures that at first blended in with the shimmering mirages of the horizon. As they approached, she could see that most of them were white structures, and a few were bright yellow. Twelve flags of various colors and patterns flanked either side of the entrance to this palace, for palace it was. A central flag shot up at the entrance, and it was forked, with long streamers of vibrant magenta, emerald, and deep, rich gold. The wind sent it stiff yet darting, like a quick and colorful tropical fish.

The vehicle stopped, and opened to reveal yet another rug, this time woven in several colors of the very flag that flew above it, deep magenta and green and gold. More of the golden beings flanked the carpet, except there were at least four times as many on either side. Galla stepped onto the carpet and stood erect, her large diamethyst blazing and warm. The little ones in her pouch felt warm to the touch, and she knew it was not from the bright sun's heat. She glanced back at Ariel, who gave her the tiniest nod. Something or someone here bore powerful psionic ability.

A being with shimmering gold and pearl-like skin wafted out to them, swirled in a meringue of pale, creamy silks. Its face was long and its neck longer and elegant, and covered in rings of various metals. Its eyes did not open very widely, but Galla could see they were downcast and large. On its head, another twisting of fabrics reached over a foot high in a sort of tightly coiled turban. Galla could see no hair on this being.

She stood erect, and a silence descended on the assembled crowd.

Finally the being spoke: "Welcome, Captain Galla-Deia, Representative of the humans and Questri. I am the High Assist of the Royal Court of Mehelkian. You and your company are our honored guests. Please follow me."

Galla gave a polite head bow and followed the High Assist through a great, ornate golden door. Her crew followed her, and when they had all entered, the door sealed shut, and they adjusted their eyes yet again. An undulation of sighs rippled through them all.

For everywhere they looked, hanging gardens and fountains and artificial waterfalls spouted, and the air was cool and sweet and free of any dust. The ceiling arched bright and open, revealing a shielded sky. Vines climbed around columns draped in deep shimmering gold curtains that made soft music when air hit them. It was a dream in the desert. Galla wondered how long it had been there.

The High Assist interrupted their admiration with a small armada of helpers, dressed much as it was, but without such high turbans. These helpers set slippers at the feet of everyone, except for Beetle, and each pair looked bespoke. Galla felt a thrill go through her. *Is there a mage here too, or is this just really good service?*

"Please follow us," said the High Assist, and it led them through more gardens and more music. Galla could not tell whether the music then came from the draperies or from musicians tucked among the foliage. Several individuals sat here and there, alongside pools or in little divans. They were all short-turbaned, and all making some sort of art. She would have liked to approach them to see what they were creating. But the High Assist waited at the end of a long hallway lined with columns. At its end, a pearl-colored, fan-shaped door opened, and yet another hallway revealed itself. Here, many doors lined the walls.

"I must ask each of you to relinquish your weapons now," said the High Assist, extending its hands out to them. The assistants opened their arms as well.

"Why?" asked Galla, the crease reforming above her nose. She could practically feel her crew bristle.

"You must understand, the security of our home is paramount, and this is necessary prior to your audience with the High Prince," the High Assist said, and bowed.

Galla raised her head and looked down her nose at the High Assist. "Very well, but we must have them back when we complete our visit. The galaxy is a dangerous place right now." She turned to the crew, and saw Jana and Rob's scowls. Ariel nodded to her.

"But of course, Lady Deia," answered the High Assist.

They brought forth their knives, pulser guns, and power tools and reluctantly set them in the arms of the assistants. Galla turned to the High Assist and smiled. She gave a little nod as if to say, "Well?"

"You are not all disarmed," the High Assist said in as polite a voice as one could imagine.

Galla shot a look at her crew. They shrugged.

"Lady Deia," the High Assist said, and it gestured to Beetle.

"I'm sorry, what?" Jana asked, staring at the High Assist.

Galla exclaimed, "Seconded! Why do you accuse Beetle, who carries no weapons?"

Beetle then clicked and chirped. Galla turned her head to look at Beetle with a disbelieving, questioning look. Beetle lowered to the ground and trundled up to her.

"I am sorry I did not tell you before," said Beetle, bowed low on its legs, "but I have a vestigial stinger."

Galla lowered her head and opened her eyes as wide as they could go.

"Seriously?" she asked.

Beetle then revealed a panel on its chest.

"This feels personal," Jana said, her voice sharp.

"I agree," said Galla, feeling the color rise in her face. "High Assist, this is not something Beetle can simply give to you."

"Then Beetle must return to your ship for the duration of the visit," answered the High Assist, with the slightest shrug.

Galla's face fell. Beetle rose on two legs next to her and folded its legs together as if in prayer.

"It is an acceptable solution," said Beetle. "I am ready to return to the ship."

"We will provide you a selection of leaves for your pleasure," soothed the High Assist. It turned to an assistant. "Please return our visitor to its ship."

"Wait. I'll go with you, Beetle," Meredith said, and she smiled warmly at the creature. Beetle raised one antenna. "I can take Paul back with me, if you like, Ariel."

Ariel nodded, and peppered little Paul with kisses before handing him to her mother.

Beetle lowered onto all its legs again. "I apologize for the trouble. Meredith and Paul can ride on my back to the transport vehicle."

A ripple of surprised laughs erupted.

Meredith climbed aboard with Paul in a sling, held onto Beetle's back spines, between its wings, and they set forth out of the palace. Paul laughed in his sweet baby voice the entire way.

Galla sighed, then turned back to the High Assist.

"You each have your own room," announced the High Assist. "Inside you will find baths, fresh clothing, whatever you need. You will be expected to wear formal attire for the evening meal tonight with the High Prince. Before then, however, feel free to explore the palace as you wish."

Galla looked at the many doors lining the hallway and said, "I thank you, High Assist. We are most grateful for the generosity of the High Prince and his staff."

The High Assist bowed, as did each assistant in turn, and they all left. The doors adjusted to everyone's size and shape, and everyone looked at Galla.

"Is this safe?" hissed Rob.

"Let's find out," Galla answered, and she opened her door and went in. The others entered their own rooms and shut the doors behind them.

Galla faced her room, which was pure white in furnishing and floor except for a deep violet lounge chair, just the color of her diamethyst. It sat at the far end of the room, in front of a curtain that fluttered. She took off her slippers and stepped with bare feet across the white quartz floor, which felt cool and sleek. She had an oblong bed, with pillows and blankets all in white. There was no artwork on the walls. But when she made her way to a long white desk, between the bed and the violet lounge, she found on its surface sheets of textured paper, little pots of paint, and water and brushes and pens.

How odd! she thought.

And yet these pleased her. She found herself sitting at the desk and trying out the supplies, and became engrossed in sketching for several minutes. It brought her a mental peace that she had not felt in a long time, not since perhaps on Perpetua, in the presence of Loreena, the Curator. *Why had I forgotten that peace? Why didn't I do something to bring it back out sooner?*

She raised her head from her work, blinked, and then noticed two doors opposite her bed. She stood, opened one door, and found inside a luxurious bathroom. A large tub began filling with bubbling, steaming water as soon as she set foot inside the room. Another pair of slippers and a robe rested on a little white chair for her. While the tub filled, she opened the other door, and inside hung a closet full of brilliantly jeweled clothing of all sorts. She sighed, reminded of her time with Aeriod on Rikiloi. But somehow these clothes looked even more exotic than anything he had provided.

Why can't I ever just have something simple and comfortable to wear in the house of a mage? she wondered. For at this point, Galla knew there must be a mage of impressive skill in the palace.

She did find a loose set of pants and a tunic, so she set those things next to her bath. She slid into the billowing foam and sighed. Galla felt herself float under the cap of bubbles, and let her hair soak and drift all around her. She found a little vial of oil, poured some onto her hand, and pulled it through her many tangles, which loosened and gave way. She floated that way for several minutes, grinning in bliss. She finally wrung her heavy hair and stood. Seeing herself in the mirror, she blushed and instinctively covered herself with a towel. Unable to understand her unease, she hastily dressed and put her slippers on. She walked to the door of the room, opened it, and stepped out into the hallway. She saw a dark shape move at the end, in the shadow of a large potted plant, and squinted her eyes. She tapped on Rob's door, which was next to hers.

He opened it, and she could smell the soap on him. His hair was fiery and spiky and shot straight up. He had also dressed himself in a simple outfit, similar to hers but with long sleeves. He stared at her, as he sometimes did, in unabashed admiration, but especially at seeing her looking so relaxed away from her usual post on the ship.

This is what she looks like when she's not around the rest of us.

In the span of seconds, he wondered what life would be like if he could take her somewhere like this place, or stay here, and just let her live in peace, away from her yoke of responsibility. *Would she be happier?* And he wished he knew, because if he knew, then maybe he could give that quiet life to her, somehow. He did not know how, as quiet life was not in his nature. But for her, he was willing to try.

He exhaled. "Yes, boss?" He looked down into her warm, shining eyes and felt his pulse throb. He wanted to lift her still-damp curls off her neck and kiss her, and work his way down...

Galla interrupted his musings in a low voice. "There's someone at the end of the hall. I suggest we check it out."

"Should we get the others?" he whispered.

"No, let them rest," she replied.

This pleased Rob. Only too glad to have a rare break from his piloting, Rob quickly joined her. They walked side by side down the hall toward the figure, which seemed to slide from the shadows and through another door. They glanced at each other and quickened their pace.

The presence flitted along shaded passageways and around columns, out of the palace, and finally into an alley. Galla looked at Rob. "Shall we?" she asked.

"Yes, Lady Deia," he said with a smirk.

6

A PRINCE AND A PROPOSAL

The alley led out of the palace and into a strangely dark set of passages. They realized that they were tunnels, leading below the bright surface of the planet. In these tunnels, markets glimmered from strung lights and bobbed with drone lamps flying throughout. The place trembled with activity and noise and diverse beings of all kinds. The captain and her pilot stayed side by side, searching.

"There," said Rob, glancing over to the right of them, and they saw movement in a stall that flashed with signs for a desert tour.

They walked over to the stall and found its curtain drawn. Rob drew it back, and Galla entered first. The air behind it was very cold and still, as if they had entered a cave. It was only a little better lit than a cave might be; a faint light shone ahead. Soon they realized this was another passageway. Something moved in front of them.

"Do not be afraid, Robert Idin," said a high whisper.

Rob jumped, and Galla looked sternly into the dark and said, "Show yourself!"

The shape moved again, and Galla felt the hairs on the back of her neck rise. It was right in front of them, yet seemed distant as well.

"What is this?" said Galla. "What do you want? We know you wanted us to follow you."

The whispering voice said, "You seek a telepath."

Galla swallowed. She wondered how this stranger knew of her plans. "Possibly. What do you know of it?"

"Your companion does not block his thoughts well," it whispered. "I can help you."

"Then come out of the shadows and show yourself, coward," Galla said in a firm voice. "Otherwise we'll leave, and we'll find what we need on another world."

The being stepped in front of them, and was dressed in dark drapings of grey and brown. It seemed a hulking thing, but was no taller than Galla. Its face was obscured, as was its head.

"I am a telepath," it said. "I am the Cogniz. I can help you."

"Can you?" asked Galla. She raised her eyebrows and crossed her arms. "Well, if you're such a good telepath, tell us why we should believe you."

The draping of the creature shifted, as if it were lifting arms that they could not see. "The telepath and the empath are attempting to block me, but your other two assistants cannot."

Galla could feel herself going pale, but said nothing.

"I know what you flee," it said in a hiss.

"I flee *nothing*," said Galla savagely. "I seek to stop the galaxy from being torn apart and eaten alive. I will go toward it, but I will never run from it!"

The being seemed taken aback.

"Now, Cogniz, what am I thinking right now?" asked Galla. "If you can tell me that, I can tell you what I need."

Another hiss. "You cannot trick the Cogniz. I cannot read you, it is true. But I can read your friend. He radiates an adoration for y—"

"Okay, that's enough, pal," muttered Rob, and he reached for the hood of the Cogniz. The being vanished.

"You'll need faster reflexes," they heard behind them. "Tell me why you need telepaths. Maybe I can better assist you."

Galla said, "I need telepaths for a mission of mine. I will not reveal more. But I can guarantee the safety of any telepaths who join me, by giving them one of these."

And she held up her pouch.

"One of these stones contains immense power," she said. "I possess several of them. They can repel Paosh Tohon, if used by a telepath."

A long whistling hiss met their ears. The figure trembled. "Power of that magnitude is difficult to find in these times. Those would bring a high price."

Galla clenched her teeth. "They're not for sale. But if I can guarantee that if a telepath joins my mission and proves to be loyal, I will give it freely."

"Why would you do this?"

She shrugged. "It's the least I can do. I want to stop this thing, and I think this is one of the pieces to the puzzle for doing that. I need telepaths to use these stones when they are called to do so, by a special signal given by my resident telepath. Not everything is in place for this, but I want to recruit telepaths now to prepare well ahead of time."

Rob huffed in frustration.

"This thing's playing games with us, Galla," he said.

Galla sighed and said, "If you're not interested, do you know of other telepaths who might be? I think the stone would be a good recruitment tool."

"You are correct," hissed the Cogniz. "I will consider this, and let you know."

"We leave tomorrow," said Galla.

She and Rob turned and left the tent, and hurried back to the palace. They met Ariel in the hallway.

She squinted at them with her bright green eyes. "Where have you two been?" she asked.

"We may have found a telepath recruit," Galla answered.

Ariel twitched her eyes to Rob, then back to Galla.

"No guarantees, I see," she said with a downturned mouth.

"Could you *not* do that?" Rob asked, exasperated.

Ariel shrugged. "You need to learn how to block me."

"I can't do that!" exclaimed Rob, turning red.

"Not with that attitude!" laughed Ariel. Then, to Galla, she said, "The High Assist has told us that dinner will be in one hour, and we are to 'dress in garb suited to the presence of His Royal Highness' at court, or some such bullshit."

"Oh, is that all," muttered Galla, rolling her eyes. "I hate wearing fancy clothes!"

Rob sighed heavily and went back to his room.

"No, it's not all," said Ariel softly, and she reached for Galla's hand. "Can I talk to you in your room?"

"Sure," said Galla. She felt frustrated, and was only too glad to speak to her friend.

She opened her door and let Ariel in. Ariel gawked at the room.

"It's so spare!" she said. "I...no offense. Our room has all kinds of things. It has a crib for Paul, all the snacks we like, and all these things we love, like—" She stopped and her eyes went huge. "Wait. Did you see Rob's room?"

"No!" said Galla, vehemently enough that Ariel appraised her with eyebrows lifted. "No, why?" she added, flustered.

"I wonder what Jana's looks like, too," mused Ariel. "Anyway, I think...maybe...our rooms are tailored to our desires. Which means...shit! Even with our blocks, someone is getting through to Dagovaby and me, and reading our minds. At least superficially, to see what we want. But no one is reading you, so...a clear, empty room."

Galla swept her gaze around her simple room. A blank slate. Except for the purple couch, and the art supplies. "The couch...it matches my stone perfectly. And the art supplies...I saw artists in the halls, and stared at them."

"So they can't read you, but they can watch you," murmured Ariel.

Both women shivered.

"I hate this place now," said Ariel. "How soon can we leave?"

Galla sighed. "I've said tomorrow morning, officially. So, if you want to do some snooping of your own, you have about twelve hours. Wait, what was it you wanted to talk about?"

"Oh!" cried Ariel, and she smiled at last. She took each of Galla's hands and looked at her with a face full of love. She leaned in and touched foreheads with Galla and said, "I'm pregnant again."

Galla threw back her head. "What! So soon! Is that...is that healthy?"

Ariel blushed. "I hope so! Dagovaby is like you, a bit worried. But other than being pukey on the ship, I feel better this time around. He's already wanting to set up the ship's microsurgery, though, and get a vasectomy, which I think is a very good idea."

Galla laughed and squeezed her dear friend's hands. "Congratulations! Is this another accelerated pregnancy?"

Ariel nodded, tucking her sleek dark hair behind her ears. The strands of silver stood out a little more in the white room. She stared at Galla, and then broke her gaze and blushed.

"Don't worry, Ariel," said Galla, assuming she knew what her friend was thinking. "You can still work as long as you feel like it. As soon as we get more telepaths, that will ease your load too, maybe."

Ariel blinked, and let go of Galla's hands.

"What is it?" Galla asked, confused.

"Hey, why don't I help you pick out your outfit?" said Ariel suddenly, looking away.

Galla groaned. "Fine. I hate this, though."

"You don't have to be a telepath to know that," Ariel called from the closet. "Oh, this one!" she squealed.

She pulled forth a spectacular copper and violet outfit, complete with headdress and elaborate jewelry. "This is you." And she burst out laughing at Galla's scowling face. "Put it on! Come on! I'll help you."

So Galla stood in front of her mirror, staring at herself in complete dismay while Ariel looked at her dreamily. Her top was deep cut so that her diamethyst rested perfectly on her bosom, and it was made of copper scales that blended into a deep violet ombré skirt, which faded to pale lavender at her feet. And on her feet she wore violet and copper shoes.

The headdress made Galla cringe. It dripped with more of the copper scales and was looped with clear violet glass beads. Ariel placed an immense choker of copper around her neck. She stood back to admire her friend, and she sighed.

"I'd better get back to Dagovaby before I propose to you right here and now," she said impishly. "You look like a queen." Then she lifted up on her toes and kissed Galla high on her cheek, and dashed out of the room.

Someone knocked on Galla's door, and she answered it to find Jana resplendent in her own outfit. She had chosen a richly embroidered gold and green cross-body top with short sleeves, green pants, and golden shoes, and her Mohawk was woven with green jewels.

"Look at us!" she exclaimed.

Galla's lips curled into a smile. "Okay, maybe this is fun after all," she admitted.

They knocked on Rob's door. He swept it open and spun around for them, and the two women guffawed. "Aw, ouch!" he howled at their reaction, clutching his heart, but he was grinning. He wore a turquoise top, similar in design to Jana's, and dark blue pants. Dagovaby and Ariel joined them. Ariel's dark hair was coiled into a bun on her head and laced with icy green gems, and her long, flowing mint-green dress was encrusted with abalone-hued scales. Dagovaby wore deep brick-red clothes, stitched with gold that matched the rings around his pupils.

"Fancy," murmured Galla, surveying her crew. They all felt a strange excitement.

The High Assist arrived then, and led them to the dining hall to their seats. The golden guards stood at every entrance and dispassionately allowed the guests inside. There, an immensely long table was set with dozens of places filled by a diverse group of beings. Flowers and vines and succulents burst out of every urn or crevice. Winged golden drones flew over their heads, trilling songs. And at the center of the table, raised on a dais above everyone else, sat His

Royal Highness, the High Prince Hazkinaut of the Twelve Planets of Mehelkian.

The High Assist announced their presence. Prince Hazkinaut looked up to see them, and opened his arms wide. His skin tone was deep gold and pearl, and his eyes were large and wide and a deep, ethereal mountain-lake blue, opaque and with tiny pupils. He had a long, very slender nose, and on his head an enormous turban was swirled in white and gold. His robes were also striped in white and gold, and his arms were covered in bangles that tinkled and flashed.

"Welcome, Lady Galla-Deia!" he announced. "You and your crew are honored guests. You will now enjoy everything you love to eat and drink!" And he held his arms up and shook his bracelets, which was the signal to eat.

Galla sat diagonally across from the Prince. He said to her, "You look splendid! Do you like your garments?"

"Um," said Galla, forgetting herself for a moment. Blushing deeply, she straightened and said, "Your Highness, thank you so much for the clothes. I am accustomed to more practical attire, but these are very...very *sparkly*."

The Prince huffed.

Suddenly, he appeared immediately next to her. She blinked at him in surprise.

"Is it so daunting for you to look fabulous?" he asked scornfully.

She twisted her mouth at the question.

"What if I don't want to look fabulous?" she asked, her head, tinkling from the headdress, lifted in disdain. "Is it so awful to want to be comfortable? To be practical and functional?"

"How provincial!" cried the Prince. "You've got to consider what others think of you, as a leader, after all."

Galla gawked at him. *Am I really being fashion-shamed by a prince?*

She could not help herself, and spilled out, "Look, I already stand out. In case you hadn't noticed my hair, which whether I like it or not reveals my mood, or frizzes at inconvenient times, or gets so tangled no brush will draw through it. And it's big. To me, that's all the attention I need!"

"This will not do!" said Prince Hazkinaut. "No, no, no. The hair is but a distraction. Treat it is as such, I say! Everyone sees it first. Cover it or dress up to move their eyes elsewhere."

"No thank you," said Galla firmly. "I have nothing to hide. Also, not every being has eyes," she reminded him.

"They may not see you," agreed the Prince. "But they will sense in you your confidence. So wear something fabulous. If you want it out of sight, still wear it. Because you will know it is there, and you can fall back on that little treasure in your mind if everything else dissolves."

Infuriating! Galla thought. *I hate when well-dressed people have a point.*

"Thank you for your suggestion, Your Royal Highness," was all she could say.

And she was shocked to see the Prince back at his dais already.

There's something strange afoot here.

"You have everything you want here," repeated the Prince. "Eat and drink well."

She looked at her food, which was very simple, yet well seasoned. Her crew were tucking into theirs with great enthusiasm, and gasping about how everything was their favorite. Ariel and Dagovaby still remained alert, and they watched the Prince while he dined. Galla took a sip of her drink.

"Ah!" she said with a sigh. She looked down into her goblet and found a deep, brilliant blue liquid in it. "I've had this before. What was it...?"

"Stroffy liqueur," answered the Prince himself. "Very rare indeed. It's a wonder you've ever had it! Enjoy, Lady Deia."

Galla looked down into the glass again and saw her crowned head reflected, and grimaced slightly. She took another drink. She felt it flood through her, and it made her feel splendid, as if she were rising up above everything in a bubble. A smile formed on her face and kept spreading. And then she looked over at Rob, who sat farther down the table.

Rob tipped back a tall, dark, frothy beer and licked his lips in satisfaction. He turned his head to look at her, and she smiled at him with openness and delight. He blinked several times. *Why is she looking at me like* that?

She laughed, whether to herself or to him, he was not sure. He tilted his head at her, and then before he could do anything, all of his food and drink vanished and reappeared next to hers. He pinched his lips together and a little scowl formed on his forehead.

He walked over and sat down next to her, and looked up to catch the Prince darting his eyes away from him.

"Hello," he said, awkwardly.

"I'm so glad you're here," she said breathlessly.

Rob turned his head back and forth and said, "Uh...thanks! All of two seats away, I know it was leagues and an eternity and all." And he waited for Galla to laugh again, but she did not. Instead, she took another drink.

She smiled and felt full of bliss. He sat perfectly still.

"What...are you doing, Galla?" he whispered.

She lowered her chin and looked up at him with her russet eyes, and he felt his blood pumping.

She's putting a lot into this, but...is it because she's on vacation, or is this her drink?

"Why don't we go for a walk?" she asked then, in such a breathy, smooth voice that he shivered from head to toe.

He cleared his throat. "We can...we can walk, sure," he said, quaking inside.

Galla took another sip of her drink and stood. So they excused themselves and left the room, and she curled her arm into his and leaned on him as they walked. They had made it just out of sight of the Prince, when she started sagging a bit.

"Rob," she said into his ear, her voice urgent but slurred, as her vision swam and her legs felt strange. "Something's happening to me —can you hold me up? I don't want anyone else to see."

"I've got you," he whispered back, glancing around. "What was it? The drink? Mine was okay. Did he poison you? Jesus! I'll beat his ass! I don't care if he's a prince!"

"No, no," protested Galla, her headdress tipping over. Rob pushed it back up and held her steady. "It's Stroffy liqueur. I...I've had it before and it...affects me in strange ways. Can you promise you'll help me, no matter what? I'm afraid I might...not behave normally."

"Understatement," said Rob bluntly. "But yeah. I promise I'll help you."

Galla steadied herself by leaning against him, her headdress bumping his forehead, and took hold of his face. The look of bliss was gone, and fear and uncertainty took its place. Rob put his own hands on hers and drew hers away.

"Let's keep walking, Galla, let's get you straight," he said, his heart racing.

He led her back toward their rooms, and she was at that point so dizzy she could barely walk at all. They stood outside their doors. She held his hands and looked at him and swayed.

Maybe we shouldn't be here right now, thought Rob in agony.

Just then an ornate little golden bot rolled up to them.

"Follow," it said.

Rob took her by the arm and followed the bot. It rolled along until it followed the same path they had taken earlier in the day, out into the alley and into the passageways. The Cogniz was waiting for them, and motioned for them to enter its tent.

Once inside, it threw off its drapes, and there stood Prince Hazkinaut in all his royal attire. Rob and Galla gasped.

"I must be quick," he told them. "Yes, I am the Cogniz. When I travel, I do so in disguise. As you can see, I am a powerful telepath." And he undid his turban to reveal the top of his head covered in long, slowly waving appendages, like a feather star's arms. "I keep these hidden, because while most of my people's are not forked, mine are. It is an immediate giveaway of my abilities. Forgive me, Galla-Deia, for the Stroffy liqueur."

"You *drugged* me?" she asked, wavering in place but still appalled.

Rob snarled, "Prince or no, I should punch you for this," and balled his fist.

"And I could toss you in the air with my mind, Robert Idin," snapped the Prince. "I am sorry for the drink's effects. They are worse than I could have imagined, for you did not have much. I was testing you; I needed to see if it were really you. There are rumors about you that you should be aware of. People are seeking information about you and your weaknesses. I recommend you take the utmost precaution from here on out. The answer is yes, by the way."

"What?" asked Galla, blinking rapidly.

"Yes, I will help you. And I do know other telepaths on other worlds. Now that I've confirmed it is you, I propose a suggestion: I will send word ahead that you aren't a threat, and you can seek them out." Then the Prince said, "I must get back. Let us speak again before you leave, particularly about the stone. Take care of her, Robert—she is more precious than you realize."

And the Prince vanished.

Rob walked her carefully back, and she started trembling uncontrollably.

"You're coming out of it, I think," he said. He watched her in alarm, for he had never seen her physically weakened like this before.

"Ohhh," she moaned, clutching her abdomen.

"Let's get you to your room," he said quietly, and he opened the door, removed her headdress, pulled her shoes off, and helped her to her bathroom. "Are you going to be sick?"

"No."

She splashed water on her face, and then drank it from her cupped palms. She looked in the mirror to see a blurry image of herself, with Rob behind her.

"You're going to be all right now," he told her. *I hope*, he thought. He walked her to her bed, and helped her get in and cover up. "Good night, Galla," he said, and he left and shut the door firmly behind him, and stared up at the arched ceiling above him before returning to his own room, alone.

7

HEART OF ACID

T he man's half-covered face shone in the flickering orange light of the fire. It gleamed off the flexible metal covering that concealed his jaw and his neck. Once, he had been called Officer Derry. He had been a loyal officer of MindSynd, which worked to keep the growing network of Earth's biological telepaths monitored. It had been a good career, until his assignment on Mandira Research Station.

There, he was injured in an attack by Paosh Tohon, manifested as former telepath Veronica. But ultimately, Veronica had given him a way out. She had made him understand that there was more than what humanity could offer, having been transformed herself into something far more powerful. She had given him an escape from the oppression of Governor Aeriod's colonies.

And here he stood, slowly becoming less human yet more powerful, a leader in his own right of Valemog, the troops that pledged their support to Paosh Tohon. Rumors persisted that the troops were coerced, that their work was done in fear and to avoid being taken by the changeable entity. Derry knew otherwise. This was the purest cause: to reshape the galaxy, rebuild it from the ashes of the lethargy and decay of the Associates' leadership. To make everything better than it was before. It was evolution, it was ascension, it was the only true route!

He surveyed the refugees, now bound in groups. He turned to his troops.

"Give them one more chance," he said silkily. "Show them I can be generous. But! Before you do that, show them what they should want to avoid, if their loyalty is questioned. If there are quills or feathers, rip them out. If there is skin, flay it. We can work with that. We can prolong their pain, so Paosh Tohon can feed."

And he took up his own invention, the acidavyper, a large, advanced gun. He turned to a thick wall. "And show them this," he said.

He sprayed the wall with barbed bullets that spun. They struck the wall and began drilling, and then erupted in bursts of acid, and the wall hissed and grew pockmarked. The scent of the acid stung his nose, but he breathed it in deeply.

"Just one little spray, spinning right into flesh and bone and shell," sighed Derry with pleasure. "Or we can make it better. It's really their choice."

8

VULNERABILITIES

G alla woke, looked at herself in all her glorious attire from the night before, touched her tangled hair, and gasped. She held herself. Anger roiled in her, but even worse, she felt mortified. Then she felt ashamed.

Her eyes stung as she tore off the fancy raiment and put her own clothes back on. She tied her hair up in a messy bun, adjusted her diamethyst on her breast, and walked out of her room in a haze of rage.

She knocked on Rob's door. He opened it, and they faced each other, and Galla's face grew hot from embarrassment.

"I'm sorry," she said, holding her palms out. "The Stroffy made me—"

Rob held his hands up and shook his head.

"You don't need to say anything. It wasn't your fault; you were drugged. Let's just...pretend it didn't happen."

"I can't do that," she said. "Can I—can I come in? I don't want to stand out here."

She looked behind her. No one else was in the hall.

Rob swallowed, and let her inside. She remembered what Ariel had said, and she looked all around the room. It looked much smaller than hers, and its walls were curved oddly, and the floors were soft under her feet. She saw little shelves of tools and other objects.

"So...this is what you wanted?" she asked him. "Your room, I mean."

"Yes," he answered, looking relieved.

She glanced up at him, and his red-gold eyelashes blinked over his blue-green eyes.

"What is it modeled on?" she asked.

"My little room on Mandira Station," he answered, with a shrug. "I'm not fancy, not really. I just...sometimes I miss my own space, you know? On the *Fithich* I...never feel at ease, because, well..." and his voice trailed off.

She nodded. *Because of Aeriod*, she thought.

Galla said, "It makes sense to me. I like it," and then they grinned at each other.

She took a breath and said, "I don't want to pretend last night didn't happen. It *did*. The Stroffy...how can I say this. It magnifies how I feel. What if I had—" and she sucked in air and hiccupped.

"Listen," said Rob, and his heart galloped in his chest, "nothing would have happened. I wouldn't have let it."

She stood close enough to smell him: clean, but with that unique, salty scent no one else had.

She took his hands and said, shaking, "Thank you. I know, it's just...I said it *magnified* how I felt."

Rob's heart pounded. He looked from her hands to her warm eyes. "And...how did...how do you feel?"

"I'm having a hard time," Galla said, fumbling over words. "I have our crew, and I have my duties, and I can't really do anything else, not right now."

Rob lifted his hands up, like he might hold his temples, and said, "I...don't know what to do with this. Is this making you happy, not letting yourself feel?"

Galla furrowed her brow. "It's not something I think about. My duty comes before everything else."

"So...now what?" he asked, and he dreaded her answer.

She closed her eyes. *I don't know what to say, but I have to be honest.*
"I'm afraid of starting something with you," she told him.
He groaned.

"Galla, I can't stand this. Why don't we go back and just pretend none of this happened? This conversation, last night, just forget it. I can't keep giving you my love and not getting anything back. I mean, I can, but it hurts, and—"

Galla's amber-hued eyes opened wide. She put her finger over his mouth. "Your *love*?"

He stared at her. "You know, right? How could you not know?"

She stepped backward.

"I'm sorry, I—I don't know what I—I'm going to go now," she stammered, and she fled into the hall.

Oh no, she thought, and she squeezed her stone in her hands and breathed in and out slowly. Ariel and Dagovaby quietly opened their door and met her in the hall. They looked at her mournfully, and she closed her eyes and turned away from them. They had no doubt read or sensed Rob's thoughts just now. Jana left her room then, and saw the looks on their faces. She glanced around.

"Where's Rob?" she asked.

Galla stood upright. "It's time we left," she told them, aloof. "The sooner we put this place behind us, the better."

Jana and Ariel and Dagovaby exchanged troubled looks. Galla motioned for all of them to assemble with her to leave.

The Prince stood waiting for her in the great hallway that led to the fountains. Galla glared at him. He took her aside and said quietly, "Lady Deia, I apologize. I did not mean for this to...I admit I learned Rob's desires, and there was one above all others, and that was not something I could give him. I did not mean to make things worse with the Stroffy."

"Can you just...shut up?" she said furiously. "Stop reading the minds of my crew! Can I count on you or not? Ariel needs to send you a signal when the time comes to activate a Device. Are you in or not?"

The Prince, shocked at her colloquial manner with him, drew

himself up. "Yes. I will help you, in all the ways I said I would. I hope our next meeting is less...fraught."

"I hope so as well, Your Highness," said Galla with eyes blazing, "because your manner of 'helping' us has caused more problems." She held out one of her small, round diamethysts to the Prince, and he took it, curling his fingers around it.

He bowed to her, and she turned away from him in disdain. She marched all the way to the doors of the palace and into the waiting vehicle. She did not look back. Ariel, Dagovaby, and Jana followed, but Rob trailed along last. He looked at no one, and put on his sunglasses and sat hunched down in his seat. His face looked pale, and Galla felt as if her insides were shrinking.

She pushed all of that away and said to Ariel, "Send the code."

Ariel asked, "Are you sure?"

"Quite sure," answered Galla. "He knows he can't hold off Paosh Tohon much longer, or he would never have taken the stone. He needs us to succeed."

Ariel nodded. She lowered her eyelids, and Galla thought she could see glints of green through them.

"Done," said Ariel. Galla nodded.

Their vehicle glided across the desert back to their ship. The golden guards had lined up outside the *Fithich* bearing gift boxes, and Galla rolled her eyes at them. "Set them in the bay," she said simply. She walked into her ship first, and Rob entered last, and they shot away from Mehelkian, unescorted.

Galla called on the comms, "I want to meet with all of you. There's something I want to discuss."

Everyone shuffled into the round room, and Paul reached out for her from Ariel's arms. "Gow-wah," he said, and everyone laughed, even Rob, who sat with his hand covering his mouth and his eyes anywhere but on Galla.

Relieved, Galla said, "I want to apologize for my behavior at dinner yesterday. I was given a drink that to humans seems like regular liquor, but to me, it works as a powerful drug. The Prince used it to test my...legitimacy."

"What the fuck!" shouted Jana. Her jaw muscles worked in her face and she clenched her fists.

"Seconded!" said Ariel.

Galla sighed. "I know. But he had a point, and he made it very well. I'm not completely invulnerable. So, keep the Stroffy liqueur away from me, if you please. But also, we *have* to be more careful. He is a strong telepath. He gave you each something you wanted, because he picked it up from your minds. That was another test, and you all failed it.

"I'm sorry, but we all have to do better. I want each of you to learn blocking, or try to. Ariel, I want you and Dagovaby to teach the others in any way you can. I know it won't be as easy without psionic abilities. But we have now given away our weaknesses. As much as I want to kick the Prince where it hurts, I have to admit, he did us a favor."

Everyone looked physically ill except for Paul, who pulled on his mother as if wanting to jump, and finally she brought him to Galla, who scooped him up. "You're getting so big and solid!" Galla exclaimed, and she kissed him and held him on her hip.

"Is there any way to keep tabs on the Prince?" Jana asked. "I don't trust him whatsoever."

Galla sighed and crinkled her nose. "Well, if we were Aeriod," she answered, "we'd put one of his silver recording diamonds on the Prince. Assuming we could even get close enough to him to do that. But we don't have access to that particular kind of tool. And Hazkinaut is a mage himself, so I'm not even sure it would work on him."

Paul pulled hard on Galla's curls and she winced, but still smiled down at him lovingly.

"Next up: we are on our way to another Device world. Jana, this time I want you to come along. But first, tell me everything you can about the place. Off to work."

Jana nodded, and Rob slipped out and left for the cockpit.

"Meredith," said Galla, for the older woman seemed very quiet, "can I talk to you in our room?"

"Sure, dear," said Meredith fondly. Galla kissed Paul's round cheek and handed him to Dagovaby.

The two women walked to their shared room. Galla sat on her beautiful quilt, made by Meredith for her before they had ever met. Meredith's plants were starting to wilt. Normally they were full and vibrant. Galla looked at the woman's hands, which trembled now so much that she no longer quilted. "My eyes are tired," she had said lately, but Galla wondered.

"What is it, Galla, is something wrong?" asked Meredith, her cheeks twitching a bit.

"I...wanted to ask you about..." Galla struggled over the words. "I think I want to convert a storage compartment into another room, for myself. Would you mind?"

Meredith laughed. "No, I don't mind. Is this about Rob?"

Galla blushed from the roots of her hair down to her chest.

Meredith fixed her with her glowing green eyes, and said, "Is it really about Aeriod?"

Galla sat down. This felt like too much for her to deal with. She would prefer to tamp it all down.

"Maybe. But that's over. And besides, I couldn't be with anyone who did what he did to you and Ariel."

Meredith nodded. "I've forgiven him," she said.

Galla gasped. "What! Why?"

Meredith shook her head and pushed her hair behind her ears, as her daughter might.

"Maybe because I'm old, and I know there are fewer days ahead. And I have Ariel with me now. It takes too much energy for me to hang onto that anger anymore. Any chance to be with Ariel again was better than no chance. He can't go back and change what happened, but I think he wishes he could. Knowing him. So I decided to let that go.

"But as for you," she said, taking Galla's hand and patting it, "you seemed very sure that it was over with him. Are you still?"

Galla lifted her chin and said, "Yes. I am." Of that she was quite certain, regardless of any feelings she might still have, deep down.

Meredith shrugged. "Then if you're ready to move forward, why wait? And don't forget what I told you. Never rule out friendship. Can you imagine spending years with Rob? Think about that. Is he your friend?"

"I—I thought he was, yes," said Galla, but she was unsure now.

"Then you have to do what you feel comfortable with. Only you know that."

Galla squeezed her hand. "Thank you. Everything you've said and done for me means so much."

And they hugged, and Galla felt the frailty of Meredith.

Why does everything feel different now?

ADMONITION

There was turbulence in the junction conduit, but nothing like before. It made Galla's room rearrangement more challenging than it might have been.

She heard the crackle of her comms. Rob's voice said flatly, "We'll be there soon. Do you want to see?"

"I'm in the middle of something—oof!" she cried as a box tumbled onto her head. Then she stubbed her toe. "Ack!"

"Where are you at?" he asked.

"I'm in the storage unit off the kitchen," Galla replied, pushing her unruly copper-gold-purple curls away from her face.

"Um, why?"

"I'm making a new room for myself," she panted.

"Oh."

"I'm moving forward," she said simply.

"Forward is good," he said in a dull tone. "See you up here?"

"Yes," she answered. She brushed her hands on the front of her pants, and left her room.

In the cockpit she felt much more herself, even with the new awkwardness around Rob. She loved flying more than most things, certainly more than being a leader. Especially just then. She fantasized briefly: *What if that was all that we did? Rob and I, flying together. Another time and another place. But not right now.*

"Here's something unique," he muttered.

"What is it?" Galla asked.

"This planet comes with a warning." He tuned a series of repeating messages in a strange language.

"Translate it," she ordered.

The ship obliged, and played back the message:

"Associate warning zero-five-nine-two-seven-seven-zero-eight-four. You are entering the Seyvelk system. All operations are offline. Avoid the sixth planet from Seyvelk, which is under quarantine. The Associates release all responsibility should you proceed. No assistance will be granted. This message will repeat. Associate warning..."

Rob shuddered visibly.

"What is it, Plague Planet?" he asked.

There's the Rob I know, thought Galla, relieved at his quip, but disturbed by its implications.

"Jana," called Galla, "what's the story here?"

Jana walked into the cockpit and said, "From what I can tell, this is one of several thousand locations the Associates quarantined in this sector of the galaxy. There may be millions, on asteroids and other planets, but I have a broken data set, so I can't be sure. This one is not listed as having a pathogen like we might understand it, though. I'm not sure *why* it's quarantined. But I did read something about it that made it sound—for lack of a better word—haunted. Shrieking voices, stuff like that."

"Oh good, *Haunted* Plague Planet," snorted Rob. "A real vacation paradise!"

Galla rubbed her eyes. "We've already been to one planet with ghosts. If we want to call them that." She shivered, thinking about how Dagovaby had almost been killed on that world. They had since nicknamed it Stormworld. She called him on her comms.

Dagovaby soon joined the rest of them, and the empath stood staring at the grey-green world.

"Can you sense anything, Dag?" she asked him.

"I'm not picking up anything at all," said Dagovaby.

Galla turned to Jana. "Are you still up for this?"

The woman rubbed her head and twisted one of her several earrings. Galla could still see threads of gold woven into Jana's hair. She looked as tired as she ever did, and doubtful.

"I said I would be, and I'm going to do what I said," she said. But she looked at Galla pointedly. "If I hear shrieking, though? I'm out."

"Good thing I'm a fast flyer," said Galla with a grin. "Rob, take us in above the Device."

Rob steered the *Fithich* past two moons and into the planet's atmosphere. It was a stormy descent. Galla watched him focus and resisted offering advice. The ship adjusted more quickly, however, to this situation than to the junction turbulence. They finally shot forth into a drizzly, foggy landscape, and could make out very little of the topography, relying completely on the ship's systems to guide them. The sensors sounded when the ship detected an indentation on the surface.

"Device sign," said Rob.

"Good," said Galla. "Jana, let's suit up." She turned and left to head to the launch bay.

Jana gave Rob a large-eyed, serious look.

He smirked. "Don't worry. She'll bring you back in one piece. You'll be a quivering mess, but you'll be once piece."

"Fuck you, Rob," she said.

"Love you too, Jana," he laughed.

The two women stood in the launch bay, suited, and set helmets on their heads. Jana peered through her visor at her captain and thought, *This had all better be worth it, someday.* She shivered when she saw Galla jump on the sky bike and pat the seat behind her.

Jana swallowed, then sat behind Galla and looped her arms around her. She thought, *I just had a delicious meal, a new outfit, and a great bath on Mehelkian. Why did I agree to this again?*

"Rob?" called Galla.

"Ready for you," he said. Jana felt Galla tense up.

"Drop time," said Galla. "You might want to hold on a bit tighter than that."

And the bay opened, and the sky bike dropped. Jana screamed, and then squeezed Galla with all her might as they plummeted down through the fog. When she finally dared to open her eyes, she saw nothing but pale grey. *Can't see what's coming. This is fun.*

Galla engaged the sky bike's engines, and they jerked ahead. Jana's teeth chattered beyond her control as they curved down and toward a great round maw in the ground. Then Galla brought the bike to a stop, peeled off Jana's gripping hands, and slid to the surface.

She said cheerfully, "We're here, and you're safe. Are you ready to go in?"

Jana tilted her head back and said, "Sure! Why not? Just had the living hell scared out of me. How bad can anything else be?"

Galla clucked her tongue. "Maybe don't ask that. Look, you may see visions in this thing. They could just be things from your past. Or they could be premonitions of a kind. It seems to be a little different for everyone."

Again, why did I agree to this? Jana wondered.

"Okay," she said, "I'm going to do this one time. One. Time. Got it? Don't ask me to do it again. Let's get it over with."

Galla nodded. "Understood."

She led Jana to a little set of stairs built into the side of the giant pit. The fog was so thick, they could not see the other side. Galla wiped the mist droplets from her visor. She adjusted her large stone inside her suit and felt its slight warmth. She patted a little pouch on her waist, where a small diamethyst sat waiting. The air smelled moldy.

"Do you feel anything from your stone?" she asked Jana.

Jana nodded. "It's a little warm."

"It might grow warmer, or even hot; it's hard to say," Galla told her. "These stones seem to know when they're ready for the Device."

"Super weird," said Jana, and she tried not to think about accidentally slipping off the little stairs and into the abyss.

A metallic scraping sound met their ears, and then a small platform appeared next to the stairs. Galla stepped onto it and held her hand out to Jana. Jana stood very still. Her eyes shone large and dark in her visor. They each turned on the headlamps of their visors then.

"Take my hand," offered Galla.

Jana did so, with both of hers, and stepped onto the platform, which bobbed.

"Sit down and hold onto me," Galla suggested.

Jana quickly complied, and the women held each other's hand tightly and gripped the platform with their free hands. And down it shot, and Jana moaned for a second. Galla squeezed her hand harder and met her eyes. Jana gawked.

"Your stone is glowing *through* your suit!" she exclaimed.

Galla looked down to see a purple light coming from the breast of her flight suit. Jana touched her own neck and said, "Mine is getting very warm. Trippy!"

"We're close, then," said Galla. "There will be a hallway, and a courtyard with many doors. And you may see strange things. Hold my hand if you need to."

Jana nodded.

The platform whined to a stop and trembled for a second. The women climbed out of it and onto the solid floor of a vast open hallway that their headlamps revealed. As they walked, lights winked on through the hall, almost like landing lights. At first it was completely silent. Then a shiver in the floor under their feet set them on edge. They were not holding hands at that point, but instinctively moved closer to each other.

They kept walking and could see ahead the courtyard, but before they reached it, large rings of light swept through the hallway around them, at first slowly and then faster and faster. Galla and Jana quickened their pace, and then everything shook.

To Jana it looked like the floor had given way, and that she was suspended in the air and surrounded by light rings all around her body. She screamed, but no sound came out, and then she could see shapes inside the rings. She hung still and watched in shock a stream of faces of people she knew: her mother, her father, her aunts...from long before Mandira, from her last time on Earth. She could even feel the sun on her neck and the sweat under her eyes, but those faces and those feelings fled quickly. Then she felt paralyzed, as if in a dream she could not awaken from, and then a grey darkness surrounded her. After that, a tear in the darkness revealed a shaft of light, and she could feel hands reaching in and pulling her toward that tear...

And then it all stopped.

She stood in the courtyard of metal floors and walls, with doors surrounding it on all sides. Galla knelt beside her, with her face in her hands. Jana moved quickly over to her.

"Did you see the same thing?" she asked, her voice high and excited. She could see Galla's large stone still glowing, but growing dimmer.

"I saw myself falling," Galla gasped. "I couldn't stop falling. And he wasn't there this time. I didn't hear his voice; I didn't feel his hand in mine."

Jana took hold of her shoulders. "You're okay now. You're not falling. Whose voice? Whose hand?"

Galla shook her head. "I don't know. I just—I know him from my other visions. He's gone." And she felt deeply sad. She could not shake the memory of the love she had felt from that person in her past visions.

"So what do we do now?" Jana asked.

Galla blinked and looked up at Jana, as if through a long tunnel, miles long, or light-years...she did not know which. She sighed shakily and opened her little pouch. With her gloved hand, she pulled out a small diamethyst and set it on the floor, and it stopped glowing. Her larger stone went dark as well. Again she felt a deep longing, for the loving voice from her other visions, from the warmth and comfort in his hands. *Will I ever hear him or feel him again?*

"My stone is cool now," said Jana, marveling. "That was all so *weird*! Kind of scary, but kind of not...I saw my ancestors. I saw Earth." She gazed off to try to return to the memory. "Wait, what's that sound?" she said suddenly.

The lights in the courtyard began to dim, and the two women began walking back along the corridor quickly toward the platform. Galla could hear it then, a high-pitched sound, at first discordant and then melodic, and she stared at Jana.

"The shrieking!" Jana cried.

"It's not shrieking, though, listen!" marveled Galla.

"No. It's music!" said Jana, and they made it to the end of the corridor and looked in wonder at what they saw.

Rising and falling in the abyss, thousands of winged creatures swirled around, their bodies and wings glowing in pale green, orange, and yellow. The phosphorescent creatures were under two feet tall, but their wings were at least twice as long, and they spun and dipped and rocketed up and down. And all the while, they sang.

Their voices blended together, and Galla thought, *Murmuration! Physical and vocal!*

"We should get on the platform," she said quickly.

"I hope they don't have teeth," said Jana in agreement, and they sat on the platform and held tightly to its surface.

The beings followed them up as the platform zoomed toward the opening of the Device. They tumbled over, and pirouetted, and trilled the whole time. One of them flew along with the two women, and hovered in front of Galla's face as they all rose.

"Hello!" said Galla, grinning, for the small being raised its four little arms into a sort of salute, while it kicked with its legs and pumped with its phosphorescent green and yellow wings. Galla crossed her eyes as the creature came right up to her face and held onto her visor, and it sang in such a haunting, mournful wail that she felt herself tear up.

"What are they singing?" asked Jana. Two other creatures encircled her head, and she looked up at them, enraptured.

"I don't know, but I wish I did," said Galla.

And then the platform stopped. The little creatures did not

continue into the light, but dove back again into the darkness, and looking over the edge of the platform, the women watched the glow of them swirl down and down, until they faded away.

"Some haunting," said Jana, with a huge smile on her face. "That was the most incredible experience I've ever had in my life!"

VICE AND VISITATION

"It's time we opened these boxes," Galla said to her crew in their meeting room. On the table, the gifts from Prince Hazkinaut were arranged in shimmering stacks.

A palpable ripple of excitement circuited the room, and their captain smiled indulgently. "I'm no fan of the tactics of the Prince, but I do appreciate his gesture. So let's see what's inside."

They had a joyful time lifting the lids on the dozens of boxes, which were in a variety of shapes. Galla appreciated the uniforms the Prince had made for them. She thought back to what he said, and how appearance mattered. Each uniform looked very similar, but they were all bespoke. The rest of the crew had black suits wrought with silver and violet stitching. *Aeriod would appreciate those*, she thought, and she liked that they matched the ship and her stone.

Hers and Rob's looked distinctly different. Rob's outfit was deep navy blue, with silver embroidered wings along the neck and on a patch on his arm that bore a picture of the *Fithich*. Galla's was deep violet, threaded with copper, and with an ornate, pleated jacket that still looked formal and assertive. Her pants were black and violet, and felt very soft and comfortable, and her boots were black with copper stitching.

"I hate to admit this," she told her crew, "but the Prince does have an eye for both style and function."

Rob coughed and slid a round box over to Galla.

"I think these are yours," he said, avoiding her eyes.

"Why, what—" she began, and she opened the box. She quickly shut it and jumped back as if stung.

Rob could not help his reaction, and he lowered his face into his arms on the table as he shook with laughter.

Jana said, "Um, Captain...your face looks like it could melt lead," and she snickered.

"What is it, what is it?" cried Ariel, craning her head with an eager expression. She held in her arms both toddler and baby clothes, along with beautiful aquamarine bracelets. Meredith looked up, grinning, from a stack of jewel-toned fabrics and a fabulous, tiny device that worked as a quilting machine.

Galla seized the round box and held it shut against her chest. She did not look at any of them.

"That's probably enough for me," she said in a high voice, and she began to make her way to her new room.

Dagovaby called, "Wait, there's something else," and he held up a gold and white flower in his hand.

They watched as its petals unfolded, and a hologram of the Prince formed above the table.

"Greetings, Lady Deia and crew," he said. "I give you these as a gesture of goodwill and as an offering for the challenges you were put through. I give you this message as well: I have sent ahead to systems with known, trusted telepaths to alert them of your coming. I am including those systems in this message; I am sure Jana Okoro can work with them. Thank you again. To the future!"

Galla raised her eyebrows.

"Well!" she said. "I guess he came through after all. At least, this time. Jana, will you find the closest world in his data?"

"On it," said Jana, admiring her new uniform and several new emerald jewelry pieces.

Galla walked rapidly back to her new room and threw the little box on her bed. It burst forth with tiny pieces of ornately woven lingerie, some violet, some copper, some black, and all of exquisite fabric. She knew without trying them on that they would all fit her perfectly. And she also knew that Rob had seen them. She blushed and covered her cheeks with her hands, thinking back to what the Prince had said: "You will know it is there..."

"Trickster!" she hissed. She stuffed the little bits of clothing back into the box and tried to get the lid to shut, but it would not, no matter what she did. So she opened up another box next to her small bunk and shoved it inside.

Jana chimed her. "Not far to the first place," she said. "He listed it as... Yaddifor's Delight, or something. It's...uh...a pleasure system?"

"A *what*?"

They soon came out of the junction and into a strange system, with a red star, two gas giants, and a large asteroid belt beyond them. Countless asteroids were converted into highly specialized centers for, as the Prince had described, pleasure and recreation, as well as commerce. One involved gambling, another aquatic adventures under domes; several hosted various concerts, shopping venues, conventions, and so on.

"So, which one is our telepath source on?" Galla wanted to know.

Jana sucked in her lips. "Take a guess."

"No," said Galla. "*No.*"

"Yes," Jana groaned.

Dagovaby grinned and turned to Ariel, who cackled.

"What is it?" Rob asked then, and the looks on their faces told him as much as he needed to know. "Ohhhhh," he said, and then he shook his head and snickered.

Beetle clicked and said, "Will there be plants there? I like the rolled and dried plants the Prince gave me. I wondered if there might be more?"

The entire crew lost it.

"Whew," said Galla finally. "My plan was for this to be a small vacation for you. Given the location, I'm not sure how practical that will be. Beetle, I apologize: there probably aren't much in the way of plants on the asteroids. I promise we'll get you some nice, fresh ones soon."

Meredith spoke up. "I'll stay here with Beetle and Paul."

"Definitely a good plan," said Galla.

"Wait, what about me?" asked Rob.

"Oh, you're going," Galla answered, one eyebrow raised. "Shore leave, I hear it's called? Captain's orders. Don't worry; it can be a working mission. Look or listen for intelligence on Valemog or Paosh Tohon, wherever you can find it. Anything useful. Ariel, you and Dagovaby need to block as well as you can, while looking for this telepath. Jana and Rob, stay vigilant. And, when you can, have fun, all of you!"

They changed into less obvious clothing, and Galla was happy to find something among their gifts from the Prince that had a hood and pockets. It was a long, dark plum coat, and she hoped it would hide enough of her volatile hair to keep her from feeling too exposed. She put it on and went to the cockpit, and sat beside Rob.

He glanced at her and said, "You look very dignified. And super beautiful," and then he looked away, his face unreadable. She stared at him and bit her lip.

"Thank you," she said softly.

He piloted the *Fithich* into one of the enormous number of bays at the Pleasure Domes. There were dozens of domes built from the inside out of this particular asteroid. It looked covered in enormous soap bubbles. They soon learned each dome had a different atmosphere, so many species could enjoy themselves. Some were immense, and some were tiny. Each dome featured catacombs filled with all sorts of activities, all for the purpose of stimulating pleasure centers. It was not simply a place of vice, but also therapeutic, with salons and spas and unnamable services Galla could only guess about. Her crew looked astounded at everything.

Ariel and Dagovaby stared at the place, wide-eyed.

"It's overwhelming," muttered Ariel, "so many minds; it's been some time since I've felt that bombardment. Maybe not since Fael'Kar."

Galla nodded. On that city-world, she had met Ariel for the first time, and they both had met Dagovaby. Galla had taken for granted the relative peace the telepath and empath couple had grown accustomed to on their ship. Even the Prince's palace seemed sparse in comparison to the pleasure domes of Yaddifor's Delight. Fewer beings meant fewer thoughts to sift through.

"Rare, true interaction! Nothing virtual, or all virtual. You decide! True pleasure awaits!" was one of the messages translated for them. They walked slowly to a sorting area, to choose their atmosphere.

Bots and beings helped guide the tourists. One willowy figure with four eyes and two whip-like tails approached them, held up a little screen, and said, "Chiefly oxygen, line four hundred and thirty-two."

"What!" Rob exclaimed. "We'll all be four hundred and thirty-two years old by the time we find it!"

Fortunately the lines were distributed everywhere like gates, and soon they found theirs. Then they all looked at each other. Jana started laughing, nervously at first, and then in fits over everyone's expressions. Galla looked curious but skeptical; Ariel looked tired but determined; Dagovaby looked amused, and Rob wavered between excited and uneasy. When it was Jana's turn to enter, she tossed a look at Galla that basically said, "I'm out of here," and she marched in, confident and ready for whatever might happen.

Galla was less sure. The experience with the Prince at Mehelkian had made her cautious now. But once inside, she admitted it was quite the sight to behold. The many subunits of their designated dome rose in all directions, and extended down into the asteroid as well. It really was a small city, and it was filled with color and light. From the uppermost ceiling, a being perched suspended, with many long arms, undulating in all directions like ribbons. With every movement of those arms, it emitted music.

There were alcoves, catacombs, swings, ropes, ladders, stairs, floating platforms, individual lifts, drones, bots, cyborgs, and beings of every type, some tiny, some almost too large for that dome. It was dizzying. She felt even more sympathy for Ariel and Dagovaby, for her own senses were overwhelmed. But she slid among all the crowds, and let the ebbing and flowing din of their voices and other sounds roll past her. She walked with her hood up and her hands in her pockets, immersed.

In addition to all the sights and sounds, she was solicited constantly. "Would you like a taste?" "How much for *you*?" "Come experience the purest pleasures!" and on and on. She kept her face emotionless, pretending she was an android like her mentor, Oni-Odi. Her many years among androids had trained her well in that regard, at least.

Do people really choose to be here? she wondered, intrigued and disturbed at the same time. She spotted a group of beings ranging in size, but all dressed similarly, huddled in worn cloaks. She casually walked over toward them. They were cooking food, right out in the open, and offering it to anyone who would take it. She decided she would try it. She chose a small loaf of something, and offered money, but they huddled away from her.

"We want others to try this, to prove it is good," said one of them.

Galla took an obliging bite, and it tasted both sweet and bitter. "It *is* good. Can I pay you now?"

But they shrank away from her.

They're refugees! she thought suddenly. She took a deep breath. *How many are there? In this dome, in every dome, on every asteroid?* And she felt a surge of anger. *Damn the Associates. What are they doing about the crisis?*

Now in deep thought about the situation, she barely noticed when someone bumped into her. It was a tall someone, dressed in a deep, brilliant yellow-green. After the individual had passed, Galla gasped and turned to look back. *Was that a human?* But the figure was gone.

More alert now, she looked around to try to find Ariel and Dagovaby. At last she spied them in a café, seated with other beings, but their mouths were not moving. This gave her a thrill. *Telepaths?* She could only hope, and moved on so as not to stare.

She heard raucous laughter from Jana, and found her among a group of beings who had raised her up above them as if she were seated. She had bev-ropes around her neck, and occasionally took a nip off one of the tubes, each filled with a colorful drink. Galla averted her eyes and smiled. Then she caught sight of a certain ginger-headed fellow in the distance, and moved closer through the throng, ignoring the constant propositions and sales pitches.

Rob was surrounded by pleasure androids, none of which looked human, but some advertised in his intrigued ear that they could become anything he wanted. Then a leggy being draped its appendages around him, and the group all leaned in and embraced him. His face was bright red, and he laughed nervously. Then he looked up and saw Galla, and he quickly tried to straighten up, but she grinned at him, and then nodded. She could see him exhale in relief, and the beings pulled him back into a green-lit catacomb.

She found a lift in the form of a small cage and stepped on it, and it sent her high above the streets below, past many pleasure bubbles. She wanted to see the scope of the place. She also wanted to be closer to the musician. When the lift stopped she stayed on it, leaned her elbows on its railing, and watched the creature loop and snap and twirl its long ribbon-like tentacles. Its notes lifted up and down, and she suspected there were some her ears could not hear. There was a breeze up here, a warm updraft, and in it she heard something flapping.

"Nothing for you, then?" a voice said behind her. She jumped.

She turned to see a figure in chartreuse green perched on a ledge with its coat rippling in the breeze, and recognized the person from earlier. It was indeed a man, or at least he looked human. He had very dark skin, which the ceiling lights of the dome shone upon and tinged with blue. His face was chiseled, his cheekbones high, his neck long, and she could see that his shoulders were broad and muscular even through his brilliant coat. His head was mostly bald, but had designs in spirals and other shapes in his hair of very short length, almost like tattoos. She spied a dark, gunmetal-colored chain that led into his shirt, but did not see what hung from it.

He swung easily over to her and into her lift cage. Looking at him, she saw immediately something different in his eyes, which were rich, deep reddish-brown. She felt goose bumps form. He was no human after all.

She whispered, "Are you...like me?"

He smiled, looking down at her.

"Let's take a walk," he said. The lift shot down to the surface streets again, and they stepped out.

They walked alongside each other, with her deep plum coat and his vivid green one standing out among the crowd. He guided her to a narrow alley, almost a slot canyon made of the small domes stacked high above.

"I don't have much time," he told her. "Yes, I am 'like you,' but only to a point. I'm a Representative."

At first, Galla stared at the man, not comprehending. Her thoughts came in little explosions. His words reverberated through her.

"Of humans!" she finally gasped. Their eyes were locked together. "I thought I was the only one!"

"No," he said, and his face looked sad. "There are not many of us, but you're not alone."

Galla sat down right in the alley. She felt thunderstruck.

"I can't believe it! Does this mean—can you do what I can do? Can you remember your training? I have so many questions!"

He held his hand out and she took it, and he lifted her back up.

"I know," he said, "and I wish I could answer them all, Galla-Deia."

Galla shook her wild curls, causing her hood to fall. "You know my name," she said, "so what's yours?"

He stared into her eyes and she felt a deep camaraderie, yet it also made her wistful.

"Call me Coniuratus," he said.

"Is that your real name?" Galla pressed him.

"Clever, Captain," he said, smirking. "I work more closely with the Associates than you do. And though I do not know everything about you, I already know you have a very different history than I. Our missions are different as well. And our abilities. I can see the question in your face, which is the most open I've ever seen, by the way: can I help you with your mission? And I regret to say I cannot, except for a few overlapping goals.

"You won't see me again for a very long time, if at all," he continued, and Galla could see again the sadness in his face. "That means I'm working. But in some ways I'll be helping you, or at least the people we represent. I hope there is a day I can stand next to you, and we can ask each other all the questions we have right now."

Galla felt her stone grow so hot that it burned her skin, and she furtively took it out. And to her amazement, Coniuratus pulled a round, faceted, deep green gem forth from his shirt. They watched their stones glow as if in communication.

He said to her, "I feel a sense of relief, like you, by meeting. It's hard. We watch the people we represent, who we love, grow and change and then fade away. I saw the young man with the red hair, and how he looked at you."

She lowered her head.

He went on, "I've loved them too. I can see why you would like him. The more vivid they are, the more alive they seem. A fire you want to hold in your hand."

"Yes," she admitted, looking into his kind, sad face.

"Just..." he said cautiously, and he took her hands in his, "don't close yourself down." He let go of her and said, "I must go now. Know this: Valemog is growing more insidious, feeding Paosh Tohon in new ways. And I have something I need to help build, or rebuild perhaps. I'll leave some sign for you from time to time. You'll know it by the color. Maybe we will meet again. Maybe we'll succeed. I hope for both."

"I do too," said Galla, feeling her eyes well up. They bowed their heads, and at that moment, Jana stepped into the alley.

"Um, Captain?" she called.

Coniuratus hid his stone, swept his coat about him, secured his hood, and walked out of the alley the opposite way they had entered, away from Jana. But her eyes were sharp.

"Who was that?" Jana asked her. "Was he...human?"

Galla looked for him, but he had gone.

She sighed and lowered her head. "No," she said. "But I can't tell you more than that. I'm sorry."

Jana's face held as many questions as Galla knew hers had, and more besides.

"Okay," she said finally. "I'm here to tell you two things. First, Ariel and Dag are ready to leave. And second, Rob is...well, he's in a decon chamber."

"What?" exclaimed Galla. "Take me to him."

They walked swiftly through the melee of tawdry activity, and finally found the entrance to the pleasure den Rob had entered. There was a clear tank in the window she had not noticed before. In it hung Rob, motionless, surrounded by spraying liquids.

"Get him out of there!" shouted Galla to the den's owners.

"He must complete his decontamination," intoned the fluttering den keeper. "It seems your companion went a bit overboard."

Jana bent over and guffawed, then drew a breath, and laughed so hard she sank down onto her knees.

Galla's lips twitched, and her throat tickled, but she held her head high and serenely said, "Very well. If you can hasten the process, we need to leave as soon as possible."

Within a few minutes, Ariel and Dagovaby found them, and Dagovaby shook his head at the sight of Rob suspended in his decon chamber. Ariel rolled her eyes.

"Success?" Galla asked.

"Yes," said Ariel. "We have a lot to talk about, though."

A whining sound came from the chamber as Rob was dried, and mercifully most of his body was shielded from view. He was taken from the chamber and placed into a too-large robe. His expression was dazed and he drooled.

"You look like a *monk*!" screamed Jana.

"He doesn't feel like one!" exclaimed Dagovaby. She and Dagovaby laughed until they cried.

Ariel began giggling then.

Galla felt her temper return.

"Okay," she said finally. "Shore leave is over. Let's head back. And Jana, I could use your assistance as a copilot for the time being. Because this guy is toast."

11

COLD

Ariel had recruited two more telepaths, but at a price. They would each get a stone of their own. Fortunately, Galla had given Ariel three of them in preparation. She wondered how they would find other telepaths. Ariel seemed optimistic.

"The Prince did as he said," she said. "So word is getting out. We just have to keep asking. Or they'll come to us."

The sound of retching reached the cockpit. Galla and Jana turned to look at each other and roll their eyes. Jana shook her head.

"Partied too hard," she muttered. "Gotta know when to say when."

"He sounds miserable," said Galla.

"I can take the wheel if you want," said Jana.

"Thank you." Galla rose and left.

She walked down the short hallway to Rob's room and chimed. He only answered by loudly retching again, so she ordered the door open. An acrid smell hit her, and she winced. He was in his small toilet, on his knees, weak and pale. She found a cloth, wet it, and gave it to him. He wiped his face and rinsed his mouth. Then he leaned back against the wall with his eyes closed and his forehead pinched.

"You need fluids and medicine," she told him. "I can't have my ace pilot down for the count."

He moaned.

"I'm sorry," he said thickly. "Mistakes were made."

She helped him up and onto his bed. "So it's my turn to help *you* out, then," she said, smoothing his brow. "We're going to another Device world. I'll take Ariel with me this time."

He nodded in silent misery.

His arms lay at his side, and she put her hand in his. Their fingers linked.

"I hate that you're seeing me like this," he muttered.

"What good would I be if I didn't see you when you're down?" she asked him, and he opened his bloodshot eyes to look at her.

He rubbed his forehead with his free hand and grimaced. "Here comes the headache. Look, before I pass out or something, I wanted to tell you. I saw some refugees there. Not in the pleasure den. But I didn't forget them. And I would guess that, if we saw some there, there must be more throughout the system. I just hope...they're safe. And they're not being taken advantage of."

"I saw some too," said Galla with a sigh. "And I had the same thought."

"I know we don't have a lot to give them, but...maybe you're right," he said, staring at the ceiling. "Maybe we can do *something*."

She gazed at him in disbelief, and looked down at his hand. *He's changing.* She thought about what Coniuratus had said. Rob was fire in her hand, and she wanted his warmth just then.

"Was it worth it?" she asked him in a soft, hushed voice. "Letting loose?"

He pulled on her hand, and she moved closer to him.

"No," he said, "not for...what I did, anyway. But...maybe for this."

"You're such a fool, Rob," she whispered, leaning closer.

"Your fool," he said, and he pressed her hand to his lips and kissed it.

She let him lie back, his face now full of color again, and pulled his blanket up for him. She stroked his head again, and her stone felt warm. She held it to his forehead. He smiled and fell asleep.

Then she dashed to her little room and changed out of her

captain suit. She looked in her mirror, and her cheeks were flushed. She could still feel the sensation of his lips on her hand. *I can't think about him right* now.

She called on her comms, "What are we looking at, Jana?"

"Breathable," she answered. "But frigid."

Galla donned layers and soon entered the cockpit. Ariel arrived behind her.

"Ice world, then?" Galla asked, watching the approach of the pale blue-white-grey world, partially ringed in clouds. The sun of that system reflected off the northern hemisphere's surface.

"Summer holiday, believe it or not," said Jana. "I'll sit this out, for more than one reason. Enjoy." And she shook her head.

The planet stood out from the more obvious part of the system, which was a sort of incomplete Dyson sphere closer to the sun. Jana reviewed the dossier from her Associates' data as well as Aeriod's scant notes. She told them the star's energy had begun to deplete, and many of the civilizations had chosen to abandon the system long ago. Now mostly nomads and miners remained, primarily on the system's other worlds. That was the official description her file revealed, anyway.

Jana scanned the surface and found a thick blue-white glacier with a strange crevasse. It was covered with great arcs and pillars of ice. She brought the *Fithich* a few hundred feet above it, and Galla recognized a circular chasm, lined by ice. She weighed their options. The platform might not reach the edge with this ice, but might be free of it farther down.

"Ariel," she said, "we could maybe rappel and wait for the platform, but that's pretty risky for you. I could take us part of the way in by the sky bike, but the Devices don't take kindly to vehicles."

Ariel looked at her with her brilliant green eyes, the hollows under them grey from fatigue. "I was hoping to fly with you again," she admitted. "I miss it."

Galla stared at her in disbelief. "You miss *my* flying?"

"Not the flying per se," Ariel replied with a short laugh. "Just flying with *you*."

Jana looked sideways at her.

"It's risky either way," cautioned Galla, oblivious to Jana's expression.

"Fly us over to the edge and let's rappel," said Ariel quickly. "Hurry, before I change my mind."

Dagovaby entered with Paul, and Galla watched him look at Ariel. Ariel stepped over to them and hugged and kissed both of them. Dagovaby then glanced at Galla, and she did not need telepathy to understand his concern.

"Mama's still asleep," said Ariel, "so when she wakes up, let her know."

"We'll be back soon," Galla reassured them.

She and Ariel went to the launch bay, suited up securely, and stowed some gear in the seat of the sky bike. They sat, and Ariel leaned against Galla and squeezed her tightly for a second before loosening her grip a bit. Galla powered the bike, signaled Jana, and the bay opened with an upsweep of snow and ice. She dropped the bike through, and Ariel whooped and laughed.

And down they went, looping around the ice overhangs of the crevasse. Galla wondered again how long the Devices had been around. Had there been glaciers at this one when it was first made? She doubted it. She shivered from the thought of the passage of time, and from the cold that crept in despite her shielded suit. She worried about Ariel's body temperature, for while Galla could handle the temperature, Ariel could not withstand the same extremes.

She circled the rim of the Device chasm, noting the enormous icicles encrusting the curving interior wall. There were only a few spots that she felt were safe enough for them to stand, and she did not want Ariel slipping. *I don't want to slip either. But I can apparently float a bit thanks to my stone. I don't know if I can carry a passenger for that, though!*

She set up the gear, screwing anchors into the ice, affixed the ropes, and attached Ariel's harness, and her friend did the same for her. With the wind whirling ice crystals all around them, they lowered themselves slowly over the side. Several feet down, the ice dripped, and then ended. Galla felt her stone warming up, and she could hear something. The platform raced into view and stopped below the ice. The women slid down onto it and unhooked. They sat down just in time for it to fly downward, into the blackness below. The platform then moved around the inside wall of the Device and aligned itself with an entrance. Galla helped Ariel out first.

"Are you ready?" she asked her friend.

"Yes," said Ariel. The women held hands.

The long hallway slowly winked on, as if its lights were too cold to want to bother. The moment they began walking, a deep thrumming sound echoed through the hall.

"Nothing yet," Ariel said. Galla nodded. They made it to the courtyard.

Then everything went blinding white.

Ariel shrieked. Galla clenched her hand tightly.

Galla could see something coming at her out of the white light, like glowing ropes, and she could see pale white branches all around her then, pulsing in all directions, like neurons firing. Then the vision changed, and she felt a crushing sadness, worse than when her beloved Oni-Odi had disappeared. The branches of light became consumed by fire, and within that fire she could see black tendrils snapping and reaching for her. She heard screaming, but not just Ariel's screams. It was a chorus of screams and shrieks and agonized moans that grew and surrounded her. Hundreds, thousands, she could not guess how many.

Paosh Tohon, she managed to think. Her stone felt as if it torched her skin.

And then it was over.

She and Ariel knelt on the smooth metallic floor of the courtyard, which shone with benign silver light, revealing the familiar spoke of doorways all around them. The pair still held hands. Ariel panted, fogging up her helmet.

Galla hugged her. "Are you okay?"

"I—I don't know," she said. "I saw something. I think it was Paosh Tohon. Black and twisting."

"Yes!" exclaimed Galla. "I saw it too. That's what it looks like, to me. What else?"

"I felt pain," gasped Ariel, her eyes round with fear. "Pain like nothing I've experienced before. And...and I felt sadness." And she started shaking. "Can we leave now?"

"Yes," said Galla firmly. She pulled open her belt pouch and brought forth the small knob of diamethyst, and in the cold air its heat steamed. She set it on the ground. The lights began to fade.

As they began walking back toward the platform, Ariel stopped her.

"I'm afraid," she said, and Galla could see she was still trembling.

"I won't let it take you," Galla told her emphatically.

"I know you won't," said Ariel. "Can you protect them too? My children."

Galla felt her face go pale. She held her hand against Ariel's shoulder.

"Of course!" she said, stunned. "Ariel, please don't worry about this."

Ariel closed her eyes.

"Thank you," she said, and then she stilled her shaking, but she was jumpy as they walked back. "Something still doesn't feel right. I feel sick."

"We're almost to the platform," Galla soothed.

The second they reached the platform, Ariel began sobbing. Not knowing what else to do, Galla put her arm around Ariel and pulled her down to sit, and held her. The platform began rising upward toward the bright white sky above, and Ariel wailed.

"Oh no! No! No!" she cried.

Their comms went off at the same time.

It was Dagovaby.

"Thank God you're in range," he said, his voice strained. "Something has happened."

Galla's entire body felt plunged into the ice itself.

"Mama!" screamed Ariel.

12

A DECISION

Dagovaby met them in the launch bay and rushed to Ariel. His face was drawn and full of sorrow.

"I can't read her! I can't read her!" she wailed, sinking to the floor, but Dagovaby lifted her up and looped his strong arms around her.

"Meredith is in a coma," he said to Galla.

Galla gasped. She threw off her helmet and stripped off her protective gear and helped Ariel out of hers. She and Dagovaby led Ariel out of the bay. As soon as they entered the main floor, they heard high-pitched wails from Paul. Ariel let out a cry and tore away at a full run. Galla and Dagovaby bounded after her.

Jana was rocking Paul in her arms, and he was fighting her. Her eyes were red.

"He hasn't stopped crying; I can't do anything to settle him. I'm so sorry, Ariel," said Jana quickly. Ariel scooped him up and pressed Jana's shoulder gratefully. Paul's cries faded to little whimpers.

Taking a deep breath, Ariel held Paul's cheek to hers and walked toward her mother's room. Rob and Beetle stood there. Rob looked haggard but alert, and somehow much older.

Ariel rushed into the room. Meredith lay in her bed, pale and still, as if asleep. Galla entered, and knelt next to Ariel.

"What happened?" she demanded, looking up at Rob.

Rob said, "Dagovaby felt something different, and then the ship picked up her health readings and alerted the rest of us just as he walked in to check on her."

Ariel stroked her mother's grey bangs away from her forehead. She did not speak. Little Paul reached over and grabbed Meredith's shoulder, and whined, "Nana!"

His sweet voice overwhelmed Jana, and she clapped her hand over her mouth and stood in the hall in tears.

Galla felt as if she had been stabbed. "When did this happen?" she asked.

"Over an hour ago," answered Dagovaby. "You've been gone about three hours."

"Oh God," whispered Ariel. "We were out of range down there... or there was interference. I couldn't have picked up on her thoughts until we were leaving."

"And you started feeling strange," murmured Galla.

She then asked, "What have you done for her?"

Jana reentered the room, composed, and answered, "I ran scans. Her brain activity is"—she looked sorrowfully at Ariel—"it's almost nil."

Ariel now lay on the bed next to her mother, her arms draped across her. Dagovaby held Paul and they leaned over Ariel.

This is unbearable. With tears in her eyes, Galla stood. "We need to get her help immediately. Set a course for Ika Nui. We'll take her to Mandira."

13

STATIC

Galla sat with her hands over her face, leaned against the console in the cockpit. Rob came in with two mugs of tea, and she gladly took one. He looked somber and still ill, but with better color to his cheeks. His jaw muscles tensed.

"You know what I'm about to do," she said to him in an even voice. "It's time."

"I know," Rob said simply. They reached across in their seats and held hands.

She spoke in a commanding voice, "Aeriod!"

She waited.

Nothing.

Several minutes passed.

She turned to stare at Rob. His face grew red.

"Aeriod!" she said again. "Please respond!"

The screen flickered and warped. Static came and went. She could see a pale white head in snatches of images, and she exhaled in relief. But that soon became worry.

"I can't get a fix," said Rob, stunned.

"How?" she cried. "We're in his ship!"

"I don't know!"

"Dammit!" said Galla. "Aeriod, we need you! If you can hear us at all, we have a medical emergency. It's Meredith! We're going to Mandira. Please respond!"

But the image flickered again and went out.

"What the fuck!" shouted Rob. "The one time we need this asshole—" but he stopped when he saw Galla's worried face.

"Something's very wrong," she said.

She stood and paced back and forth behind Rob's chair.

"Two more hours to Ika Nui," he told her. "I'll contact them on final approach."

"Good call," she answered. "We don't need to risk anyone picking up our transmissions."

It was the longest two hours anyone on the ship had ever experienced. And they all dreaded its finally coming to an end.

14

INTRODUCTIONS

Galla-Deia squinted up at the bright sky and the small cumulus clouds expanding in the heat. There was no sign of a shuttle. Relieved, she gathered up the last huge cycad frond and laid it carefully on a stack of them heaped shoulder-high. A rustling sound came from behind the pile, so she stepped over to look.

A man had left the underbrush and began tying the great pile into a tight bundle. He was closely shaven, with tattoos on his light umber face, neck, and arms, which shone from sweat. At first he did not see Galla. So she watched, fascinated, as he worked efficiently, his muscles taut from pulling ropes around the frond bundle.

Finally she called out, "Thank you!"

The man looked up in surprise and then broke into a bright smile.

"Hello! Didn't see you there!" he called, and he wiped his hands on his leaf-stained paints and stepped forward. He shook her hand with a strong grip. "You must be Captain Galla-Deia," he said.

"I am," she answered.

The man bowed his head.

"The name's Guru Pahue," he told her. "Finally get to meet you! It's an honor."

She dipped her head. "Call me Galla."

"Call me Guru," he said cheerfully. "Do you think this will be enough? Should we dry some?"

She eyed the now compact bundle.

"I wish I knew," she sighed. "Beetle is offworld. So I'll have to hope for the best."

Guru laughed. "I might once have said this is the craziest thing I've ever done, wrapping up treats for a giant bug. But Ika Nui is wilder than that!"

His dark eyes swept along the turquoise horizon, as if searching for something.

Galla reached for the pile, but Guru swept up the entire thing and carried it on his head along the beach. She smirked and walked by his side. Off to their left, white sand blended into pale blue water, which stretched for some distance before dropping off the continental shelf of that land. There the deep sea beckoned in cobalt blue. It all looked so tranquil to her, but she felt volatile inside.

She had heard of Guru from Ariel. He seemed interesting, so Galla wondered why Ariel had not spoken of him much. She watched him slip back into the bush, and she followed him on a well-worn path.

"Too hot in the sun," he called. "And no rain for a few hours. So it goes."

The coastline receded behind them, and eventually they padded on the sandy path to a clearing. A small hut stood there, and she smelled something strong but pleasant coming from it. Guru set the brush pile down and walked up to the hut. An elderly man stood there, watching her closely. He had white hair, a white mustache, and reddish-brown skin, and he held a mug in his hand.

"Is that who I think it is?" he bellowed. Galla raised her eyebrows, looked behind her, and looked back again at the older man.

Guru grinned. "Captain Galla-Deia—Galla—this is Troy Pinedo, coffee connoisseur."

Troy bounded out from behind his stand and bowed low before Galla. He took her small hands in his weathered old paws and shook them heartily.

"Well, I'll be damned! *You're* the lady with the stone!"

Galla laughed. "I do have a stone," she replied, and she pulled from her shirt her large purple crystal. Troy whistled and Guru leaned in for a closer look.

"I don't remember that one!" exclaimed Troy. "Just a little tiny one, about so big," and he pinched his thumb and forefinger to reflect the size.

"That was Aeriod's," Galla said, very evenly.

Still, Guru searched her eyes, which looked amber in the bright sun.

"Was," he murmured.

Troy puckered up his mouth and whistled again.

"Well, we can keep that story for some other time," he said. "How about a cup of coffee? I know it's as hot as Satan's butt pimples here, but I've got this brew you just *have* to try."

Galla snickered despite her troubled mental state. Troy served her a cup of the strong brew, and she took one sip and swallowed the acrid liquid dutifully.

"Try this in it," Guru whispered, handing her a short, cream-colored stem. She took the stem and stirred her drink. She sipped again and nodded to him in gratitude.

"Thank you!" she chirped to Troy. "It's very...bracing!"

Troy beamed at her. "You should try it with Guru's rum!"

Guru's mouth stretched to one side. "At this hour?" he answered lightly. Troy shrugged. "Now, Galla, what do you think? Should we give Beetle some other kinds of food? Troy saved his coffee grounds and we've made them into logs. I also have some canes I use to make my rum with."

Galla answered, "Beetle will probably just be glad to have something different from what the ship can produce. I think we all will be!"

Guru nodded and gathered up some of the coffee logs. He made a neat stack of them, then walked over to cut off some large, reed-like plants. He laid those on top of the frond bundle and tied them up as well.

"Beetle will like these, I think," she said, appraising the pile.

Troy said softly, "I sure wish Merry was down here sharing a cup with us. She was always more into tea, though."

Guru turned to Galla. "Any word?"

She breathed in deeply. The sea air and the smell of vegetation and coffee comingled, and she felt disoriented by it all. She looked up at the sky again.

"I don't know if anything's changed," she admitted. "Ella Varis says she is very weak."

Guru followed her gaze. Above the clouds, Mandira Research Station orbited the planet like a great conch shell. On board, Ariel, Dagovaby, and Paul waited to see how Meredith was responding to treatment for her coma. Coming to Ika Nui was a great risk, but Galla was determined they give Meredith a place where she could rest comfortably, and hopefully heal.

"I'll see what I can do," Guru said very quietly to her. "I'm a botanist. I'll send up some things I've been working on."

Galla searched his face with sad yet hopeful eyes. "Anything you can do, we would all appreciate."

"Why did you come down here, alone?" Guru asked.

She looked down and sighed.

"I needed to be away from the ship. Just for a little bit. Jana was going to come down, but I think she's engrossed in getting some of Mandira's tech." Galla managed a smile. "She also wanted to see her girlfriend." Jana was, as ever, resourceful, no matter the situation.

"What about Rob? What's he up to?" asked Guru. "I'm surprised he's not down here too. At least for my rum!"

Galla dug her toes into patterns on the sand. She shrugged.

"Hmm," said Guru. "Well, I'll send a bottle or two up when the shuttle comes back." He watched her face as she fought her emotional turmoil. *There is a strangeness to her, but a depth*, he thought. *I like her.* He knew she wasn't human, but living on an alien world as he had for the past few years, he knew also that he had an affinity for those who were out of the ordinary. Like Forster and Ariel.

He smirked over the memory of Forster, or "Thinking Man," as he liked to call him in the bar on Mandira. Galla was quite different from Forster, but Guru guessed, watching her copper eyes shine in the bright sunlight, that she could brood as well as his old friend had.

It would be easy to fall for someone with such an open nature, he mused. He was an observant man, so he quickly surmised from her emotive face that she was a complicated woman, full of loves and hurts and responsibilities that weighed upon her. He almost had to look away from her, for her beauty astounded him. She was slender yet curvy, and her magnificent, multi-hued hair twisted and drifted uncertainly right now. What would it be like to hold such a creature, and for her to look at him with loving eyes? He entertained the idea for a few seconds, and then simply shut his mind to it. He wanted to know Galla, but in many ways he knew he was better suited to being alone. Maybe he could help her, though. She looked as though she needed a friend.

Galla blushed under the man's unflinching gaze. She also felt she should look away from him, and given her ambivalence about Rob and her lingering thoughts of Aeriod, she did not dare contemplate anything with someone else. She felt as though Guru knew too much about everyone. Including her. It unnerved her. But also, she felt an unavoidable topic would soon come up, and she dreaded it. Trent Korba had lived on Mandira, and later Ika Nui. His wife had perished in the wild on the planet. And under Galla's watch, on Beetle's world, Trent had died as well.

"Try this," Guru said, and he handed her a small cup.

She sniffed its contents, and while it burned her nostrils, its underlying notes were sweet and rich. She took a sip and felt the liquid race down her throat with fire in its wake.

"That's my aged rum," he explained.

Galla's shoulders relaxed. It did not have the same effect on her as Stroffy liqueur, for which she was glad. But she now felt relaxed enough that she could talk.

"I'm sorry," she managed to say. "Trent was our friend, and I let him down."

Guru glanced at her.

"I asked Rob what happened. I knew Trent, but not as well as I knew his wife, Phoebe," he remarked. "I felt responsible for *her* death. It was my expedition."

"That was just a horrible accident."

"Yes, and Trent's was an outright attack," replied Guru. "Neither of us expected these things. But here we are."

They sat in silence under the shade of the tropical trees, and Guru poured more rum for Galla and some for himself. Troy was whistling and singing, alternately. Finally, Guru set down his empty cup.

"How long do you think the defenses will hold here?" he asked quietly, so Troy could not hear him.

She shuddered. "I don't know," she answered. "I'm not sure how strong they still are."

"Aeriod runs a tight ship, so to speak," Guru mused. "But obviously he has some lapses in judgment. So I'm just going to assume that, sooner or later, the fight will come to us."

"What will you do?" Galla asked, her innards feeling light from the rum.

Still, a stab of concern made its way through her, thinking of her crew. Sooner or later she knew she would have to leave and continue her task. And Meredith would have to stay behind. Galla was not ready for this. She felt her ship was the safest place to be. At least they could get away, with the *Fithich*. The idea of staying on any planet too long disturbed her.

"We have some older ships, a few down here, some up at Mandira," said Guru. "Aeriod retrofitted them, and there are a few of his as well. As for weapons, I don't know what we could use against Paosh Tohon."

Galla lifted her stone. This one purple gem represented her only defense against the crawling nightmare that lurked in deep space. At that moment, her Task of stopping the dual disasters of the Event and

Paosh Tohon seemed so far out of reach. And yet the jewel in her hand held the key. She needed to harness it soon. She was Questri. Instead of waiting for the fight to come to her, at some point she had to take it to the monster in the void.

Their comms went off. Galla looked at Guru.

The message said simply, "Come back now."

15

EVENTIDE

G alla walked quickly down the corridors of Mandira Station with Guru beside her. Even in the unsettling panic of the moment, she thought, *These floors feel very strange.*

She was not sure what to think; she just felt the urge to *move*.

Get to Ariel. Get to Ariel. That's all that matters.

And finally she sprinted ahead of Guru, who followed with long steps.

She found the hall to the medical facilities on Mid Deck and saw a small cluster of people outside. There was a bright ginger head visible among them.

"Rob!" she called, and it felt as if her voice had been muffled, and that he was too far away from her.

He turned and walked slowly toward her, his arms outstretched, his brilliant blue eyes reddened and sunken and full of nothing she wanted to know just then. She stopped in the hall, stock still, and refused to budge.

If I don't move, neither will time. Please, Universe.

So he came to her, and he put his arms around her.

"She's gone," he said into her ear.

Galla felt as if everything had tilted and she was falling. She would land on her side and look up, and it would only be her that was wrong. She had heard wrong. That was all.

But she did not fall. Guru caught up with them, and she looked at him and Rob.

"Where is Aeriod?" she asked.

The two men blinked at her.

"He's not here, Galla," Rob said slowly.

"Why? Why isn't he here?" Her voice came in chops.

Rob shook his head.

Galla wheeled around, dazed, and held onto the wall and stared at the people outside the med bay. She felt her way forward and thought, absurdly, *I really hate these soft floors.*

She had made it to the entrance, and it was all strange; she knew no one there, and felt like no one else there either. *Because I'm not human. I'm other to them. They can tell. I can tell.*

But she ignored them and entered anyway. A pale turquoise medic bot cruised up to her, and she stared up and down at it. *A bot! That's better*, was all she could register.

"Captain Deia," it intoned, "right this way."

I am following a bot again. My lot in life.

The bot led her to a dim hallway, soothing in light but in no other way that she could tell. And into a pleasant room, with soft, rushing water sounds, the bot guided her.

"Gow-wah!" called a little soft voice.

It was Paul.

She watched the dark-haired toddler stumble over to her and seize her by her legs. And she looked down into the same green eyes as his mother's, and her mother's. And Galla wept.

And Ariel rose from her mother's side and locked eyes with Galla. She began crying again as well.

Then they were all together, Ariel and Paul and Dagovaby and Galla, looking down at Meredith's face, her eyelids closed, her color gone. Galla took a gentle hold of her hand, and it felt cold and hard. *Like a bot's*, she thought dully. *I lost the only person who was ever a father to me, in Oni-Odi. And now I've lost a mother too.*

Ariel looped an arm around Galla and leaned her head on her shoulder. Galla smoothed her dark hair and put her arm around her as well. She could feel Ariel's bump, which had grown rapidly, just as when she had been pregnant with Paul.

The baby will never know Meredith, she realized suddenly. She let out a small cry.

It seemed years that they stood there, and it was the strangest moment Galla had yet experienced, of wanting to leave and wanting to stay and wanting to reverse time. She felt so completely powerless. *I can take away pain, but not this kind of pain.*

16

BOTTOM DECK

She turned away at last and saw the kind face of Ella Varis, a black woman in her sixties. Her eyes looked hollow from crying as well. Galla understood then that Meredith's life had touched many people. Mandira had been her home for decades. And it had also been Aeriod's.

She asked Ella quietly, "Did you hear nothing from Aeriod?"

Ella shook her head. "We tried to contact him on every channel. There's a lot of interference out there, I understand."

"Yes," said Galla. "It's due to the Event. We saw him briefly. Why didn't he make it in time?"

Ella looked at her with a face full of sympathy.

"Captain Deia—"

"Please, call me Galla," she insisted.

"Galla," said Ella, "I'm not sure there's anything he could have done. She was comatose. And upon sampling her tissue, we found she was undergoing a rapidly degenerative disease. It must have begun some time ago, and then cascaded at the end."

Galla felt nauseated. "She...she had tremors, and she was less energetic."

"She may have hidden the severity of it from you," said Ella sadly. "Knowing her, I can imagine that."

"Was there no cure?" asked Galla, searching for anything, any line of logic, anything that made sense.

"No," said Ella. "This is a recent disease, one that appears in only some carriers of the telepath gene. It manifests in carriers, and not in telepaths. It's fairly rare. Caught earlier, the effects might have been mitigated, but then again there were no guarantees of that either."

Galla dipped her head. "Thank you for everything, Ella."

"I'm so sorry we had to meet like this," Ella said with a shaky sigh. "I'll let you know about funeral arrangements."

Galla nodded, unable to speak. She walked out of the room, and there stood Rob waiting for her. Behind him, a small crowd had gathered, including Troy, who was inconsolable, with Guru's arm around his shoulders, and two elderly gentlemen whose faces were wet from tears.

Rob took her hand and introduced her.

"Galla, this is Pop, and this is Burgess," he said. She shook their hands. "And Troy."

"I've met Troy," said Galla. She reached out and held her hand to Troy's face, and he patted it affectionately, sniffing and stuttering.

"Meredith was the best of us. Shit!" said Pop.

Burgess nodded, his sleepy eyes nearly swollen shut from tears.

"Yes," murmured Galla, head bowed. "The very best."

Rob led her on, and the hallway seemed too bright. They stopped at a lift.

"Where are you taking me?" she asked him suddenly.

"I'm taking you home," he said, and the lift opened. When it closed, they turned to each other, embraced, and cried again. Then they held hands as the lift swiftly descended.

"Bottom Deck," chimed the elevator. The door slid open.

This lowermost section of Mandira extended to a point. All through its length, Bottom Deck was pocked with small to medium docking bays. The station's power and gyre were managed there as well. Everywhere she looked, Galla could see industrial equipment and the inner guts of the station: pipes and control panels snaked along ceilings and walls. It reminded her of a rudimentary bowel of Demetraan, where she had spent her early life. There were young people here and there, all roughly Rob's age, in their early to mid twenties. And trundling along or climbing about, several bots whirred and whizzed.

For a moment, she felt a sense of comfort.

Some of the workers saw Rob then and converged on him, patting his back and shaking his hand.

"Not too good for us after all, eh?" roared one of them.

Rob smiled, but did not laugh. He said, "I'd like you to meet someone." The group all made cooing sounds, and then he led Galla forward.

"This is Galla-Deia, ship's captain, and keeper of the stone."

They all stared at her in silence, and then focused on the large diamethyst around her neck. Her skin crawled. She felt as though she were being examined. *Not everyone here wanted to move across the galaxy*, she thought, and she shivered, remembering what had happened to Officer Derry.

"Hello!" she said, as cheerfully as she could manage.

Rob glared at them until they each came forward to shake her hand. Some genuinely wanted to meet her, but she could tell Rob mirrored her feelings. She would not be universally loved. But she knew that.

The group all chatted with Rob, and their voices rose and fell, talking about Meredith, who some of them knew a little. They also begged Rob to tell them about his adventures. He started telling them about the planets he had been to, and the species he had seen, and Galla could see he was energetic and excited, and momentarily distracted from grief.

So she slipped away.

She wandered around Bottom Deck, and found an alcove with charging and cleaning stations for bots. She looked up at the various tubes and pipes twisting around the ceiling above her. She sighed.

This was where Rob had spent the past few years. She wondered how much he missed it.

She heard little beeps, and turned around to see an assortment of bots all in an arc surrounding her. Her lips curled into a smile.

"Hi there!" she said to them all.

"Hi there!" said a few of them back.

Galla laughed in delight, and sat down on the floor in front of them. They moved in close to her, and were joined by other bots and even drones.

"Tell me your names or numbers, and what you do," she said to them.

And each bot spoke to her in turn, or made other indications if they were not vocal. She understood them all. It reminded her so much of Demetraan that she felt very at home all of a sudden.

"I grew up in a city of bots," she told them breathlessly. "It was"— she caught herself—"is called Demetraan. And it is led by the android Oni-Odi, who has been around for millions of years."

Galla looked at the scuffed floor in front of her and said, "I can draw it for you." She used the fire blade on her wrist to sketch a picture of Demetraan into the floor itself. "Don't worry, we can smooth it when I'm finished."

She completed her sketch, and the bots all rotated around it to get different views. She felt very tired then, and her sadness returned. The bots moved next to her, and they felt warm. She curled up on the floor among them and promptly fell to sleep.

Rob found her there and stood still to watch her, surrounded by the little bots. He could see the sketch she had made. His presence startled the bots, and they all screeched or blipped or peeped, and they fled promptly. He chuckled. He leaned over Galla, who lay on her side, and could see the shimmer of pale violet crystals from tears on her cheeks. He wiped them off.

"Galla," he said, and she sat up sharply.

"The floors are soft everywhere but here," she groaned, rubbing her side.

"Right?" he said with a small laugh.

Disoriented, she looked around. Then it all came crashing into her again. Meredith was gone.

Rob sighed and pulled her to her feet.

"Come with me," he said. "I'll show you my old quarters, and something else."

She lifted one eyebrow at him.

His eyes sparkled, and he took her hand. He led her to a hallway lined with doors on one side; the other side faced space, and had no windows. He stopped at one of the doors and put his hand up to it, and it opened. The lights came on.

"Welcome, Rob," said a soothing voice from his room intercom.

He led Galla in, and held out his arms and turned around.

"A humble little shithole," he announced with a grin. "But it's *my* shithole."

Galla turned to look at it and nodded.

"The Prince really did mimic it well, didn't he?" she said, impressed. "And anyway, it's a fine room. I like it. Except for the soft floors."

"Can't have everything," said Rob. He examined the objects on his shelves, picking some up and putting them back. "It's so weird to be here after all this time. I thought I would miss it more. But now that I'm back, I don't know..."

She understood. When she had returned after decades on Bitikk to Aeriod's floating palace, she had felt like a stranger. Yet for a little while, Rikiloi had been her home. Rob turned to her, and they stood apart but looked at each other.

Galla asked in a cracked voice, "So...what was the 'something else' you wanted to show me?"

She noticed she was breathing more quickly, so she slowed her breath.

Rob laughed. "It's not here," he said.

"Oh," she said, and she exhaled.

He stepped over to her, took hold of her hand again, and led her back out of his room. "This way," he said in a whisper.

He led her farther down the hall, toward an exit. This led into a storage facility that meandered around. It was dim, but he knew where to go, and he took her to a little flight of stairs. She followed him up it, and they finally stopped at a landing. There was a ladder that went up to a hole in the ceiling above. He started climbing, and motioned for her to climb as well.

At last they stopped. He pulled her down to crawl under some low-hanging pipes, and there, incredibly, was a little window.

"Whoever built this place had a sense of humor," said Rob, "because there's no need for this little window. Or hell, even this little room. But look!"

They sat in front of the window next to each other on the floor, and Galla looked out. There shone Ika Nui, the planet below, beautiful and blue and green and white. She gasped. She then felt her tears return. *What had Meredith thought, when she first saw this world? I wish I could've asked, and now I never can.*

"I thought you'd like it," Rob said softly, and she looked to see tears in his eyes as well, spilling onto his cheeks. "I'm just...I'm just so glad you're here."

His fingers crisscrossed with hers.

She felt a thrill then, and a shiver of fear, and a simmering sensation in her body. He was very close to her, and she could feel his body heat. And the coldness and sadness in her from the terrible day thawed just a little, and she put her arms around him, and they kissed.

17

DUNNAGE

alla left Rob to his friends and his room, and rode up the lift to Mid Deck. As she stepped off the lift, a message from Jana chimed on her wrist.

"He's here," was all that it said, but it made Galla go cold all over.

She found Aeriod slumped onto the floor of the Dome Car observatory, in the dark, with Ika Nui's night side now facing the station. She stood absolutely still, clutching her throat, thinking for a fleeting moment he might be dead. But she breathed through that thought, knowing better, and entered the room. She stepped quietly across the floor and approached him. He lay on his side, curled into a ball, his cape wrapped around him and his hair limp and puddled on the floor.

She sat on her knees and looked at Aeriod, at his sharp face, his silver eyes dull grey, staring out at the planet. Turmoil swirled in her. She wanted to comfort him but feared his response. And, she admitted to herself, she feared her reaction to anything he did. Hesitantly, she reached out her hand and touched his shoulder.

His arms shot out and seized her around the waist, and she fell back and caught herself. He laid his head in her lap. She found herself stroking his long, straight white hair away from his pointed ears, and he turned to look up at her.

"I used to tell her about you," he said, and his eyes gleamed silver then. Galla looked away from him, and she swallowed.

"She told me," murmured Galla.

"She was the only person I could really talk to here," Aeriod told her. "And I couldn't talk about—about the damned mission," he said, and his voice broke. "I should have. I should have got Ariel sooner, I should have—"

"Stop," said Galla firmly. "Stop. You can't undo what happened."

"I'll never forgive myself," said Aeriod bitterly.

Galla looked at him with solemn eyes.

"She forgave you," she said to him. His eyes widened and he blinked.

"What?" he asked, and he rose to sit next to Galla, and took her hands in his.

Galla teared up. "We spoke. Before she—before she—she went into the coma," she choked out. "She said that—she said that she couldn't hold onto her anger," she said as she shook the tears off her face, "but that she forgave you. Aeriod, I am sorry."

Aeriod bowed his head. He looked haggard. Galla looked down at his long, pale fingers wrapped around her small hands. She remembered her first night on Rikiloi, when she had shivered in fear and excitement and cold, and he had blown into her hands to make her warm. She had been afraid of him then, and attracted to him at the same time. The smoky-spicy scent of incense on his cape was faint, and she recalled those days with him long ago. Now she only felt sadness. For Meredith, for him, for what was gone and could never be rekindled.

"Ariel wouldn't even look at me," he told her.

"She's distraught," said Galla quietly. *She's enraged too, I am sure. But he doesn't need to know that.* "She needs time."

"Galla," said Aeriod softly, "I know she needs time to grieve, but will she be able to continue, do you think?"

She stiffened. "She will when she is ready," Galla said curtly.

"What if she's never ready?" asked Aeriod.

She furrowed her brow at him. "She's Ariel. She'll be ready."

I hope.

"They're more vulnerable than you think," Aeriod said. "I fear this will weaken her, and she will not be able to help you."

"She isn't alone," Galla said. "And I believe in her. They're stronger than *you* think."

Aeriod sighed. "I hope you're right. I'm late because I was given chase getting to a junction. How they found me, I don't know. Valemog *trash*. I had to slip through another junction to get away so they wouldn't track me here. Then the interference from the Event was so terrible, I couldn't communicate properly. Things are falling apart out there. I've been on the front lines of things I hoped I would never see in all my long life. And it's happening so quickly...It won't hold much longer, no matter what the Associates do."

"We'll hold the line and do what needs to be done," said Galla, and she clung to that belief. But she was troubled, and she could tell he knew it. "Do we have any advantage?"

"As long as you're here, there's an advantage," Aeriod replied, his platinum eyes earnest.

"Aeriod, I don't—" Galla began.

Aeriod smiled sadly. "No, I know," he said in a quiet voice. "But what I mean is, when you trained with Bitikk—"

Galla made a disgusted sound.

He nodded. "I'm sorry," he said. "But when you were there, you did not have your diamethysts."

Galla raised an eyebrow. "Good thing," she said, "but I could maybe have used some training with them."

"I'm not sure they would have known what to do with them," Aeriod remarked. "But at least Paosh Tohon will not gain any of that knowledge. And I think that's what Oni-Odi had in mind."

Galla started. "What do you mean? You've not—"

"No, dearest," Aeriod interrupted her, looking deeply into her copper eyes. "I would have told you. Surely you know that?"

Galla looked away.

He went on, "I just mean that it makes sense, in retrospect, that Oni-Odi only gave me a code. No instructions, no history...only the code. He knew that I would give the geode to you. He was always looking out for you."

Galla fought back tears. Her missing Meredith was so raw, yet always she grieved the disappearance of Oni-Odi too. She did not know how to cope with this kind of pain.

Aeriod watched her. She sighed and said, "Paosh Tohon knows I have a crystal, and obviously knows about yours as well. They don't know my full capability with the diamethysts, or how many I have. Since the beings on Bitikk didn't know they existed while I trained with them, that information won't be hacked from them, should Paosh Tohon or Valemog attempt such a thing."

"That would be quite something, wouldn't it?" he speculated.

Something made a faint, metallic tinkling sound, like a little chime. Galla caught sight of a sparkling little shape that had fallen out of Aeriod's sleeve: one of his flat, silver recording diamonds, perhaps an inch long. She knew he used these to record conversations with others, usually by placing them directly on an individual's body, which would absorb the diamond into the skin until its work was complete. She remembered considering whether Prince Hazkinaut could be tracked with such a thing. For a fleeting second, she wondered if Aeriod had ever applied one of the diamonds without someone's consent. He swiftly scooped up the flat little diamond shape from the floor and tucked it back up his sleeve.

"What was that for?" Galla asked, her brow creased.

"Oh, it's insurance," Aeriod responded lightly, with a smirk. "You never know when you'll need one of these!"

She tilted her head, and her vibrant hair drifted away from him.

Ever mercurial, she thought. *I do not know that I can ever trust him again.*

Galla sighed. "What will you do now?"

"I have much to do," said Aeriod. They looked at each other, fingers entwined.

"Do you love him?" he asked suddenly.

Galla threw her head up, and her hair twisted upward and outward. She blushed.

"Why are you asking me this?" she demanded.

Aeriod reached for one of her locks and wounded it around his finger, as he might have done long ago.

"You see what it means to lose one of them that you love," he told her.

Galla stood quickly, and Aeriod joined her. Her cheeks burned.

"It's none of your concern who I love," she hissed.

"I don't want you to hurt for so long," Aeriod protested. "You're a passionate, caring person, and I fear—"

"Aeriod," Galla told him, "I've heard enough. I do think it is a good idea for you to leave."

"Wait. Tell me this: why do you care about all of them so much?" he asked her.

She looked at him quizzically. "I'm their Representative," she said instantly. "This is my Task."

Aeriod took hold of her chin. "But why do you *care*?"

Galla lifted an eyebrow. "There's no why about it. I care. I love them."

Aeriod blinked. "You might not feel that way if you met the rest of them, out there."

Galla rolled her eyes. "Well, I've *not* met them all, and I don't suppose I ever will, though I wouldn't mind the chance."

"You've got other things to focus on, and certainly don't need their species as a distraction," said Aeriod with disdain.

"Why do *you* care about them, then?" she asked him suddenly.

He stared at her, and looked her up and down. "Because of you," he answered.

Galla swallowed, with scarlet cheeks and crossed arms. "Please leave," she said curtly. She held her breath so that she would not smell any more of his smoky-spicy incense scent, lest it tempt her all over again.

Aeriod sighed heavily, his brow creased, his mouth pulled down.

"Very well, Galla-Deia. You can still reach me if you need to."

And he stepped back, bowed, and walked in long strides away from her, as she stood in the darkness. Mandira's orbit shifted to reveal a thin sliver of the day side of Ika Nui, and the arc of reflected sunlight burst into the Dome Car. *The first day without Meredith in it,* she thought.

18

ENMITY

A eriod slipped away quickly and quietly through the halls of Mid Deck. He dodged his old quarters and the old hallway where he, Meredith, Forster, and their coworkers had spent so much time. He simply did not need to see that area again. He slid along to the bar, peeked in, saw no one he knew, and kept going. He called a lift and swept into it before anyone could see him. He arrived at Bottom Deck and looked around the bay to where his ship was perched. The sleek *Fithich* sat across from it, and he found what he was looking for: the bright ginger hair of its pilot shone in the floodlights of the bay.

Rob stood with his eyes closed and his arms crossed, wearing a dark blue T-shirt and black pants with several pockets, his back to the open door of the ship.

"Hello," said Aeriod.

Rob stood up straight, his arms shot to his sides, and his fingers curled into fists.

"Hello," Rob returned, his voice brusque, his blue eyes hard. "Leaving so soon?"

"Duty calls," said Aeriod in an icy tone. "Might I have a word before we part ways again? I know you're devastated I'm leaving. So let's have a little chat."

"Why?" asked Rob coldly.

"It's time we talked about your dear captain," said Aeriod in a hiss.

"I'm not talking to you about Galla," retorted Rob. "Nice try, Space Mage Fuckface."

Aeriod's mouth curled into a grin.

"You've come a long way, then, I see," he said almost out of hearing range. He stepped toward Rob slowly, arms out and his palms up. His black cape swayed as he approached. "I mean no ill will. I'm glad to see you've got some sense of respect for her now, at least."

"Of course I respect her!" Rob snapped. "She's my captain."

"Is that all she is?" Aeriod asked, his eyes glinting.

Rob rolled his eyes. "Really? Mind your goddamn business."

"Touchy!" exclaimed Aeriod. "So you do have feelings for her. But I wonder, Rob Idin, if you understand what it would mean if you entered a relationship with Galla."

"Why don't you let us figure that out?" spat Rob. He dug his fingernails into his palms. "Go on back to your ship. You're not needed here."

Aeriod held up a hand. "I can see you're defensive. But I want you to listen to me. Not for my sake, but for yours and for hers."

Rob shifted on his feet, uncertain, his eyes never leaving Aeriod's face. His own face and ears glowed red.

"Galla is ageless," Aeriod told him. "That does not mean she cannot be destroyed, but she can never age. But you, being human, obviously will."

"No kidding," snarled Rob.

"She will watch you age and crumple and eventually die," Aeriod continued, nonchalantly. "And then she will live on, grieving you for a time, but she will persevere."

"That's what I would want," said Rob with a shrug. "I don't see the problem."

"So you don't mind becoming an old man while she remains young?" asked Aeriod, unblinking. "You'll be nothing to her."

"I don't believe that," said Rob frankly. "Galla's not like that."

"Ah, well. If you're quite certain," said Aeriod silkily, "then may I offer you congratulations?"

And he stepped forward and held out his hand to shake Rob's. Rob did not take it. So Aeriod moved closer, towered over him, and gripped the young man's forearm in his hand. He pulled Rob forward to whisper in his ear.

"You're better off not getting involved," Aeriod said. "She's a person of fire, not warmth, and she will never need you."

Rob shoved Aeriod with all his might, so that the mage skipped a bit where he stood.

"You're wrong about her," Rob declared. He swallowed and went for it: "She's the most loving person I've ever met. Unlike you. It's no wonder she doesn't want to be with you anymore. Go back to your high tower. Alone."

Aeriod shook back his mane of pale hair and laughed. He made a great, showy bow to Rob, and swept around, his cape whirling after, and strode to his ship. Rob stared at him with loathing and gasped with relief when he left.

19

THE HEALER

Dagovaby watched Ariel put Paul in a little bed next to theirs, which Ella Varis had ordered set up for them. Five days had passed, and Meredith's funeral had come and gone. In that time Ariel's shimmering green eyes had gone dull and flat, and almost grey. He could feel her freezing up, and shutting him out mentally and physically. She ate only because he insisted that she did, and she would chew her food methodically. Her interaction with Paul was muted as well, and that was when Dagovaby grew more concerned. The only time she seemed to return to her old self was whenever Galla appeared.

And then he watched his wife, fascinated.

Whereas everyone else on the station broadcast their thoughts casually, Galla did not. She was the only quiet person, mentally. He suspected she was much more turbulent than she seemed, given her fiery nature, but he could not sense her, and Ariel could not read her. She was a living pillar of silence to them.

That's why she's drawn to Galla, he thought.

But Jana had guessed something he had not, because Ariel had hidden it from him too well. So when Galla came into his wife's view, color returned to her pale face, and vivacity as well.

Galla, for her part, felt an obligation to check on Ariel whenever she could, which was not as often as she had hoped. She had been meeting with Ella and her husband, Darren, as well as Dr. Vinita Singh, former head of Mandira, to get a sense of their capabilities, and to see if they could take on refugees. They also spoke about Paosh Tohon, and Valemog, and what to do to prepare for the worst.

When Galla was not in meetings, Rob would steal her away and give her tours of the station. Dagovaby knew from Rob's emotional radiation the level of his adoration for her, for he put no effort in hiding it. But as for Ariel, he wondered why she would shut him off, and not Galla, who could not know her feelings.

Or could she? he wondered.

She sat in their small living room on the couch with Ariel. The two of them were, to him, a beautiful sight, with Ariel's long dark hair and green eyes, and Galla's billowing mass of hair in all its colors, and her warm face and eyes like embers. They animated each other, and Dagovaby could not help but love seeing their interaction. Ariel let Galla put her hand on her growing belly. She began crying then, and Galla draped her arms around her friend. Dagovaby sighed. She would not let him do this for her, but he was glad she would let *someone.*

Grief, to him, was a part of his very existence. His own mother had conceived him without truly knowing his father, for his father was unknowable. She would never tell him much about his father, as she insisted it would endanger him. So they had never had his presence in their lives while he grew up.

Much of his youth had been a haze of sorts, which always puzzled him. He felt drawn to a place where he and his mother had lived briefly, and sometimes at night he would remember flashes of it: bright auroras overhead, a strange dark room full of crystals that acted like candles.

He later learned she was there for a healer, and only after they had left and he entered his teens did he realize his mother had been slowly dying the whole time. He was on his own in the galaxy, and the way back to that world was perilous, but sometimes he wanted to try to find it again. He knew a contact that claimed to travel there from time to time. If only he could go there, he could maybe understand the mother he had lost, and maybe learn about the father he had never known. It was only when he found Ariel on Fael'Kar that he felt anything like a home. She had drawn him to her, and vice versa.

And so when Ariel pushed him away after her own mother's death, he felt derailed. No one else could have blocked his empathic skill so effectively. It hurt him terribly to experience it from her.

Yet here she was, alive and vibrant again, and all because of Galla.

"Did you seriously kiss him!" exclaimed Ariel.

"Yes," said Galla, blushing.

Ariel smacked herself on the forehead, and Dagovaby smiled. *There she is!*

"Ohhhh, Galla," she said with a sigh. "Well, he must be happy!"

"I think so," said Galla. She cast her eyes down, but she grinned.

"He'd better be," said Ariel severely. "He's broadcast his feelings for you high and low *forever*. Oh, don't act coy about it! You knew he was into you! Anyway, he'd better treat you like the goddess you are."

"Oh stop," said Galla, laughing.

"I'm being very serious," said Ariel. Dagovaby coughed, and she glanced at him. She said quickly, "But if *you're* happy, then so be it. I'm happy for you. But," and she lowered her voice, "have you...?"

Galla then rolled her eyes. "No!" she said firmly. "I—we—there's no time for that or—or place, for that matter."

Ariel laughed, startling both Galla and Dagovaby. "You could start in a closet, like we did," she suggested, and she finally looked at her husband, with his dark brown eyes and their gold-rimmed pupils, watching her incessantly, lovingly. Her gaze wavered and fell away from him and sought Galla again, and she took her friend's face in her hands and touched her nose to hers. She looked at Dagovaby again, and there was a light in her eyes he had not seen in some time.

She stood.

"Excuse me, Galla," she said hastily, and she stepped over to her husband, seized his hand, and pulled him to his feet. "We have some-where to go."

Dagovaby looked down at his wife and put his arms around her. He mouthed to Galla over his shoulder, "*Thank you!*" and she looked all around and wondered what had happened, and left their suite.

She then walked to the conservatory, entering its air showers and locks, and found herself breathing in the smell of trees and flowers and fruits in the balmy air. Little worker bots and gardeners still worked there, though some of the former staff now worked on Ika Nui. Again she felt reminded of Demetraan, and its vast gardens. She missed it keenly here on Mandira, though the two were strikingly different in most respects. She pondered all this, when a deep voice brought her out of her reverie.

"You must be Galla-Deia," it said, and she looked up into the face of a massive man. "Er—I mean Captain Deia," he quickly adjusted. He had a haunted look about him.

"I am," she said, "but please, call me Galla."

"I'm Spears," he answered in his baritone.

"Oh!" she said. "I remember who you are. A survivor of Paosh Tohon!"

"Well, yes," he said, rubbing his shaved head. "I used to be a captain myself. But I think those days are over."

"Why?" she asked. "I love flying. I can't imagine not doing it again."

The large man sat next to her on a bench. "Well, being attacked kind of killed that for me. Just took it all right out of me."

Galla looked at him sadly. "I'm so sorry."

"I heard it was you whose stone moved us all," he said.

"It was one of them," she agreed. "With Ariel and Forster's help. I have more, and I plan to use them to stop Paosh Tohon."

The man nodded. "Good."

She tilted her head. "How are you now, other than not flying?"

He sighed. "I'm still not right. I mean, my body is healed, but my mind, you know? That shit scarred me."

"What"— Galla began, delicately testing the words in her mind before speaking them—"what was it like, when you were attacked? Or—or would you rather not say?"

He shook his head. "No point in hiding it. I would rather folks know. It was like all the worst nightmares you ever had, combined with all your worst fears, and all the worst pain—and I've broken bones, mind you—and yet, somehow, it was all compounded and *so much worse*. And it didn't stop. Like, I knew, on some level, that I was still alive. And I never, ever in my life had ever wished I was dead, until then."

Galla shuddered.

He went on, "I still have moments. Sometimes I think I'm trapped again. In that moment right before I wake up, I slip right back there, and feel this twisting in my mind. Like teeth digging into my brain, eating..." He shivered.

"Oh," she said, helplessly. "How awful! I am so sorry this happened to you. I've got to stop this from happening to anyone else!"

Spears took a deep breath. "I don't know how you can, with one stone, or twenty, or however many. I hope you can, though."

Not knowing what else to do, Galla pulled out her large diamethyst from where it had lain on her breast, concealed. Spears' eyes bulged at the sight of it. She held it in her hands, and it glowed, and felt warm to her, but not hot. She then stood and placed a flat side of it against Spears' forehead. He sat still, head bent, as if receiving a medal. After a few minutes, the stone went cool. And then he stepped away, and stared at her with wide eyes and his mouth agape.

"I—I feel better!" he exclaimed. "I could feel—warmth, going into me, into my thoughts!" He lunged forward and seized Galla and hugged her, lifting her off the ground. "Thank you, thank you!"

Then he set her down, embarrassed, and she laughed, so he laughed too, in great booms that echoed through the conservatory.

And for the first time since Meredith's death, Galla felt hope again.

20

THE CONCH AND THE RAVEN

A riel opened up more. She still cried from time to time, but her cheeks grew rosy again, and her eyes brightened. Dagovaby was ever at her side, and Paul on her hip or around her legs, unless she wanted to be alone, or go to Galla.

Galla could tell from the streaks on her face that Ariel had been crying one day. The green irises of her eyes were more offset by the red around them too. Galla quaked with sympathy.

"How are you?" she asked gently, in some ways afraid to ask anything at all for fear she would hurt her friend more.

"I'm tired," Ariel said. "So tired. I—I keep thinking I need to be more motivated, help with Paul, and still...I'm making this new baby on top of everything. I'm just wiped out."

Galla embraced her friend. "You're doing more than enough," she reassured her. "Take all the time you need."

"There's not much time, is there?" asked Ariel, her head on Galla's shoulder.

"I don't think so, no," said Galla reluctantly.

Ariel straightened up and pushed her hair behind her ears. Galla noticed more silver strands in her dark hair. She felt bittersweet then, for she knew what was coming.

"Galla, I want to keep going," Ariel said earnestly. "But Dagovaby thinks I should not right now, and even though you know I would totally go..." She blinked her puffy eyes.

"It's all right," said Galla. "I think you're better off staying here."

"Just until he's born," said Ariel quickly.

"As long as you like," said Galla warmly. She reached out and cupped her friend's cheek.

"And after that, I wonder..." Ariel murmured. Her eyes grew glassy. She said very quietly, "Would it make sense just to give her what she wants?"

Galla sat straight up and stared into Ariel's leaf-green eyes. "What did you say?" she asked.

Ariel yawned. "Hmm? Oh nothing, I think maybe I dozed off for a second." She shook herself.

Galla felt a gnawing sense of dread, and she grew nauseated. *What did she mean by saying that?*

"I'll give Beetle the code," Ariel said eagerly, more alert. "He can transmit it to other telepaths, and you can keep going."

"It might be tricky," Galla said, grimacing, "since none of us is a telepath."

"You'll figure it out," insisted Ariel. "And anyway, Prince Hazkinaut owes you several favors. So call on him. Once you get a couple of them—us?—on your team, you'll be fine until I can rejoin you."

Galla felt sick. She did not want to leave Ariel, especially now.

"I don't want to miss his birth," she said sadly.

Ariel smoothed her rapidly growing belly. As with her pregnancy with Paul, this baby was growing much faster than a normal human would. "I know." She began crying again. "You helped take the pain away, last time."

Galla bent forward and seized Ariel, and they rocked back and forth. She knew Ariel must feel Meredith's loss even more keenly, now that she would not be there for her second grandchild's birth. It seemed cruel to leave.

"It's okay," mumbled Ariel into Galla's moody hair. "I'll be okay. Go kick some ass for me, will ya?"

"Oh, I will," said Galla firmly, smiling through tears. "I will for all of you."

She felt every soft step as she walked through Mid Deck.

I can't imagine not having Ariel with me, she thought. She felt bewildered.

She found herself walking past the bar and spied Guru behind it. He waved.

"Getting a bit of a throwback vibe over here," he called. "It's been a long time since I tended bar. Come, I'll fix you something!"

She entered, and took in the low ceiling and broad expanse of tables and chairs, and the dim lighting. The bar, however, was well lit, and full of Guru's own bottles of liquor, some of which he had saved over time before Mandira moved. Others were new, such as the rum he had distilled from new plants on the planet below. He eyed her, and considered.

"Hmm," he said. "You're a bit low right now, I can see," he observed, and he reached for a little crystal glass dish. "I know just the thing!" And then he bent down out of sight behind the bar. She sat on a stool and craned her neck to watch him, but he was too far down, and she could only see his back. He rose, holding a small jar with dark brown contents.

"What is that?" she asked. He did not look at her, but instead smiled as he worked.

He took the dish and placed it under a little tap, and she heard a *whish*, and watched a creamy mound form in the dish. Then he opened the jar, scooped out little brown chunks, and added them to the top. He opened another jar full of small red fruits, and he put one on top. He stuck a spoon into the dish and gave it to her.

"That's...not a drink," she said, her eyes large and curious.

"Try it," he urged her, grinning. "And get everything in one bite. Wait...like this." He took her spoon and gathered some of the creamy substance, the brown pieces, and the fruit onto it and handed it to her. She put it in her mouth and he laughed at her expression, with her eyebrows bouncing, and then her eyes rolling back as she chewed.

"Mmm! What is it?"

"It's a sundae," Guru answered. "I don't have everything here I would like to put on it...but it'll have to do. You like it?"

Galla could not speak, and instead focused all her attention on the dish. But after a few minutes, she finally asked, "What is this part?"

"Ice cream."

"This?"

"Well, it's not a cherry, but it's a little similar, so I'll call it a cherry."

"And what are *these*?" Galla spooned up the little deep brown, broken bits and looked at them dreamily. She ate several at once, and held her hand over her mouth as her cheeks bulged.

Guru threw back his head and roared with laughter.

"That's chocolate!" he said at last. "Easy, though! No need to gorge. I have a secret stash. Please don't tell anyone. I've kept it hidden for years in cold storage!"

"So," Galla said, looking at the lines in his forehead and the tattoos he wore, and his dark hair with bits of grey, "you're good at keeping secrets, then."

Guru's eyes scrunched up. "I'm a bartender. Or...was. So, yes."

"What else are you good at?" she asked, then blushed and said, "I mean, what are your skills?"

He threw a towel over his shoulder and leaned on the bar and said, "Well, I was a botanist, once upon a time. I've been helping on the surface identifying plants and other organisms. I can make boats and surfboards. I'm pretty good at navigation, and that's in my DNA. My ancestors on Earth were the greatest navigators at sea! Hmm. I'm good in a fight. I'm not afraid of much."

"Well, Guru," said Galla slowly, reaching the end of her treat and feeling a bit sorrowful about it, "I need a new crew member. The Brant-Ambronos are staying here at least until the new baby arrives. I could use someone resourceful. Would you be interested?"

He gawked at her. "The sundae wasn't *that* good!"

"It was," said Galla. "But you're better. Think about it? We need to leave tomorrow. I still have more Device worlds to deliver to, and more telepaths to meet. I can bring you up to speed."

"I'll speak to Ella," Guru replied, but his demeanor had changed, and he seemed charged with energy.

By the next morning, she watched Guru come up to her with a pack on his shoulder. "I'm good to go," he said, "Captain Deia." He then opened his pack, pushed aside a couple of his rum bottles, and showed her a jar full of chocolate. He whispered, "For emergencies," and she beamed at him.

So the goodbyes began, and Galla held Paul to her cheek and fought her tears, determined to keep her face even and calm. She hugged and shook hands and looked at the blur of faces among the Mandira crew. Dagovaby gave her a tight hug, his eyes full of gratitude and love. Troy had brought her a gift of several bags of coffee, and she kissed him twice on each temple, which sent him into a singing fit. Ella and Darren and Vinita wished her well, and assured her they would maintain a relationship and keep each other alerted as best they could. She watched Ariel lean her head against Beetle's, and though neither made a sound, Galla knew Ariel was sending him the code to give to other telepaths. Ariel then embraced her, and they said nothing, for both women were overcome. She felt herself crumple inside.

Jana, meanwhile, steeled herself. Everything had changed: Meredith was gone, the galaxy was sliding toward chaos. Mandira was no longer a remnant of Earth. It was a survivor of the galaxy. And it held the woman she loved.

Jana knew then that she could never stay. Misun Hae, the love of her life, would never leave Mandira. So Jana would love her from afar, as she had done before. They had lived independently of each other, and rarely intersected. That did not stop Jana from caring. Jana would do everything she could to save Misun, to honor their love and friendship. No other plan made sense.

Galla watched Jana closely as she lingered with Misun at the ramp of the *Fithich*. Jana avoided her eyes. She knew Galla was no telepath, but her naivety made it easier for her to recognize emotions in others. Her copper eyes felt like telescopes looking into Jana's soul.

Galla waited until their embrace ended, then stepped toward Misun. She held out her hands, from which a necklace dangled, with a small diamethyst gleaming in the dim light of the bay. Misun stared with wide eyes at the lady with the billowing, warm hair and amber eyes.

"Everyone else will have one soon," Galla said to Misun. "But I wanted to give this to you personally, as an honorary crew member. You are always welcome on any ship I command, and also as a friend."

Misun blinked several times, and finally nodded. "Thank you," she said. "Bring her back to me, okay?"

"*Oakay*," Galla replied with a shy smile.

And she left the two for their final goodbye.

She walked with her crew to the *Fithich*, and tried not to think about how four of them were not coming with her, one who was gone forever. She turned, with Rob on one side of her, Jana on the other, and Guru and Beetle behind them, and saluted Ella, who saluted her as well. A little cadre of bots rolled up then, and sang, "Goodbye, Galla-Deia!" Chuckles and sniffles coursed through the bay.

And they entered the great raven of a ship with heavy hearts, and it took them away from gleaming Mandira and tranquil Ika Nui, to what dark vales between the stars they could not guess.

21

THE SIREN

Her voice sang in their minds, luxurious, lilting, and altering for each species to trigger their brains' pleasure centers:

"I am your victory, your greatest ally, your dreams made real, your nightmares harnessed."

She altered her image as well, to suit them. To Derry, she was voluptuous, dark-haired, violet-eyed, and tall, with long legs...just as she had been in her days as a full human, years ago. He was her servant, though he did not realize it. He commanded his own troops of beings now, for Valemog.

And though she enjoyed her role in flaying the thoughts of those she tortured along the fringes of the Event, she sought for more. Paosh Tohon indulged her hunger, for they were one and the same, and through her, it flourished. She was its most adaptable manifestation. Yet she wanted something she did not have. One final prize remained, and then nothing would stand in the way of domination.

That prize was not the keeper of the diamethysts, whom she loathed and feared, but ultimately could not use to her end: it was Ariel Brant. And as long as Galla protected Ariel, Veronica could not have her.

Whispers flew in the wake of the mage governor's ship. And through space and its many networks, she called, for she was the siren of Paosh Tohon.

22

LINES OF COMMUNICATION

Guru made an ideal new crew member, quickly learning the idiosyncrasies of the *Fithich*. It helped that Rob and Jana already knew him from Mandira. Galla felt satisfied with the arrangement, as much as she could. The loss of Meredith and the absence of her family left her raw.

They set off toward a star cluster between the Horseshoe of Device systems, in search of more telepaths. Prince Hazkinaut stayed true to his promise, and they now had a list of telepaths to work off of as they laced their way back and forth between Device worlds.

The Prince cautioned Galla in a message, "Some of these contacts might seem a bit brusque, or distant, or completely enigmatic. I cannot guarantee you will be able to recruit them. Should you have any trouble, alert me at once."

"Understood," Galla responded crisply. She still felt uncomfortable dealing with the Prince and his methods. She wanted to be able to trust him, but her experience with him had heightened her insecurities.

Guru watched Galla's hair flow outward and partially upward, and he laughed.

"You're like a cockatoo!" he said.

Galla stared at him. "A what?" she demanded.

"A cockatoo. A parrot...a bird with a huge crest. You can tell when a cockatoo is excited by its crest!"

She walked over to him, arms crossed, face doubtful, and said, "Show me."

He accessed Earth's records: "Earth, cockatoo images, cockatoo crest," and soon had brought up for her footage of a splendid white, winged animal with bright eyes and a yellow feather crest that rose when it was particularly feisty.

He watched her slyly, and when she let out a whoop of laughter, he relaxed.

"I love it!" she said. "And...yes. I think you're right!"

"It's a good indicator," he noted. "Gives us all a bit a warning."

"Good point," she conceded.

"Shift change coming up," Guru noted, lowering his eyelids coyly. "I can take it from here if you need to go."

She nodded. "Thank you."

He's very accommodating, she thought. *A good sort of crew member to have.*

And she headed back to her room. Rob was waiting for her.

"So...about the things the Prince gave you," he said, with a deep red face, and she blushed then as well.

She walked over to the box of lingerie, and Rob watched her choose something out of it.

"One day," she said, swinging the tiny outfit in front of her.

"I hope it's soon," he said with a laugh, and they wrestled play-fully for a bit before settling into a session of kisses. She then looked at him seriously, and he gave her a questioning lift of his eyebrow.

"I just feel...a little uncomfortable," she admitted.

"Oh," he said, his voice even. He glanced around the room. "Tight space?"

"In a way," she said. "A little closed in and a little too—too close to —oh dammit. This place just crawls with Aeriod."

Rob sat up on his elbow. "Oh," he said again. He sighed. "Well, yeah. It was his ship. But...it's yours now." But he shivered. *He can't keep track of what we do, can he?* Rob wondered.

Before he could continue that thought, his comms chimed, and he rose and put on his jacket. He quickly kissed Galla and said, "Good night, see you in the morning," and left for his shift. And that was how they managed over the days and weeks.

GALLA TOOK no one with her for several of the remaining Device drops. She needed to be alone, sometimes to think more clearly. Sometimes she wanted to seek again the loving voice she had heard in her visions in the past, but he was not present. What had happened to him? Who was he, and why had he spoken to her in the past, and yet was silent now? She could not guess. And in some ways, wondering about him undermined her growing feelings for Rob.

One of the Device worlds was underwater. So she adjusted her suit and helmet and sank down into the dark depths, holding her platform and watching bubbles escape her suit. She felt the pressure of the water squeeze her on all sides as she descended. The platform halted at a door, as it had done on every other Device world. The door opened but did not flood the hallway. The Device had made a barrier of the water. Galla walked along the hall and dripped. Again she had a vision of the branching, white other place, and then she saw the city made of copper, as she had before. But most disturbing were a pair of diamond eyes, breaking through the white space. After that, she felt unsettled for days. Not for the first time, she worried about Ariel.

WHEN GALLA and her crew met a telepath guild on Tartiph 7, she approached them with caution and anxiety. She and Guru and Beetle met with the group, and they were unlike other telepaths she had encountered. There were six of them, each helmeted and suited in armor, and they worked as a kind of hive-mind, not speaking, but interacting with each other in a manner Galla could not discern.

"Beetle," she said, "can you work as a translator for us?"

The great insect twitched its antennae. "I assumed I would. We have been conversing about the quality of plants on their homeworld. I have been assured that—"

Galla cleared her throat, and Guru stifled a laugh.

"Beetle," she said, with utmost patience, "let's focus on the task at hand. Can you please let them know we need their help, and can repay them however they wish, and we can promise them stones to protect them?"

"I did this already," said Beetle placidly. "They are only concerned about being separated on different planets."

"It's necessary," she replied. "I also want them to be prepared for various climates. We can tell them which worlds to go to, and give them each a stone of their own to protect them, meanwhile."

She watched as Beetle and the consortium of telepaths sat silently but gesticulated in little movements. Finally, Beetle turned to Galla and said in a flat voice, "They agree to the terms."

Then Beetle turned to Guru and told him, "They want you to know, the answer is 'no.'"

Guru avoided Galla's inquisitive look.

"What was the question?" Galla wanted to know. Guru's ears turned red.

Beetle made a popping sound and said, "Guru wanted to know if all six of them can—"

Guru said quickly, "It's not important. Sorry." Galla lifted her right eyebrow at him. He shrugged.

"Do they have information on refugees?" she asked.

Beetle said, "The Associates have been seen ferrying refugees from the Event in some systems. But Valemog apparently is recruiting some refugees by threats, or outright seizing them to take to Paosh Tohon. The guild says Paosh Tohon is particularly keen on recruiting any telepaths it finds."

Hearing this message in Beetle's neutral voice sent shivers up and down both Galla and Guru's spines. They looked at each other in alarm. Galla stood and brought out six of her small diamethysts, and gave one to each member of the guild. They stood then, and arranged themselves in an arc around her, in a kind of salute. Galla bowed to them and returned to her ship, with Guru and Beetle in tow.

On board the *Fithich*, Galla made a decision.

"It's time we contacted the Associates," she announced. Rob and Jana looked at her in surprise.

"I hope they don't mind that I hacked their system!" exclaimed Jana. She bit her lip.

"Don't worry about that," said Galla. "They sound like they have a lot of other issues to distract them. Open a channel to Ezeldae."

Rob did so. There was a great deal of static, and the receiver's voice was warped.

More Event interference, thought Galla.

"This is Captain Galla-Deia, Representative, requesting an audience with Ushalda," she said.

Several minutes passed, but it worked. The long, slender face of the Associate, Ushalda, flickered into view. The distortion of the signal maddened Galla.

"Ushalda, I regret the circumstances and interference. If you can hear me, and adjust on your end, I have intelligence about Valemog."

"Galla-Deia," said Ushalda, "we welcome your contact and are relieved you are well. It is likely we have all the information we need."

Galla gritted her teeth and thought about her new contact, Coniuratus.

"You should know, Paosh Tohon is recruiting telepaths. I also need them to complete my Task. Anything you can do to provide protection for telepaths would be a good idea. I'm going to help in any way I can. Also, we are seeing and hearing of more refugees, including some working in unpleasant conditions."

Ushalda stopped her. "That will do, Galla-Deia. The Associates are working to mitigate the problems. I suggest you do your part."

"Where do I send the refugees I find?" demanded Galla. "It's not enough that they should have to wait for an Associate ship. Suppose they're attacked or enslaved?"

"I assure you, we have the ability to assist them. They should contact us."

"What if they don't want to? What if they're afraid, or don't have the resources?" pressed Galla.

"You will have to trust the system we have put in place for far longer than you have been a Representative," Ushalda said coldly.

"Thanks for nothing, then," spat Galla. She motioned Rob to cut the line.

"What the *fuck*?" he said.

"Exactly," said Galla. "Oh, this is bad. They're completely out of their depth, and they don't even know it!"

23

GLAD TIDINGS

"Good morning," a voice woke her up. She opened her eyes to see Rob leaning over her, smiling in the dim light.

"Already?" she protested. "It's too early!"

"It's for a good reason," he said, kissing her nose. "Come and see!"

Galla dressed and followed him to the cockpit.

"Oh!" she cried, reaching for the screen. It was Ariel, holding a tiny baby up to her shoulder, patting his back, and looking flush and radiant, yet exhausted too.

"Here's our new boy!" she said, and already the infant held his head upright and strong, and swiveled it, looking over his mother's shoulder. "Ack, I can't get him to look at you!" she said. "He's such a sweet baby, so calm," she said softly. "I'm sorry I didn't get through to you sooner. I tried a couple of times, but there was too much interference. So I thought I would wait a few days and try again."

She sighed.

"Is everything all right?" Galla asked her.

Ariel shrugged her free shoulder. "It's fine. We'll head out soon, and we'll meet up with you, and we'll get this thing done. And then I want to settle down for a while."

"Good idea," said Galla, nodding. That appealed to her very

much, the idea of settling down instead of constantly being on the move. She knew it would be a long road to such a time, if in fact it could ever happen at all. She thought briefly of Rob, and wondered what it would be like to spend many years with him, watching his eyes grow crinkly and his hair turn white. She shook herself.

"What is his name?" she asked.

"We're still figuring that out. He's not told us yet," she added, winking at Galla.

"I hope to see you soon in person," said Galla. "But first: I love you!" She blew a kiss to her friend.

"I love you, Galla," said Ariel with a wry grin, and she leaned forward in her image as if to kiss Galla, but her baby squawked, so she quickly leaned back. She waved to Galla, then her image vanished.

Galla leaned back, propping her feet upon the console as Rob might. He kissed her neck and went back to their room to sleep. Soon the cockpit sat quiet, the crew asleep. And it was such a small crew now: Jana, Guru, Beetle, and Rob. Away from them all, Galla let her tears spill then. Tears for Meredith, tears for the dear Brant-Ambrono family she missed so much already. Space seemed so much emptier without them.

24

RETICENCE

Dagovaby could feel his wife shutting him out again. She was staring at the stars outside the station, which was turned away from Ika Nui just then. He had caught her doing this several times lately, and it troubled him, but he did not know why. The greater mystery was her coldness toward him.

"Is this...are you doing this because of your mama?" he asked finally.

In a high-pitched voice, Paul chirped, "Mama!" and slapped Ariel's thighs. She bent to pick him up, groaned, kissed him, and set him back down.

"You're a lot heavier than a newborn, sweet baby!" she said, smiling down at him. "I forgot what it was like!"

"You're ignoring me," said Dagovaby, and his jaw muscles worked.

She turned to look at him with great, marble-like green eyes.

"I see," said Dagovaby. He put his hands behind his head. "Why block me? Why hide? Just...help me understand."

"I'm tired," said Ariel. "How many times do I have to tell you? Do you want to feel my exhaustion all the time? I doubt it! I wouldn't wish it on you." She pushed her dark hair behind her ears. A few more grey hairs flickered in the light.

"You're telling me part of the reason, but not all," he responded. He picked Paul up and bounced him on his legs, and the toddler screamed with joy. "And when will we name him?"

He watched Ariel pick up their new son, who was paler than his brother yet with a darker complexion than his mother's. He was healthy, but more slender than Paul had been at the same age. His hair was soft and fine, very like Ariel's. His eyes were dark like his father's, rather than green, yet they bore no gold rings around their pupils like Dagovaby's.

"I still don't know what to call him," she answered. "He's so different from Paul. And he doesn't seem to want to read me. I think he's maybe more like my parents, with no psionic ability. I can read his sweet little thoughts, and he is a very curious and precocious baby. For now he's just Baby Ambrono. Baby A."

"Bay-bee ayyy," said Paul, grabbing for his tiny brother.

"Gentle!" said his father in a soft warning. Ariel looked into Paul's eyes, speaking to him silently with her mind, and the wee boy snatched back his hand.

"Just...promise me," said Ariel, as she nursed the infant, "that we can have a place to go, to keep them safe, just in case."

Dagovaby looked at her stony face with sadness. "I'll see what I can do."

25

FIRE IN THE HAND

J ana translated the description for the next Device world as they approached it. "Fairly clean air over most of it. Breathable. A lot of ancient ruins, and newer retreats. It's basically a planet-wide commune."

"Sounds like a hippie paradise," quipped Rob.

Galla tutted. "Want to see for yourself?" she asked.

"I wasn't suggesting—"

"You'll be my companion this time," she told him.

"Oh, I'm being voluntold," said Rob, crossing his arms and swiveling in his seat.

"I mean, you could stay," said Galla, and she leaned down and let her hair tickle his face.

Jana said, "You know I'm still in this room, right?" and she glared at them.

Galla jumped, and looked back at Rob, whose ears had gone pink, and she said, "We'll leave immediately."

He did not have to be told twice.

They suited up, hopped on the sky bike, and dropped from the ship. Rob yelled and Galla laughed at him, and then she engaged her engines and shot ahead and swooped through the air. They circled over treetops stained with autumn color and around large, monolithic boulders. Off in the distance, they could see a haze of smoke from a village. But the Device was removed from it, burrowed next to the base of an ancient, weathered mountain.

The ruddy and golden canopy of trees was too thick for Galla to weave through on the sky bike, so she flew to the nearest clearing. Hopping off, she removed her helmet and let the fresh breeze catch her hair. Rob took his own helmet off and looked disheveled and wild-eyed.

"You really are crazy on that thing," he said to her, looking at the bike. She curtsied, her smile impish.

"Before we go to the Device," she said, "I have to tell you what I do everyone: that you might experience strange things inside there. Visions, sounds—it varies."

Rob shrugged. "It can't be any weirder than anything else we've seen."

She raised an eyebrow. "Oh yes. It really can."

They began their trek back toward the Device. Little thatched domes rose from the ground here and there, long abandoned by some animal or prehistoric civilization. Their shapes made Galla think of overturned nests. She peered into the golden woods at one, and could just make out an opening. It looked almost as tall as she was.

She liked the sound of her boots shuffling through the fallen leaves: *shiiiiifff, shiiiiifff*. All around her the trees glowed in shades of bright yellow, orange, mottled green and gold, scarlet, deep crimson, and pale violet. The slant of the morning sun shone on Rob's hair and set it ablaze. He seemed to blend into the woods, wearing a dark olive outfit, with his red hair matching the trees. His bright blue eyes stood out, though, and Galla could not look away from them. She felt herself shiver. He saw her look, and she blinked.

I am afraid, she thought. *Why am I so afraid? If he was the voice in all my visions over the years...but he isn't. I still want to be with him.*

And Rob knew for certain then. *It's real*, he thought, and he had never felt happier in his life. He looked at her, this beautiful creature he had loved for so long, with her shining eyes and wry little smile, her many-colored coils of hair flickering in the autumn dawn, and marveled.

He took her hand, and she could feel his rapid pulse in hers. His eyes were wide, and his pupils began to dilate. The sun glinted off the gold-red hairs in his growing stubble. The barest crinkles formed at the corners of his eyes, and his lips twitched, as if he wanted to smile, but was afraid to.

He's afraid too, she realized. She took Rob's other hand.

"We're finally alone," she said. "Away from everyone."

Rob took a deep breath, and breathed it back out through his mouth into a cloud in the brisk air. She smiled, and did the same. It was cold, but the sun warmed everything as it rose. It seemed to Galla to take a long time in doing so.

"I love you, Galla," he said to her, suddenly shy and serious.

"I love you," she murmured, blinking rapidly.

Then Rob kissed her, warm and soft, though his nose was cold at the tip. She looked into his eyes and kissed him back. He put his hands up under her hair to cradle her head, and he kissed her temple, down her cheek, lingered where her jaw met her ear and met her skin with his tongue.

Galla pulled away and looked coquettishly at him. She took his hand and drew him off the path. Golden leaves twirled in the wind above them and some drifted down around, but she barely noticed them. His blue eyes never left her copper gaze, and she led him to one of the little huts. They ducked their heads a bit to enter, to find a small space that smelled of dry leaves. The floor was soft, padded by moss-like vegetation that had dried long ago. Sunlight glinted in slivers between the worn thatching.

"I'm turning my comms off," she said, looking at him with lowered eyes. She dropped hers outside the entry to the dome and asked him with a half-smile, "Want to join me?"

His eyes widened, and he dropped his comms link next to hers, grinning. "Oh yes," he answered. She pulled him into the hut.

She ran her hands along his brow, down his funny upturned nose, to his scruffy chin. Her hair twisted up and around his shoulders. They both shook, and not from the cool air.

Rob took off his coat and laid it on the floor, and Galla did the same. They fumbled with fastenings and laughed and shivered. And then they stared at each other's bodies, kissing and touching every-thing, as they lay on their sides on top of the coats. She wrapped her arms and legs around him; he felt hot to her, and his pulse bounced in his neck where she kissed him. She tasted the salt of his sweat. They bound themselves together, trembling, slow at first, and then they were frenzied. Pushing and pulling and rolling, they did not care if anyone or anything saw or heard them then. And then they lay spent, flushed and ecstatic, holding each other.

Rob stared at Galla in awe. He caressed her from her lips and neck to her breasts and her hips, and thought, *I could stay right here, forever, and never move from this spot.*

As for Galla, she felt as though she had experienced something elemental and natural, surrounded by the wind and the land and the golden leaves. She lay mesmerized by Rob, and her own state of bliss, and she draped herself around him. He held her close, holding her face, and kissed her again.

Knowing they needed to go on, they soon dressed and clasped hands, and sighed. They grabbed their comms, snapped them on their wrists, and slipped in the leaves from shaking legs. And they walked back to the path hand in hand, stealing glances at each other, cheeks and noses red, and plucked bits of leaf and twig from each other's hair and clothes. Rob laughed at Galla's tangled hair, and she grinned at him and brushed off his outfit.

And then Galla sobered, mostly, except for the shaky smile she gave Rob. She had not known what to expect from him. He was different from Aeriod in almost every way. Again Rob felt to her so very alive, with a fire inside him. She knew every part of him now, and already wanted to feel his warmth and strength again. Their bodies were well suited to each other, but somehow she felt more vulnerable now. *Why do I still feel so frightened?* she wondered. She squeezed his hand, and he lifted hers to kiss it.

They walked along, and the ground sloped downward. Galla knew they must be close to the Device. But when they arrived at the space where the chasm should be, with trees arching overhead, they found only a broad circle covered by dirt.

"What!" exclaimed Galla. "That's a new one."

Rob stood behind her and held her around her waist, and she leaned against him.

"What do we do?" he asked.

She took out her stone, and it felt cool. So she walked to what should have been the edge of the pit and waited. Rob followed her. They heard shuffling sounds. All around them, figures emerged from the woods, and they approached slowly. Some were very tall, half as tall as the trees, and others were human-sized, and still others were tiny. They all were covered in mottled outfits that blended in with the surroundings.

"Um, hello," said Galla.

They pressed in closer, and Rob grew anxious and reached for his belt.

"No," she said to him firmly. She addressed the approaching crowd.

"We mean no harm. We are here on a mission, and we will leave as soon as it is over," she called to them.

Whispers and hisses rose and fell among the throng, until two beings moved closer to the pair. "Who are you?" they asked in unison.

Galla's stone grew warm, and then hot, and she took it and held it aloft. The sun caught it and sent violet shards of light throughout the circle.

"I am Galla-Deia, keeper of the diamethyst, Questri. I am here to prepare the Device. This is Rob Idin, and he is also Questri."

Her diamethyst then radiated bright purple light and cast her entire body in its glow. She looked down to see her feet dangling above the ground, and she gasped, but held tightly to her stone.

Rob looked at her with his mouth wide open, and the crowd of beings made a cacophony of noises. Some fell to the ground, some bowed, and the two who had spoken raised their arms and appendages high.

"Welcome at last!" they said together, and the ground over the Device disappeared, leaving Rob teetering at its edge and Galla fully suspended over the darkness of the abyss below.

"Oh!" she exclaimed, looking below her. "Okay!" She did not know what to do, but willed the stone to carry her over to the edge, and found that this worked.

She settled her feet gladly onto the ground and seized Rob around his neck. The stone stopped glowing and cooled to lukewarm. The two beings came closer.

"We have long awaited this day," they said together. "We have kept the watch, as our ancestors told us, and we have kept it secret."

Galla lowered her head and held her hands out.

"I thank you for your service," she said. "I trust, when I leave, you will keep the watch again? There will be a day when others come to enter the Device. You will know it is safe to allow them, for they will give a special message to you. Will you help?"

"We will maintain the vigil for all that time allows," they answered.

She nodded. "You have my gratitude. Now we must enter the Device."

The beings retreated, but the group surrounded the entire circumference of the chasm, and they watched in silence as Galla traversed the edge. She held Rob's hand and made her way to the stairs toward the platform.

"Ready?" she asked him, as they sat down.

"I'm ready for more of *you*," he said quietly with a wink, and he kissed her.

"Later, lover," she replied with a grin, and they shot down on the platform into the black depths.

The platform shuddered to a stop at the door, and they entered to darkness and silence. The light did not wink on, or turn on automatically, but gradually grew brighter, and was pale orange. They looked at each other. Rob's face began glowing, and his hair shone like fire-light. As they walked toward the courtyard, Galla wondered if this time, things might be tamer.

Until everything burst into flames.

Galla screamed, and looked all around her, but could not see Rob. He had let go of her hand, and she felt the fire burning her, though her skin looked intact, and thought in horror, *It's burning him!*

"Rob! Rob!" But the fire lashed away her words and burned her mouth.

She looked down at her stone, and it glowed, but it was not hot to the touch like the flames around her. Despite the flames, her clothes had not burned.

"It's not a real fire, Rob!" she shrieked, hoping that he heard. *I hope I'm right about this!*

Something punched her, right in her abdomen, causing her to groan. She saw nothing, but the feeling it left her with made her so desperately sad that she wept uncontrollably. She managed to stagger to her feet.

She shouted, "Enough!" into the fire, and abruptly, it vanished. And she slid and crumpled onto the floor, her face pressed against its surface, and it was cool. Pale, golden light flooded the courtyard.

"Rob," she croaked, and she looked around, and found him intact. She let out a relieved yelp and crawled over to him. He was on his side, shaking, holding himself.

"Rob," she said again, arms around him, and he did not acknowledge her at first. She put her diamethyst against his fore-head, and he jolted once, then stilled. He uncurled, and she helped him sit up.

He stared at her as if he did not recognize her, and then seized her, and sobbed into her neck.

"You're all right," he moaned. "You're all right."

"Yes!" she said. "Are you?"

"Get me—get us out of here," he said, clambering to his feet, his shoes squeaking against the floor.

"I will," said Galla, and she took out her small, egg-shaped lump of diamethyst and set it on the floor. "Hurry, before the light is gone."

They pelted back to the platform, and Galla helped the weakened Rob onto it, and they hurtled upward. The look in Rob's beautiful eyes sent a stab of cold through Galla.

What did the fire take from him?

26

VEILS

The wake of the Device experience left them shaken.

"It wasn't a real fire," Galla said. "I know it was terrifying, and seemed real, but everything turned out fine."

Rob shook his head. "You don't understand. It wasn't just a fire. Is that all you saw?"

"Y—yes," she said. "You saw something else?"

He put his head in his hands. "I saw the fire. I saw you *in* the fire, screaming. Crying and screaming. And...floating."

She put her arms around his neck and rubbed her nose against his. "It's over. Everything is okay."

"Tell me," Rob said urgently, seizing her, "is it the future?"

She blinked. "I—I don't know," she admitted. "It could be something from my past. From my time on Bitikk." And she hoped that it was. She shuddered, for she still could not remember all of that traumatic era.

"Did they *burn* you?" he cried.

Galla began shivering. "Yes," she answered. "They were...I think they were testing me. My limits."

He moaned and held her close.

"I'm so sorry," he said. His tension had gone, though. "That must have been what I saw."

But there was something else, a shadow, some difference in Rob's face. Galla hoped it would go away soon. She decided the best thing to do was to keep Rob occupied in as many ways as she could.

I'm going to let go of any awkwardness I feel about being with him on this ship, starting now, she decided. So the moment his shift was up, she coaxed him into her room.

"We...didn't have much time, before," she said, surprised to find herself feeling shy with Rob all over again. "Want to continue?"

And Rob smirked and knelt in front of her and helped her out of her clothes, while she pulled his off as well. He worked his way up the inside of her thighs, and reached under her and took hold of her hips. She reached for something to hold on to.

"What—what are you—" but she could not form any more words then, and every thought was an exclamation. After that, she took her own journey up and down his body, and Rob could not focus either.

For at least an hour, their ordeal on the planet was forgotten.

In the cockpit, Jana's eyes grew large. The ship's acoustics left little to the imagination.

"Whew," said Jana. The corner of her mouth twitched. She glanced at Guru, who looked her way at the exact moment, and they both laughed.

"It's not gonna end well," she gasped, covering her mouth.

"No," agreed Guru. "But for now, it seems to be going *very* well."

Beetle waddled in quickly, antennae swiveling, wings shivering.

"Are Captain Galla and Rob hurting?" Beetle said in a rush, with pops and crackles interspersed in its words.

Jana bent her head down between her legs and roared with laughter.

Guru strained to speak coherently, and his eyes watered. "No, Beetle. They are not...hurting. They are"—he coughed—"enjoying each other."

Beetle's antennae bent forward toward Guru and Jana, and then shot straight in the air and twitched.

"I understand now. They are producing a larva."

Guru and Jana guffawed.

"I should prepare a pupa," Beetle hooted in excitement. "Or perhaps I should prepare several. It sounds as if there will be many larvae."

Jana slid onto the floor.

Between spasms, Guru gasped, "I—don't think—they will produce—any, Beetle. They...aren't the same species."

Beetle lowered its head.

"That is true. That is too bad. I enjoy making pupae. But if they will not produce larvae, why are they so energetic?"

Jana pointed to the door, her face streaked with tears, and she wheezed, "Beetle. Mind your own business. Cover your...ear holes, or whatever, if you need to. That's what I'm going to do."

Beetle's antennae wavered to and fro for several seconds. Finally the giant insect shuffled out of the cockpit. "I will cover my ear holes."

27

CLANDESTINE

They skimmed through the bomboro of particle waves, another Event phenomenon that wreaked havoc on smaller ships. Turbulence grew more frequent, and so Galla would sometimes pilot the *Fithich* through the worst of it. But Rob, Jana, and Guru soon got the hang of it as well. Their next rendezvous with telepaths involved several security checks, to reach the planet Ixinerro. As they finally reached its pale blue atmosphere, Galla appraised her small crew.

"Beetle," she called, and watched the creature scurry in and stand on two if its legs. "Are you ready?"

"I am prepared to perform my duty," answered Beetle, clicking, and its antennae stood erect.

"Good. Guru, I would like for you to come along," she said, and he nodded. She briefly touched Rob's shoulder, but he did not react. His expression had changed, and he seemed not to know she was there. She sighed, and furrowed her brow.

"See you soon," said Jana, and she sat next to Rob in the cockpit. She looked over at him, but he was unresponsive, staring ahead.

"What the hell is wrong with you?" she hissed.

When he turned his head slowly to look at Jana, she felt chilled.

He was not really looking at her, but at something else, or somewhere else, as if a curtain hung between them.

"What?" he asked, shrugging then, and he turned back. "I'm just the pilot."

Jana's eyes darted from him, to the controls, and back. *I wonder if you should be, right now.*

"Look, if you need a break—" she began.

"I don't," he answered curtly.

She shook her head.

The little shuttle took Galla, Guru, and Beetle to a port city where the docks perched high in the air on thousands of long stalks, natural structures that grew out of the ground of Ixinerro. Jana had told them these were fossilized remains of an organism, and given their great height, Guru visibly cringed.

"What kind of creature was *that*?" he wondered.

"Perhaps it merely molted," Beetle suddenly declared, "and the creature is still out there, in a larger form."

Jana squirmed at that remark.

"Okay, I'm staying on the ship this time, thanks," she declared.

Once Galla walked into the port, she realized how high up they were, and Guru glanced at her with a worried look. But she had lived on an asteroid trained to orbit just above the planet Rikiloi, so to her, it did not seem that unusual. She did not, however, want to think about Beetle's suggestion. If it was right, where, indeed, had that creature gone?

Ixinerro served as a commerce and special interest world, and as such its skies hummed with the comings and goings of many crafts. The trio was put through another security check just inside the port. They were halted by a bot, a boxy little thing that walked in jerking steps.

"That cannot enter here," it said, indicating Beetle. It shone one eye-camera onto Beetle.

"Beetle comes with us," Galla corrected him, "and is necessary to our task."

The bot squawked in response, but Galla stared it down. Guru said in her ear, "I can take Beetle back," but she shook her head.

"Only Beetle can transmit the code to the telepaths, assuming they go for this," she whispered. "We have to bring Beetle."

Another two bots, sleeker and more ovoid in shape, hovered over to the first bot.

"We must relocate that," they said, aimed at Beetle.

Beetle stood firmly on its legs and said, "I will not leave my captain. I am ordered to accompany her. I do not wish for there to be an altercation."

Grinning nervously, Galla said to the bots, "What Beetle means to say is, we absolutely must use its particular skill set to do business here."

"We cannot allow that—" began the three bots, and then Beetle flicked its wings up and out over them like great umbrellas, and they whined and squealed.

Galla and Guru watched Beetle in amazement.

"I'm not sure this is going well," Guru observed, pulling on his tattooed chin.

"No," Galla agreed. "Beetle, please! Fold your wings. If we cannot do business here, we will leave." She looked darkly at the bots. "You can be sure I will broadcast our treatment here today, for all traders to know."

And Beetle tucked its wings back.

A hooded figure appeared next to the giant insect then, and Beetle's antennae zipped forward and down. It trilled.

"Beetle?" asked Galla, watching.

"We are to follow," said Beetle simply, and the hooded figure led them away from the bots, who followed cautiously.

Once away from the building lines behind them, the being in the hood made a movement, and the bots beeped, turned around, and made off somewhere else in great haste. Galla's eyes met Guru's.

"What—" he began.

"I don't know you," said the figure to Guru. "Come, Lady Deia."

She gasped at the sound of his voice: it was Prince Hazkinaut, disguised as the Cogniz.

She motioned for Guru and Beetle to follow him, and he walked onto a terrace with a ceiling open to the soft blue-grey sky above, brushed with cirrus clouds. He sat on a white, round, cushioned seat, large enough for all of them. Beetle climbed on top and sat down, resting.

"I could see you were having trouble," said the Prince, still covered. "I cannot reveal myself, you understand," he said quickly, brushing his simple robes and adjusting his enormous hood.

"Of course," said Galla. "This is Guru, by the way. A new crew member. You can trust him."

"Hmm," said the Cogniz, "not much of a thought spill with this one," to which Guru squinted at him. "Your thoughts, they're very well secured. Yet you're no telepath. I'm impressed!"

He turned to Galla again. "Where is Ariel?"

And at that, Guru's eyes opened a bit, and the Prince nodded. "Ah," he said. "Felicitations, then. But will you manage with just Beetle? This incident gives me pause."

"Pri—Cogniz," said Galla, "where are the telepaths we are supposed to meet?"

"Right in front of you!" he exclaimed.

"Excuse me!" she said loudly, then cleared her throat. "What do you mean? Are you being serious?"

She watched the Prince twist his secretive robes around.

"Well, obviously you need me," he said. "You're down a telepath! So I was right to trust my instincts and find you again."

"How—how can you leave your people?" she said. She felt uneasy, remembering all too well a goblet of Stroffy liqueur.

He fluffed his robes as if shrugging indifferently. "The High Assist is well suited to my long excursions. Contrary to what you might think, I am no stay-at-home prince."

Then he said in a low voice, "It only made sense. I took on the responsibility and the honor of wearing a stone of yours," and he flicked open his robes long enough to reveal a small purple stone, fixed onto a long, pearl-colored chain. "The least I can do now is ensure you get everyone you need. Not too many more, yes?"

"Not too many," agreed Galla. "But listen, I hear things are getting worse out there, and we're a bit removed, but not by much."

"I hope you've assumed things will grow more hostile," said the Prince.

"Yes."

"Will you accept my aid?" he asked, grandiosely bowing.

Galla sighed. "I suppose you would be useful. Yes, you may join us. For now. But if you cause trouble, that's subject to change."

"Good. Then let's be off. Something about this planet disturbs me, as if it listens to us," said the Prince, twitching.

Guru shuddered. "I'm with this guy," he said.

"That's Prince Hazkinaut to you," sniffed the Prince.

Guru set his mouth into a firm line. "I think we're in for an interesting ride," he said dryly.

28

THE DERELICT

The arrival of Prince Hazkinaut on the *Fithich* upended their routine immediately. For Guru, that did not matter overly much, because he was still new. Galla could see in his face the doubt he had about the Prince, but he kept his opinions to himself. Jana had reservations, but ultimately she shook her head and thought the arrangement could work. His arrival was the first thing to bring Rob out of his reverie.

"You!" he said, vacillating between shock, rage, and disappointment.

The Prince looked at him for a long time.

"What happened?" he asked, and then he sprang back, as if he'd been shocked.

"Stop. Reading. Me," Rob said through gritted teeth.

"Well, that's just it," said the Prince slowly. "I can't read you as well anymore. I saw something, and—well, I apologize."

Rob squinted at him in surprise.

"At least," whispered the Prince, "you did get what you wanted, yes?" and he looked at their captain, who stood in the doorway of the cockpit with her arms crossed and her jaw set.

"Shift change," said Galla, and Rob jumped to his feet.

He rushed at her and grabbed her hand. "Oh!" she said, and the Prince gave her a sly look as they quickly left.

She took a moment and said on her comms to Guru, "Do you think you guys can handle things tonight?"

"Sure thing," said Guru, and she could tell in his voice that he was smiling.

"Let me know if you need anything," she said.

IN HER ROOM, Rob was very alert and present, not distant as he had been before in the cockpit.

"I didn't know," she murmured, gripping him, "that it could be like this."

"I didn't either," he said, kissing her.

This time, they stifled their sounds as best they could, but ended up laughing. Galla was relieved to see him behaving normally. They finally slept through most of the night together, with Rob curled up behind her, clutching her close, as if afraid she might slip away. But she later woke to find him gone, and so she rose and dressed, and went to look for him.

After several minutes, she found him replacing a panel down in the launch bay.

"Um..." she said, and he looked up casually at her. "What are you doing?"

"Checking things," he said, and then he rose and kissed her.

"In the middle of the night? After...after that?" she said, bewildered.

"Just making sure everything is fine," he said, his face bland.

And that strange look swam in his eyes, the same look she had seen after he had recovered from the Device visions. Part of her felt as if she had been pummeled, as she had been in the vision. *What happened to him?*

"Come back to bed," she urged. He shrugged and followed her back, and once he climbed into their bed, he promptly fell asleep.

Galla watched him sleep, and she trembled. He had been so present, and then seemed so far away.

With shaking hands, she made her way to the cockpit, and found Guru still there.

He was a man who had seen the faces of many people in his life, confessing many things. And although he knew Galla was no human, her face told him so much just then that it hurt to look at her.

"I can keep an eye on him," he said quietly, standing to leave. "Fair winds, Captain."

She shook herself out of her worry and looked at him gratefully. "Thank you," she said.

Alone, she held her knees in her pilot seat and chewed her lip.

Meredith is gone, Ariel and Dagovaby and Paul are gone, and Rob seems to be changing too.

She had little time to dwell on this, however, for the proximity alert went off. She silenced it and waited. Something was just ahead of them in the junction. She projected the image and took a long look at it. It was a ship, mostly rectangular, utilitarian, maybe four times longer than it was wide, and pocked with holes. She stood quickly.

"Everyone, get to the round room," she ordered on the comms.

Jana, Guru, the Prince, and Beetle sat in the meeting room. Rob entered, looking exhausted, and Galla projected the image of the ship above the table.

"We'll overtake this ship soon," she told them. "Look at the sides." She enhanced the image.

"Shot?" asked Guru.

"Maybe," said Galla.

"Have you hailed?" asked Rob.

"Not yet," she answered. "I wanted you to see first."

"Can you pick up anything on it, Your Highness?" she asked the Prince archly.

He drew himself up. "I can only sense life forms, at this range," he answered, twitching.

She lowered her eyelids at him and said, "Well, if you're quite sure. Let's go."

She and Rob headed to the cockpit and took their seats, and she glanced over to see him completely focused as of old. She said, "Unveil us, and open a channel."

Their ship flashed into visibility.

"Unknown craft, this is the *Fithich*. Can you identify yourselves?" Rob said.

There was quiet static.

Galla nodded for him to try again, so he did, and she stood and paced, arms crossed.

"Are you in need of assistance?" he asked the ship. Still no response.

"Can you bring us alongside?" Galla suggested.

Rob maneuvered the *Fithich* so that it sped beside the damaged ship. "It seems to be on autopilot," he said.

"And no response," Galla muttered. She said over the comms, "Guru, Cogniz, meet me in the launch bay."

"What's the plan?" Rob asked her, and she appreciated his lucidity just then.

"We're going in. Hover over anything resembling a hatch on that thing. Open the bay at my order."

"You're gonna cut through?" he asked, jumping up.

"We'll see," she answered.

In the launch bay, Galla and Guru suited up, and she glared at the Prince.

"You don't expect *me* to come with you?" he asked, aghast.

"I do. You're a member of my crew now, and I am ordering you to suit up. Then we'll see just how good your telepathy really is," she said, adding with a downturned mouth, "and whether or not you're telling the truth."

He stared at the suits. "How will I ever get this helmet on my head? What if the suit doesn't fit? These aren't my things."

"Lucky for you, they're adjustable," grumbled Galla.

The Prince dodged behind a bin and changed, and when he emerged, Galla and Guru had to turn away from him for a moment to avoid guffawing. He was a very slender being, with a large head even without his appendages. With the fitted flight suit and the helmet adjusted to size, he looked like a doorknob on sticks.

I'm glad Rob is not seeing this right now, she thought.

"The indignity! I look absurd!" he cried.

"So," Galla managed in a strangled voice, "you could...um...put your robes *over* the suit then."

With something resembling a whine, the Prince obliged.

"Rob," she called. "Now."

The bay opened, and Galla said, "Engage grav boots," and her crewmates said the same to their suits. The Prince huffed, struggling to lift his legs from the floor of the bay.

"I'll go first. Cogniz, you go after me, and Guru, after him," Galla said. Guru nodded. "Get us really close, Rob."

"Not scraping the paint, though," he said in a light voice. "Good luck." In her helmet speaker only, he said in a low voice, "Be safe. I love you."

The bay opened. Galla took her gravity-enhanced steps to the edge and stared at the ship several feet below. She sat down, slid her feet over the edge, and let go. She landed on the ship with a disturbing jolt through her body, splayed her hands on its surface, and then looked up. Guru had his hands on the shoulders of the Prince, who visibly recoiled from the opening.

"I really object to this!" he shouted in their helmet comms speakers.

"Then maybe you should be more truthful!" she called back. "Jump! I've got you."

She readied herself. The Prince, with his great bulbous helmet, clumsily slid over the side of the open bay. Just then, the ships hit turbulence in the junction, and their synchronous flights were thrown off, leaving the Prince dangling by his hands several feet away from Galla. He shrieked uncontrollably.

"Rob!" she shouted. "Move us back together!"

Slowly, the *Fithich* moved back into position over Galla.

"Lower!" she ordered.

"That's gonna be pretty close," Rob replied.

"Do it!"

And he did, so Galla seized the legs of the Prince.

"Let! Go!" she yelled, her face inflamed with frustration.

Squealing, he did so, and Galla set him down feet first onto the ship's surface. His huge helmet struck hers, and they both sat down abruptly on their behinds. After that, Guru leapt down sleekly.

I'm glad I can count on one *of you at least!* Galla thought, rolling her eyes.

"We're on," she gasped to Rob. "Move away until I say."

The Prince was breathing heavily, so Guru put a hand on his shoulder to reassure him.

"Now," Galla said to them, "we need to get in. This could be a hatch; I'm not sure."

They walked heavily around a circular indentation in the ship's surface.

"Guru," she called, "can you walk around and see if there's anything else of interest?"

"Yes," he answered.

"You okay with this?" she asked. "I know you've never done this before."

"I can handle it," he said cheerfully, and he stomped away.

"Cogniz," she then said, turning to the Prince, who looked very strange indeed in his frozen robes in the junction space, "do you see anything I'm missing? A control panel, anything?"

"No," replied the Prince.

Guru returned. He announced, "It's a pretty battered ship. Parts of it are torn up from whatever hit it. There are cauterized areas where there might have been doors and ramps."

"Then let's cut through here," said Galla. "Three of us can work to get this done."

She and Guru swiveled forth their suit's tools and worked with laser torches in the circular groove. These barely made a scorch mark and did not penetrate the surface.

"What is this thing made of?" Galla wondered.

Hazkinaut stood watching, not using his torch. She stared at him.

"Why aren't you helping?" demanded Galla.

"Torches won't work," he said.

"Why not?" she asked, leaning toward him with hands on her hips.

The Prince threw out his arms and then placed his hands on his bulbous helmet.

He said in an exasperated tone, "It's psychically sealed from within."

"It's *what*?" Guru exclaimed.

Galla faced the Prince.

"You *knew* about this?" she shouted.

The Prince smacked his helmet lightly.

"I didn't know it would be sealed like this, no," he replied. "Now that I'm here, I can tell."

"Okay," said Galla, and she fogged up her helmet with a great exhalation. "How can we break the seal?"

"You can't, because someone with telepathic ability is keeping it shut," he answered.

"There has to be some way of getting this open," said Galla, frustrated.

Guru said, "If your stones can move space stations, surely they can open this seal!"

"Good point," Galla answered brightly. She unzipped part of her suit, and out drifted the diamethyst. She grasped it in her gloved hands, and they all watched it begin to glow. "I don't know if this is going to work," she told them, "but I'm gonna try."

She put all of her focus into her stone, and the tip began to shine brightly. "Look away," she warned them, and they did so, except for sneak peeks.

She knelt down and tried plunging the stone's brilliant tip into the surface of the ship. It scraped and partially burned the surface, but did not penetrate further. She sat and pondered the situation.

"Ariel said they used the stone by focusing on it and visualizing what they needed to do...with Aeriod's help," she muttered. She looked up at the Prince.

"You're a telepath," she said slowly.

The Prince scoffed. "Congratulations, brilliant Lady Deia."

"And you're also a mage, aren't you?" Galla continued, her eyes narrowed.

Prince Hazkinaut said nothing.

"You're not to the level of Aeriod in skill," said Galla, and the Prince twitched. "But if you can put your focus and concentration on my stone, what would happen?"

The Prince made an exhausted sound, and said, "Fine. I'll play this little game, but I don't expect it will work."

He knelt beside her. She positioned the stone on the groove, held it steady, and focused on it again. Once again it shone at the tip, and felt hot even through her gloves. The Prince could not look at it for long, but he put his mental focus on it as well, and held his hands above Galla's.

Guru gasped. The stone sank into the ship as though it were putty. Galla then twisted and dragged her stone all around the grooved seal, and finally at the last remaining bit, she stopped. Then she pushed down on the circle with her grav boots and strained and pushed again. It opened downward like the lid of a can.

She looked up at the Prince with a tired smile. "We did it, Your Highness! Thank you!"

But the Prince merely nodded, clearly exhausted as well. He stared at the hole with unease.

What remaining air had been inside the ship's space below came soaring out, with bits of debris along with it. Then she waved at her companions.

"Let's see who's hiding from us," Galla said in a low voice, and she and Guru and the Prince lowered into the darkness.

29

FORSAKEN

Their helmet lamps cut triangles of light inside the dim ship. Above them, the junction flow pulsed, giving some light from plasma. But the empty space within the ship stretched for a long distance on either side, for it was a large vessel. They walked around and searched for any airlock door they could find, and at first their slow plodding with their grav boots yielded nothing. Galla noticed the Prince hanging back, however.

"Cogniz," she hissed, "I notice you're not up here with us. I take it that means we're headed in the right direction."

"I am not really sure," he answered.

Galla could feel her temper rising.

"You can direct us, or we can go ahead without you," she responded forcefully. "Go climb back through that opening and back up into the *Fithich* if you like."

The Prince made a clucking sound and moved up closer to Galla and Guru. She glared at him, daring him to say anything.

"What do you think they were carrying?" Guru wondered as they stepped forward, their legs pulled to the floor by their boots.

Galla shivered. *Whatever it was, it's gone now. Maybe.*

"There," said Prince Hazkinaut finally, gesturing into the bleak, black-brown depths illuminated by their helmets.

Galla surged ahead, and soon they found a large door, sealed off. They all looked around its edges for any buttons or panels. Galla fingered her stone. "Shall we?" she asked.

"Let's not cut it!" urged the Prince. "If it's an airlock, we need it to work again once we're inside."

"Then how do we get in?" wondered Galla.

She leaned against the door with her palms. And then it opened with a great rush of air and particles. "Ah," she said.

"They let us in," said the Prince, and all three of them shivered then.

They stepped through, and the airlock shut behind them. Absolute darkness surrounded them, and they were grateful that they could at least see each other with their helmet lights. A rushing sound met their ears. Galla moved away from her companions and found the other door. It opened, and they entered this new space, and the airlock closed.

A dim, rounded hallway met their eyes, and Galla was grateful for some light. But it was spastic, flickering in dull yellow track lights along the floor and on the ceiling. At times they would go out altogether. She walked ahead, still plodding.

"No gravity here either," she noted.

She noticed dark smears of something on the walls, and blast marks, and long, snaking cables hanging from the ceiling. At one point she tripped over something, and looked down to find a coil of clothing.

It's empty, thankfully. But where is the being it belonged to? Feeling unease dance up and down her spine, she kept moving forward.

"Nothing good happened in this hallway," she murmured.

"No shit," said Guru, leaning in to look at more smudges on the walls. He pointed down. Gouge marks and more dark stains crisscrossed the floor beneath them. "Something dragged them out of here."

The Prince made an odd yip and they both turned swiftly to stare at him.

"Keep going," he gasped. "If you must."

And so they did, moving ever forward in the long vessel. They reached a large mass of tangled cables and equipment, piled in front of them, blocking the hallway.

"It looks collapsed," said Galla.

The Prince said in a disquieting voice, "Continue."

"But it's blocked," she protested.

"*Just. Continue,*" said the Prince in a whisper. His large, ethereal eyes shone from inside his helmet.

So they walked up to the wreckage, and Galla and Guru reached out to start moving the pieces, but then they both fell forward onto their faces.

"Urgh," groaned Guru.

"There's nothing there!" marveled Galla, and she noticed the Prince looked smug. "Ah. A powerful telepath," she said. He bowed his head. She noticed he did not want to look her in the eyes.

What is creating this fear in him? I can almost smell it!

She turned around and saw what she assumed was the ship's cockpit. Its rounded panels flickered on and off, just as the lights in the hallways had. More stains and rips and destruction met them. *But no bodies.*

One panel gleamed continuously, so she approached it.

"Guidance," she whispered to herself. "It *is* on autopilot."

She turned to Guru and the Prince and said, "I think the ship can be taken off autopilot. We can get this thing out of the junction, at least. Now, Cogniz, tell me. Where are the passengers?"

The Prince looked beyond her, at nothing, so far as she could tell. She felt another surge of irritation well up in her. Once, long ago, she might have fanned that spark of rage. Now she swallowed and pushed it down. For the moment. She was not sure how much longer she could cap the flame, for the Prince tested her.

But she could see his hesitation, and something more. Sadness? Dread? She wished, not for the first time, that she had his skills, and could read his thoughts. With Guru, she already felt secure; she knew where he stood on everything. With Prince Hazkinaut, scenarios seemed fluid and unreliable. But seeing someone with such a powerful ability look daunted at anything gave her pause.

After taking long, slow breaths, and continuing to stare past Galla and Guru, the Prince at last gestured with his outstretched hand. His companions turned their gaze into the darkness ahead.

Galla saw a tiny, almost imperceptible shiver in Guru. She sympathized.

"Very well," she said, her voice cracking. "Let's move forward."

Their lights scattered as they pushed ahead. They found the door to the cockpit, tall and formidable and sealed shut.

"Another telepathic seal?" she asked Hazkinaut.

"Yes," he murmured. He watched her grasp her diamethyst, and it began to glow. "Lady Galla," he said then, gently touching her arm. "This is painful. I am afraid."

She stared at him with wide eyes. Such an admission from him sobered her as nothing else had.

"We are all afraid," she answered firmly. "But we must do this. Will you help me cut the seal?"

The Prince's breath came out in short, quick puffs. "Yes," he replied.

Galla held her stone in her hands, and the Prince hovered in front of it. He focused his mind on the purple sparkles in the hexagonal crystal, and it grew brighter. She thrust the stone into the lip of the door, and it fizzed and sparked and grew molten.

Guru watched in awe as Galla dragged the stone all around the perimeter of the door, and the Prince's feathery head swayed as he harnessed his mental power. At last they finished, and they both sagged to the floor, exhausted, panting.

Guru knelt beside them. "Are you all right?"

Galla nodded. "Can you open the door?" she asked him in a feeble voice.

The Prince let his head fall onto his knees, his appendages twitching and sagging inside his helmet.

Guru pushed and kicked until the door made a ghastly screech of metal, and he shoved it open wide enough to let them in. On the other side, darkness lay. But the air seemed moist.

Galla and the Prince recovered enough to help each other up. Guru offered his arms to them, but they both refused. Galla smoothed her outfit, placed her stone back around her neck, and reached over to clasp Hazkinaut's hand. *Ariel would have done this for me,* she thought. *I will do it for him.* He took it, and his appendages swirled back together again. He gave her a short nod, and they walked ahead into the darkness.

Inside, the three of them swept their lights to and fro, finding nothing at first except more signs of struggle. They could smell something both sweet and acrid through their helmet filters. Galla watched Guru's mouth turn down, as he clearly did not like the scent. She did not either, but she forged ahead. They could see nothing but blank screens, chair-like objects hanging from above, and filth on the floor.

Galla was just about to ask where the passengers were, when Guru's light arced upward and he jumped back and struck it against the wall with a horrible crash.

"Fuck," he said under his breath, which Galla could hear wheezing. He scrambled about and seized his light, then held it up again, and she and Hazkinaut watched his eyes water and his throat bob in near panic.

They slowly lifted their eyes, and there they were: the huge, black, tilted eyes...eyes from her dream long ago... *"...our children..."* Aeriod's voice whispered in the dream memory.

For above them hung at least a dozen small bodies, upside down, staring at them all with large, lidless eyes.

30
THE CHILDREN

I n the glinting dark of the eyes of the hanging creatures, Galla
saw her own diamethyst reflected. She took in her breath
slowly, then released it.

"Jana," she said softly into her comms.

"I'm here," the other woman's low voice responded.

"Record everything starting now," Galla instructed.

"Got it," replied Jana.

Galla blinked back her unease and turned to the Prince, who
trembled, and whose feathery appendages twitched and twisted.
Galla could feel her own hair responding, going flat in her unease.

"Your Highness," she said to him, "can you speak to them?"

Hazkinaut stared at the shapes above and dipped his head. "Yes,"
he replied.

"Tell them," Galla continued, "that they are safe, we will not harm
them. We are here to help."

She watched the Prince take a deep breath, and his tendrils
unfurled halfway, like fiddlehead ferns. He stared up at the hanging
figures, and Galla felt a swell of pride. *Good for you*, she thought. *You're
doing it.*

And Guru, who stood a few feet back, now stepped forward and shone the light away from the eyes of the beings above. One by one they dropped easily to the floor, and sat with webbed arms wrapped around their knees.

"They really are like bats!" Guru whispered to Galla. She cocked her head to one side, not understanding the comparison, for she had never seen a bat. He saw her confused look, and said softly, "A bit different from cockatoos. I will show you bats when I can."

Galla nodded and smirked.

"That one," said the Prince suddenly, "that's the telepath," and he gestured toward a slender figure with dark gold-brown fur. It stared at him with its great, glinting eyes.

Galla could sense the tension in Hazkinaut. But this was a child: what reason could he have to fear a child?

"I'll address the children," she said firmly. "You can translate telepathically as you see fit." The Prince bowed his head, with a look of displeasure.

She said to them, "I want you to know, you are safe with us. If you want to come on our ship, you may. We will need to land somewhere to make that safer. If you can tell us anything about what happened, please do, so we can help."

She noticed Hazkinaut bristle.

"And if you are not ready," she went on, furrowing her brow at him, "that is fine as well. We just want to help you."

She watched as the Prince focused his gaze on the telepathic youth. That young individual lifted its arms a bit, and a sort of cough-squawk emerged. Chattering sounds rose from the others. Galla looked at each of them in turn, her eyes soft and her spirit thrilled. *I was wrong to fear them, ever. I want to help them, if they will let me.*

The Prince looked drained, and he said to Galla and Guru, "They lost their parents to Valemog."

Galla cried out, and covered her mouth with her hands. Guru shook his head.

"Their parents fought..." the Prince continued, and he shook as he did so, "and did all they could to protect their...children." The Prince knelt in front of the telepathic child. "Silderay, here, says their parents were either taken or killed by Paosh Tohon. The children do not know for sure. So Silderay hid the children with his mind. Made the ship seem like a derelict. Even tricked their parents into thinking they'd vanished, so the parents could never reveal their secret."

Hazkinaut slid to the floor in front of Silderay. Galla pressed her hand onto his shoulder, and tears pooled in her eyes.

Guru asked in a murmur, "What should we do now, Captain?"

Galla looked up at him. "I want you to return to the *Fithich*. And I want to stay here and pilot the derelict. Rob and Jana need to find us a safe world where we can land, and give these children a chance to board our ship."

"On it," said Guru, nodding. He stepped back into the shadows, his light swaying.

Galla said to the Prince, "Tell them what we are doing, and that they should strap themselves in. It could be bumpy."

"With you as a pilot?" said the Prince. "I expect it." Galla rolled her eyes.

Several minutes passed, and Rob spoke through Galla's comms: "Guru's on board. We've found a world we can go to. Follow my lead."

Galla sat at the dim controls, and Silderay crept up to her and passed its hands across the panels. They activated.

"Silderay shut down that too," said Hazkinaut, his voice grim. Galla wondered at his tone.

"That's marvelous work," she said warmly to Silderay, who did not understand her, could not read her thoughts, but somehow sensed her kindness, and relaxed.

With the controls working, Galla called to Rob, "I'm ready."

Within moments, the junction burst open in a bright spindle, and the ships shot through, the *Fithich* leading. Out of the netherworld of the junction, empty space shocked them. But among the dark spaces, a long, brilliant finger, like a stretched nebula, sparkled and burned. It stretched far into the distance, in a great corkscrew.

"What is that?" Galla breathed. "Rob, where's the planet?"

"Fuck!" cried Rob through the comms. "It's gone. The Event!"

"The terminus!" Galla gasped.

And the comms stopped working. "Rob," she called again. "Rob!"

And at that moment the void of space erupted into several spindles, as ship after ship came through junctions.

"Oh no," whispered Galla.

Silderay shrieked, and the other children followed suit.

"Valemog!" cried Hazkinaut.

Long forks of yellow light leapt forth from multiple ships toward the derelict. The *Fithich* was nowhere to be seen, and Galla knew it was cloaked. She frantically looked around the controls.

"We need a junction! Now!"

The Prince communicated with Silderay, and then shook his head.

"Doesn't know how," said the Prince.

"Rob!" Galla shouted into her comms. A crackle. *Please work!*

"Rob! Junction!"

And there, just off the port side of the ship, the brilliant scintillation of an opening portal burst forth. Galla could just see the shadow of a birdlike shape at its opening. She sighed in relief.

"Going through!" she cried, and at that moment a blast from a Valemog ship sliced into the derelict. A horrific groan sounded from behind her, and she and Hazkinaut were thrown forward to the floor on their knees. Their boots still anchored them, and they both winced in pain.

"It's been cut in half!" cried Galla.

"Can you still pilot it through?" asked Hazkinaut, on the verge of panic.

"I'll try," she said, and she aimed the ship at the junction. She reached its edge, and the remaining engine whined.

Then the spindle caught the ship, seized it, and pulled it through. More blades of light tore through the space, but the ship had vanished from Valemog's sight.

31

TRANSFERS AND TRANSFORMATIONS

A nother junction hop and they were out again, in blank space, with only distant stars. Galla took a deep breath and let it out with a groan. She turned to look at the children and at the Prince.

"We're safe now," she told them. "I am sorry...I should have guessed nothing would be straightforward anymore, with the Event. Systems destroyed. Communications scrambled. Valemog swooping in to take advantage."

"Galla," called Rob from the *Fithich*. "What's your status?"

"I don't think I can land," she said ruefully. "I can't risk it; the damage is too great. We don't need a crash landing."

"We're not in a junction, so we need to figure out a way to get everyone over here," he said. "Can I do the same thing as before?"

"I think it's risky," said Galla. "The connection is not good enough between that damaged door and the *Fithich*. I don't need to lose any children."

Rob sighed. "So now what?"

"I don't know. Does Jana have any ideas?"

Jana spoke. "I'm not sure. If we could somehow make a connector between the ships, to make it safer...but with what?"

Galla said, "Hmm. I don't know. Let's think on it a bit more."

She heard a pop and some rustling sounds.

"Beetle, *goddammit*," snarled Rob, "can you get off me?"

A crackle sounded through the comms.

"Captain Galla-Deia," said Beetle.

Galla raised her eyebrows. "Yes, Beetle?"

"I can help you," said the great insect in a musical voice.

"How so?" she asked it.

"I can weave a connection tube," Beetle announced. "It should work. You would still need suits and helmets, but it would keep anyone from floating away if we hook the ships together."

"What!" cried Galla. "Beetle! Yes! Brilliant! Get started!"

She clapped her hands together and smiled. She turned to Hazkinaut. "I really do have the best crew," she said, her smile radiant. Hazkinaut scowled, loath to participate in the transference from the derelict to the *Fithich*.

Nevertheless, he worked with Galla to find protective gear for each child, and once everyone was suited up, they waited. Finally, Rob said, "It's ready. I've never seen anything like it...Beetle worked so fast, he *blurred*."

"Beetle's not a *he*," pointed out Galla.

"Okay, *it* blurred," sighed Rob.

Jana connected two rods to the diaphanous web-tube Beetle had made, to stabilize it. She and Guru donned suits and helmets inside the bay. She called up to Rob, "Get the hatches lined up—we're ready down here."

"On it," called Rob.

Galla listened in and waited. The derelict essentially floated now, its last engine sputtering, so Rob aligned the *Fithich* with the drifting vessel.

"Lined up," called Rob.

Galla rose, and turned to Hazkinaut. "I'll go first, just to lead us out, and then you can bring up the rear, and make sure everyone is accounted for. Tell Silderay to let the others know we are going to another ship, and to stay close together."

She stepped forward into the darkness, out of the melted door-way, and eventually made her way back to the first door they had entered. The damage from the earlier attack was more obvious now, and she realized how close they had all come to being sliced into bits.

She shuddered. Valemog's agents were getting bolder. The derelict would not have survived another hit, and would soon be found again, since it did not have the *Fithich*'s security. Galla shivered when she realized Valemog might have seen evidence of the *Fithich*. She hoped they had not.

The hatch above opened into darkness, but the lights of the *Fithich* flashed on, illuminating the hatch and the room beneath it. Galla squinted as she looked up. She jumped, released the gravity boots from the floor, grabbed the edge of the hatch, and swung herself until she was able to get an elbow over the edge. She felt her legs drift, but she hung onto the lip of the hatch. She looked up and saw two rods extend toward her, pinning down a pale, gossamer tube. She saw the helmeted faces of Guru and Jana just beyond it, and she sighed in relief.

She took hold of one rod, pulled it down, and shoved it into the hatch. Then she took the other and did the same. "Get hold of those and pull," she called to the Prince. He obliged, and she found herself inside the tube, blinking.

"Can we attach those rods to something so they don't float out? Can we bend them?" she asked. Hazkinaut pulled on one.

"Not bendable. I will hold the rods and the children can climb up."

Galla looked at him with wide eyes. "Are you *sure*?" she asked, amazed.

"No," conceded the Prince. "But I will try."

"Thank you," said Galla, relieved and pleased. "Now tell them each to reach up for me, and I will pull them through and help get them through the tube."

And slowly, she worked to do this. At last the final child, Silderay, emerged, and she looked down at the Prince as she helped the child move beyond her.

"You ready to come up?" she called.

"The rods," said the Prince, nervous at letting them go.

"Reach for me," said Galla, "and I'll bring you with me."

Hesitant, the Prince released the rods and watched them drift. Galla reached down to him, her body partially extended up the tube. He made the leap, and she caught his hands.

"Pull us up," called Galla, and the two entered the tube, and the entire thing was brought up inside the *Fithich*.

The lock closed, and Galla and Hazkinaut wrestled against the webbed tube, and fought their way out at last. Then they all stood looking at each other: Galla, the Prince, the children, Jana, and Guru. Rob emerged, and took one look at Galla, bounded over to her, and lifted her off her feet.

"Thank *God*," he said, his voice muffled in her now-loosed hair.

The children did not know what to think about any of it. So Hazkinaut reluctantly told Silderay everyone's names and ranks, and Silderay passed the information on to the other children. Galla motioned for them all to follow her, and she disentangled herself from Rob with a smirk. "Back to the cockpit, pilot," she said to him in a gently chiding voice. He nodded and winked at her. The others all lined up behind her as she walked to the round room.

Smoothing her flight suit, Galla said to them all, "Thank you, Beetle, for the wonderful creation that helped us out of a strange situation." Beetle bowed its antennae. "Jana, Guru, thank you for the assist.

"We have refugees on board: children. Their parents are dead or missing. I am offering them sanctuary on board this ship, until we can maybe, just *maybe*, get an Associate ship to take them to safety. For now, they are our guests, and they need a place to sleep and food to eat, such as we can offer."

Galla pushed her tangled hair out of her eyes and sighed. "I think it's safe to say we are all very tired. I say we eat and get some rest as soon as possible."

Her feet dragged as she headed back toward her quarters, and she grabbed clean clothes before heading to the bathroom. She had had little time to think of anything for several long hours, and she felt disoriented by the journey and the ordeal. And yet she knew what she felt must pale in comparison to what the children had gone through. She sighed heavily.

How do I help them best? I know I can't count on Aeriod. I'm not sure I can trust the Associates, but then again, I don't think there's much choice. She straightened up. *I stink,* she realized, and she blushed to think of Rob seizing her in her filthy state.

She cleaned herself and headed to her bed. Rob was waiting for her, under the bedcovers, shirtless. She stared at him in surprise.

"Jana gave me the night off," he explained.

"Oh," she said, blushing.

Rob patted the bed beside him.

"I'm not sure we should..." Galla began, but Rob reached for her with his arms wide, and she felt herself grow hot. She slipped out of her clothes and into his arms, and then she forgot why she had hesitated.

Later, in what served as their night, she awoke to find Rob had gone again. She blinked, rubbed her eyes, and put on her clothes. She walked to the cockpit, where she found Jana engrossed in something on her viewscreen. Rob was not there. So Galla quietly slid back into the hall and went looking for him, as she had before.

She found him in the tail section of the ship, running through simulations.

"Rob," she said, and he jumped. "What are you doing?"

"Just checking up on things," he answered, shrugging. She caught sight of his eyes, and there was that blank expression again, distant, as if he were looking at her through thick glass.

Her throat seized up. *It's happening again with him.*

"Why, Rob, why in the middle of the night?" asked Galla. "Why sneak out of *our bed* and do this?"

He blinked. "You said a long time ago I should find out this ship's potential. So that's what I've been doing."

Galla swallowed, remembering that conversation with some shame. Still, she felt frustrated.

"Is that all?" she demanded, arms crossed, a stern crinkle in her forehead.

"Yes."

"Then why sneak around when everyone else is asleep?"

"Don't you trust me?" implored Rob, and the strange light in his eyes flickered.

Galla fought back the chill that crept down her back. She told him, "I want to, but you're not acting like yourself. I feel like you're holding something back from me."

Rob closed his eyes, shook his head, and then looked at Galla.

"I just want to make sure this is the safest ship there is. We've got precious cargo. And I'm not just talking about those kids," he said, and then his eyes cleared up.

Galla looked at him with a feeling of physical pain.

"You don't need to do this in secret. Go through whatever checks you want, but please...stop sneaking around," said Galla. "It's not...it's not right. And it's unnecessary. And it's...it's not...*oakay*."

Rob snickered. "Fine, fine, Space Princess," he said, soothing her. "I still have a couple hours left before my shift change. Why don't we go back to bed, and I'll make you forget *all about* this."

Galla looked at him skeptically but hopefully, and took his hands. He led her back to their quarters, and knelt before her, and soon she did, in fact, forget everything, including how to breathe, as she gasped and grabbed for something to hold onto. Rob afterward pressed his face against her abdomen and looked up at her.

"Better?" he asked, with a rakish grin.

"Much," she exhaled.

32

THE KEY

Galla woke, stretched, and smiled. She lay alone, but knew Rob's piloting shift had begun. She tried not to dwell on his strange nighttime activities for the time being. She chose instead to think of the pleasure he had given her. And then she sighed, and brushed those thoughts away as well, and readied for her day as captain.

She entered the round room and blinked. There perched all the children from the derelict, and they turned their immense, black, glittering eyes to her. *Do not react*, she told herself. The long-distant dream on Rikiloi returned to her briefly. She steeled herself and looked at them openly.

The Prince shuffled in, disheveled, and Galla felt a flicker of sympathy. He looked exhausted, and she realized it must be from his constant thought bombardment from everyone on board the ship except her.

She recognized his expression of relief when he looked at her, because she had seen it on Ariel and Dagovaby's faces as well. *I'm an oasis for telepaths*, she mused. *Well, at least for now.*

"Lady Galla-Deia," said Hazkinaut formally, "I think it best that we contact the Associates. I can travel with the children, and get a transport back to Mehelkian."

Galla stared. "Really! I'm impressed and pleased, Prince. What then?" she asked. "We still need more telepaths."

Silderay clucked.

"*Absolutely not!*" cried Hazkinaut suddenly.

Galla stood very straight. "Excuse me?" she asked, eyebrow cocked.

"Not you, Lady," said Hazkinaut, and he groaned. "Silderay suggested he be one of your telepaths. I refused."

"Agreed!" exclaimed Galla, but she smiled at Silderay. "Tell this wonderful child I am grateful, but we must only have adults for this task."

"I already did," said the Prince with a sniff.

Galla sighed. "Then we must try to contact the Associates. I'll ask Jana to try and get a clear, secure channel open. But the interference—"

Silderay rasped and made small, chirp-like sounds, and twitched its hands toward Galla.

The Prince stared at the child. "What!" he cried.

Galla squinted. "Yes?"'

"Silderay...are you *certain*?" asked Hazkinaut, his eyes piercing the child. It did not flinch. The Prince looked up at Galla in alarm.

"Lady Deia," he said in a low voice. "Silderay says...they knew about you. They...they wanted to know if...if their parents had seen you."

Galla felt her hair drop, as if pinned by icicles.

"They?" whispered Galla. "Valemog?"

"Yes," answered Hazkinaut. "And, Galla, I regret to inform you: you have a bounty on your head now."

Galla gasped.

"Jana!" she called.

"Yes?" responded Jana.

"Please open a secure channel to the Associates. We need to get these children to safety immediately. Rob, keep an eye on anything unusual."

Guru popped in and asked, "Is everything all right?"

"No," said Galla, biting her lip. "I'm a target. You're all in danger."

"Oh, well," said Guru with a smirk, "if that's all..."

Galla clucked her tongue and paced. "We have to make sure these children are placed with the right people, in as safe a place as possible. Immediately."

"How can I help?" asked Guru. Galla glanced at him with her forehead pinched. She kept walking.

"I don't know," she admitted. "I have to find some way to defend everyone. I don't know how. I wish I could remember...all of my training. I feel so useless right now! I'm locked up!"

"Can we help you remember?" Guru asked.

Galla whipped her head around to look at him. "How?" she wanted to know. She had not thought of this before. Other than looking at the recordings, she did not know a way to remember anything from her time on Bitikk.

"You've got footage," Guru commented.

"Yes, but that didn't help me," snapped Galla. She folded her arms.

"But what if you approached it from a different angle?" asked Guru calmly. "What if...what if we went somewhere, a safe space. A training ground. And you could try to remember there? Maybe we could test you!"

Galla's hair shot in all directions around her.

"Could you?" she asked, her eyes agog and her fingers clasped under her chin, making her look childlike.

"It's worth a try, don't you think?" asked Guru with a crooked grin.

"I'm afraid to look at those recordings again," Galla said suddenly. "And Jana won't."

"I will," promised Guru.

Rob stepped into the room. "And so will I."

Beetle waddled in just then and stood up on its legs. "Captain Deia, I shall assist you in your training."

Galla beamed.

"You would all do this?" she asked. "There's a lot of risk involved."

"You need us," Rob pointed out, "and we need you."

"You said you're locked. We're your key," said Guru.

Galla closed her eyes, her hands still clasped. She felt an extraordinary sense of hope and gratitude, and when she opened her eyes again, she knew she was ready.

33

EMISSION

They sat around the round table while Jana prepared the viewing material. Galla made sure none of the children could see, by closing off the doors to the room. They were given a chance to play and explore the rest of the ship.

"Like I said," Jana reminded Galla, "I'm not watching this again. But I'll get it ready for you. Then I'm taking the helm."

Galla reached her hand out to Jana, and Jana bowed her Mohawk-crowned head and squeezed Galla's hand in return. "I'm so grateful for you," said Galla.

Jana sighed. "I hope this isn't too much for you. But I guess I have to agree, you need to see what you can and can't do. I'm still searching for more info on you, but I think I've combed through all the data I have at the moment."

"You've done your best," Galla told her. Jana nodded, then left for the cockpit.

Rob sat on one side of Galla, and Guru and the Prince sat on the other. Beetle stood on its hind legs behind Rob to watch. Jana had enlarged the recordings, making Galla appear one-third her actual size. The effect chilled each of them, even before the playback began.

Galla felt as though she were being hung over an abyss, one far greater in depth and width than a Device. Her fear and shame at being tortured returned, and she trembled where she sat. Her friends, however, reached to her, clasped her hand, put an arm around her shoulders, stroked her hair, or touched her with antennae, in Beetle's case. It helped still a deep ache in her, a longing for Meredith's warmth, or Ariel's support. And at a more primordial level, she thought sadly of Oni-Odi. Those feelings of loss still reverberated through her. She missed each of them so much.

She swallowed, and let the images play.

When they came to the point at which Galla was set on fire, Rob cried out as if punched in the gut. He held onto Galla, who blinked back hot tears. She could not remember the exact sensation of the plasma fires. She had blocked it. But there was something deeply awful about it—the visions in the Devices came back to her. Rob's own visions seemed to come alive in these images. But Galla wondered again...had he seen her past, or her future?

Guru said slowly, "So you can withstand a considerable amount of heat and fire without being burned."

Galla nodded.

They watched more, and Galla in one segment was pummeled between machines, and this disturbed her friends so much that she stopped the recording.

"I remember the pain afterward," she told them. "I don't remember how I felt after the fire. But the hits...I remember those. I was bruised. I couldn't sleep well. You don't have to keep watching."

"We're here with you," said Rob, and he kissed her temple and put his arm around her waist. She leaned against him.

"You can bruise," observed Guru, "but can you be *cut*?"

He soon found his answer. Galla had been dropped into a turbine of blades, and then subjected to lasers. Nothing broke her skin. In one scene, four beings fought her and held her down, then attempted to cut off her hair. Their implements all broke.

"Indestructible head material!" exclaimed Beetle, and nervous chuckles responded.

"Maybe," answered Galla, with a sigh and a little smirk. "Sometimes I wish otherwise, because my hair gives too much of me away."

There was one recording that Galla played back several times. She could not understand what she was looking at, and neither could anyone else. She was standing with her arms above her head. Voice commands came sharply, and she put her hands together high above her, and a great column of white and violet light shot straight up from them.

"What do you think?" she asked in a soft voice. She froze the image so they could see the great beam coming from her.

The Prince stared at the image a long time. He said slowly, "I think it might be like the cutting of the derelict door."

"What do you mean?" asked Galla.

"You had your crystal with you on the derelict," the Prince continued, "but I don't see it in these recordings."

"I left it on Rikiloi," Galla replied. "They didn't know I even had my geode. Aeriod never told them. So they didn't know about my crystals until—until Mandira!" And she gasped. "Somehow... somehow they got me to channel my power."

"Well," Rob pointed out, "you said yourself: *you* are diamethyst. You're made of the same stuff as your stone. More or less—because you"—he coughed—"are anything but *hard*."

Galla blushed crimson and nudged him, but she grinned.

"So," Galla said, biting her lower lip, "somehow they triggered this from me. How?"

Hazkinaut said, "There had to have been at least one telepath present. Maybe several."

Galla stood up in a rush. "Your Highness," she said, her breath coming quickly, "can we test this out—without my crystal—using *you*?"

Prince Hazkinaut visibly shrank down into his seat, and his head-appendages curled tightly against his scalp, making his turbaned head look as though it had shrunk.

"What might it do to me?" he asked, his voice shaky.

Galla grimaced. "I don't know. We can't tell from these recordings if anyone else was around."

"I think someone was," said the Prince. "What happened to that being, or beings, though? You might have killed them!"

Galla gasped.

"Jesus fucking *Christ*, Prince Has-Been," snarled Rob. "Way to make her feel *worse*."

"But she doesn't know," pressed the Prince.

Galla put her head in her hands. "No, I don't know. I won't risk hurting you. I am sorry."

Rob's fists clenched and he glared at the Prince. The Prince shrank back down in his chair at first. Then he looked again at the image of Galla emitting a great beam. He shook himself, then sat upright.

"No. No. I'll do it. We need to know," he said, and he stood up. "Take us to a place we can practice. That way you'll have some idea for what to do with the Device. If one tiny stone can be channeled using telepathic power, what can an entire person made of it do? You have to know. This has to be the answer."

Galla stood again. "If you're willing, then, let's do this immediately. We have to get those children away from me as soon as possible, and you'll have to go with them. We need to find a suitable world. It's training time."

Galla approached Jana in the cockpit. Jana looked up at her with sunken eyes. Galla could tell she had not ceased her research. *She never stops.*

"I need your help, Jana. I've decided it's time to test my abilities. I need a place where I can do this without incurring risk to any nearby civilization. Can you find us a world that's desolate *enough*, that we can still work with? It doesn't have to be suitable for all of us. We can suit up. But having decent gravity would be good, so maybe not an asteroid."

Jana nodded and twisted one of her emerald earrings. "I'll see what I can find. And Galla," she said, looking warmly up at the lady, whose hair swirled and whose brow furrowed anxiously, "I'm sorry I didn't sit with you in there."

Galla shook her head and cast aside her errant thoughts. "I wouldn't ask you to do that again. You sat with me before, and you gave me courage then. Thank you for that, Jana."

Jana nodded, said, "You're welcome," and swiveled back in her seat.

And Galla thought, for maybe the thousandth time, that Jana might be her most resourceful crew member. She sighed in relief and gratitude.

It took a long time for Jana to sift through worlds and clear them with Galla.

"There are only three left anywhere close to our mission zone," declared Jana. "One of them is full of defunct old mining operations. I guess someone plundered and left. Only a few scattered settlements there. The second one has a significant underwater population, but its land areas aren't very big. Still, they could be useful test sites— think desert islands, that kind of thing. The third...I don't know. It seems ideal. It's a tundra world, basically. It has almost no population. But what *is* there is strange. It has some sort of other life signature I'm not recognizing."

"Can you show me?" Galla asked.

Jana brought the world onscreen. "Here's the population I'm reading. But then look here," she said, pointing at strange streaks on the planet's surface.

"What are those?" Galla wondered.

"They seem like frozen lakes, glacial lakes. Not all of them are frozen. But there's some sort of life in them. And it looks extensive."

Galla stared for several minutes at the screen. *Beings in lakes.* That was not particularly exotic. Except on Perpetua, where a being in a lake had contacted her and told her to find the Device worlds, to try and stop Paosh Tohon. *Could there be more like that?* Her diamethyst felt warm to her chest just then. She held on to it and bowed her head.

"Let's try it," she said suddenly. If there were more such beings on that world, maybe they could help her.

Jana looked up at her doubtfully. "Personally, I think the mining planet might be best," she said. "It's warmer. And you could practice against the equipment."

"Maybe," admitted Galla, drumming her fingers on her chin. "But I think we should at least give this tundra world a try."

Jana nodded. "Okay, I'll set the course."

"I'll tell the crew," said Galla.

And she walked back to the round room. She felt exposed. She had shown them her own torture. Just before she entered the room, she closed her eyes. She remembered an old sensation, of someone's hand finding hers. *I waited for you*, he had said.

But who are you, who were you? she wondered. She peeked around the edge of the door and saw Rob's fiery red head. He was leaned back, his arms behind his head, his feet propped on the table, and he was laughing with Guru about something. She felt a gush of love for him, and fondness for Guru as well. Beetle was cleaning its antennae, and she found she adored this as well. *My crew. I am so lucky. I don't want to let you down.*

"Yeah, well, one thing's for sure," Rob was saying to Guru, the pitch of his voice lowering. "I'm not being taken by them alive. You know what they did to Spears."

"Like teeth in his brain, he told me," Guru muttered in agreement. He turned his head and listened, and then he put a finger to his mouth to hush Rob.

Galla entered the room and felt her hair coiling around her, reflecting a sensation of both anxiety and hope. The two men glanced at each other, and then at Galla.

"We've found a place," she announced. "I'm going to train."

The Prince turned and looked up at her with tired eyes, but he appeared determined.

He said, "Lady Deia, we will help you."

And they all stood and bowed to her. She blushed, and smiled at them.

"If I fail spectacularly," she said in a shaky voice, "what will you think of me?"

Rob smirked. "We'll think you might just be human after all."

34

VIOLET

Ariel lay curled on her side, facing her infant. He slept soundly, miraculous for such a small child. He had awakened earlier to nurse, but promptly fell back asleep.

He's so content, she had marveled.

It was as if the little fellow knew his mother needed all the support she could get, so he would not ask for more than he needed. He never fussed unless he needed changing. Or perhaps he was just so different from his older brother, Paul, that it only seemed he was a calm baby. For Paul was vocal and on the go, and nearly wore his parents out.

But the peace of the new baby's sleeping patterns helped them all to rest. And Ariel needed it most: for her grieving, for her postpartum recovery, for her sanity. So she was grateful for an easygoing child.

She slept, and she dreamed. She drifted across time and space.

And in her ear, a melodious voice whispered.

"We were the only two. They changed us, and they feared us."

No. That was your doing, thought Ariel.

She could almost feel Veronica's lips on her neck.

"Nobody made me feel more beautiful, you know. Not even

Dunstan, and he treated me like a goddess. But *you*. If only. He was my consolation prize."

You chose all of that. You shut out everyone.

"No, you shut *me* out. Why? Why did you bury this? Was I that awful to you?"

You weren't. Until you were.

"Why didn't you help me?"

Hot tears flowed from violet-blue eyes. The beautiful woman pushed her dark, wispy hair from her temples and stared at Ariel.

"Why, Ariel?"

Ariel jerked awake.

Fuck, she thought.

Dagovaby stirred next to her, and she quickly put up a mental block against him. She felt sick.

I did this. I played a role in all this. I have to make it right.

35

THE LAKE

Kein walked all through his house. He stared at every single object on every shelf. His eyes traced a small crack in the plaster of a wall, which he usually forgot about because Rez had placed a tall potted plant in front of it. He breathed in deeply through his nose, to smell it all. Home. He was memorizing home.

Everything was tidy. Rez had cleaned the day before, while Kein was out staring at his kayak, stopping his relentless polishing to sink back into sadness. Rez had called him for dinner, and Kein had stood blinking, staring at his plate, and all the clean surfaces. He could not eat then. He wanted to lean over and vomit, or roll onto the floor and curl into a ball. He avoided the grey eyes of his husband, who watched him. Rez sighed.

"You may as well eat," he had said, his voice level. "A good idea for any journey, right?"

Kein had pulled his eyes back to his husband's bearded face, and he studied the wiry grey curling in that ginger beard. They were getting older.

Kein opened his mouth, but Rez stopped him by saying, "You can't back out. Stop it."

And Kein's voice cracked. "I don't fucking want to go," he said, his teeth grinding. "I know I *have* to go."

"We've been over this," sighed Rez. "Why be like this *now*? Now is the time to say goodbye to everything and everyone."

That shut Kein up.

He managed to force his food down, then he abruptly scooted his chair back from the table. It made a barking sound.

He zipped up a raincoat and left, marching into the drenching dusk.

Well. I won't miss the weather.

And so he made the rounds, dropping by the co-op, speaking to the folks at the hangar. He even waved at a group of Veeldt-Ka, the other bipedal, sentient species that resided on Perpetua, but if they noticed him, he could not tell. And then he began to walk back home. He stopped by Auna's Rock, and thought fondly of Galla. He also thought about Auna, and wished anew that he could have known her.

"You followed Great Granddad all the way out here," he muttered, sitting where she had sat many years ago, feeling a new world's wind in her face. "You built something. And now I have to leave it. But if I don't...well, it would all have been for nothing, right?"

And then he inhaled the scent of the sea, and let the rain fall on his face. *Convenient. Hides the tears.*

And then he turned to go home, saying goodbye mentally to everything. The trees, the small town, and every step took him both closer to his home and farther away from it, for he could not guess where the journey would lead next. That was his last night on Perpetua.

Now he turned at last to the back deck. Rez sat outside, waiting, staring into the forest. The forest Kein must enter, and never come back to Rez again.

Rez rose and pulled him into his massive arms, and Kein felt his determination slip. He clenched his teeth. Rez simply held him.

Finally he said to Kein, "I packed your bag for you. I knew you'd be in a mood."

Kein gave him a clipped laugh that ended in a choke.

"I'll look for you forever," he said, and then he could not speak.

"I'll wait until you find me, somehow, somewhere," Rez answered. "I love you, and I believe in you."

"I love you," said Kein, his voice rasping.

He walked down the stairs, away from his home and his husband, and shouldered his bag. They looked at each other again, but then Kein could not bear it, and finally he turned toward the path. Each footfall seemed a crash, a calamity, a disaster to take him from the love of his life.

How can anything be worse than leaving him? And yet I know it is. I've got to stop that thing out there from taking the people who love each other apart.

And soon he was enveloped in a cavernous silence, the dark evergreens bending over him as if they had been waiting for years. He had not been this far along the path since his youth, when the lake had whispered to him, and he had run full-tilt away from it back home. The nightmares followed for years: someone whispering, "Kein, Kein, Kein," slowly, and other whispers he could not interpret. Voices folding in on each other, incomprehensible.

Yet now, silence. The light grew dimmer the farther he walked. He was beyond sight and sound of the house he had lived in his entire life. He kept walking.

And there, at the base of a long, curved line of tree trunks, a flat expanse stretched back beyond sight. And it began to glow.

The lake.

He froze, and felt his bag slide off his shoulder. It hit the ground with a too-loud *FOOMP* and he jumped. Ripples spread in the pale blue glow of the lake, ripples coming toward *him*.

Oh fuck.

One ripple stretched out of the banks of the lake with a little *gloop* and then grew into a phosphorescent tendril. It hissed along the ground toward him, and he felt as if his legs were rooted. And there it was, at his ankles. It touched him.

He wanted to scream, but could not. His mind flashed with pulses of light, with images whirling, faces familiar and yet not so. And then he felt himself falling, and the tendril wrapped itself around him and held him above the water so that he did not sink face-first into the lake.

Not comprehending, Kein shook, and he drooled, as more images flashed. A face emerged from the blue light of the lake, his own face! Or was it? It was a man, and he looked very like Kein ten years prior, though his forehead was narrower, and he wore a beard.

"*Kein,*" the man said. And the name echoed through the woods: *Kein, Kein, Kein.*

When and where am I? Kein managed to think, as he hovered over the water, held aloft by the lake creature, staring at what should have been his reflection, but was someone else's from long ago.

"*You're in the Innervation,*" said the man, answering his thoughts. "*Pay attention.*"

And Kein watched the face fade, and beheld a city with copper spires and buildings and floors that curved ever so slightly into a giant bowl. Above it, auroras twitched and roiled. The image faded, and a great purple facet reflected his face. *It looks like Galla's crystal!*

At that moment a great downdraft of wind splayed the trees above him, and the lake creature released him and slipped at great speed back into the water. The lake darkened.

"Wait!" he cried, almost wading into the lake, but then he looked up. It was a ship.

The Associates' ship, he thought. It was time to go.

But when the ship landed, Kein stared at it. He felt confused.

Not the Associates' ship?

For he had never seen anything like it. It was sleek, and silvery green, and seamless, like a great droplet. A panel opened, large enough to stand in.

"Who are you?" Kein called, but only the hissing of the wind in the trees answered him. He glanced back at the lake, and it sat dark and quiet.

Curiosity got the better of him. He approached the ship and peered inside. There was a seat, just the right size for him. Otherwise it was spare, but somehow beautiful to Kein. There was something about it, ancient yet new, and he marveled. He entered and found he could stand to his full height. He let the bag slide onto the pristine pale green floor. The door shut softly behind him. The controls glowed, and they again were unlike any he had ever seen before.

"Wow," he said aloud, "I guess this is my ride. The Associates have really upgraded things."

He sat in the chair, and it adjusted to him and made him feel safe and secure, which really did not make sense to him. And yet that was how he felt. He felt that things would be, as Galla might say, *"Oakay."*

The engine made no sound as the ship powered up and rose above the trees. Part of it became transparent, so he could see below, and he held his hands over his mouth as he saw Rez waving goodbye. He waved then too, frantically, and blew him a kiss.

And the ship shot up with great speed away from Perpetua, before Kein could take in one long look back at his homeworld. The ship shielded his view then, and Kein knew to secure himself, for there would be junctions to travel through...and he had heard of turbulence and disruption. He was not prepared for the number of junctions the ship bounced through. He was too unnerved to sleep through any of it, and so he grew exhausted.

He felt nauseated, wondering when it would all end. And then quite suddenly the ship stopped, seemingly through a final junction.

"Can I see out?" he asked aloud. The ship did not oblige him. It drifted a bit, until something seized it.

"Oh shit," he muttered. "What's happening?"

And then he felt the crush of intense gravity. Something pulled hard at the ship. He secured himself in his seat, and felt his body pulse and sweat from fear.

"Am I going to crash?" he wondered, but then quite suddenly he felt himself droop, and he began to fall asleep.

Kein. Kein. Kein.

36

LITTLE TOWERS

"**N**ow," urged Ariel. "Send it now."

"Ariel," sighed Dagovaby. "Why *now*?"

"Just do it. Trust me. They're not safe. Neither are we."

Dagovaby looked at the wan face of his wife, her hair limp and dark, taking in all light. Her brilliant green eyes stared at him, hooded, shadowed by something he could not discern. He felt deep down that he was losing her, and he did not know what to do. But he knew the urgency in her voice meant his family was in danger.

"I will send the signal," he said to her.

Ariel sifted through their clothing and began packing quickly. She found a little box in the bottom of a duffle, under her mother's quilts. At first she stared at it, not comprehending. She picked it up and studied its ornate silver scrollwork.

Aeriod's picture box, she thought. She opened it just a bit. She saw Forster's face, and she slammed it shut instantly. She shoved it back into the duffle and felt tears form in her eyes. *I don't know what else to do, old buddy. Sort of wish I could ask you.*

She tucked the two quilts around the box and wiped her eyes and nose on her sleeve. Then a little form crashed into her back and threw its fat little arms around her neck.

"Mama!" cried Paul, and he kissed her on her wet cheeks. She laughed through her tears and swept him into her arms, and squeezed him until he squealed and laughed, and then he pushed away from her. "Blankets?" he asked.

Ariel swallowed back tears. "Quilts. From Mammaw."

"Mine," said Paul authoritatively, patting the top quilt. He pushed his wee hand underneath and found the second quilt. "Baby A's."

At that, Ariel began to shut herself down. She picked up her infant son and held him on her lap, and she pulled Paul onto her left leg. She looked at them solemnly.

And she looked deep into their eyes, past an initial surprise. Deeper, into their sweet little minds. *Listen to me*, she told them. *Listen to me, and then forget. You know how you build little towers, Paul? I want you to build little towers. In your head. Watch me. I will show you how. Inside the little towers I have something. A treasure. It's only for you two. No one else. You'll know when you need it.*

Too soon, a ship arrived, hovering alongside theirs. It was nondescript. Softly pearl-colored, it bore a script on it that looked quite like a golden tree to Ariel.

"You're sure," she choked, her face in Dagovaby's neck.

"Ariel," he said, his voice cracking, "it's all I had."

And the strange emissary who boarded, hooded and short, held out pale lavender hands to the children. Paul ran to squeeze his mother around the legs, and she and Dagovaby looked lovingly down at him and his baby brother. With a small squawk, the infant rubbed his wee nose on Ariel's cheek. She held him out to the emissary, who took him gently. The baby turned to look at Ariel and Dagovaby, and Paul took the emissary's hands.

"'Bye!" Paul shouted at his parents. And the emissary took the boys onto its ship. The ship vanished instantly.

Ariel dropped to her knees and wailed. Dagovaby joined her, putting his arms around her, and they sobbed. Finally they quieted, rocking back and forth.

"That was the hardest thing I have ever done in my life," Ariel whispered.

Dagovaby spoke in a low murmur. "That makes two of us. If you're wrong, they're orphans."

"And if I'm right, we have a chance."

Ariel held Dagovaby's face in her hands and stared into his dark, almost black eyes, their gold pupil rings vibrant. "There's one more thing I have to do. But before that...I love you. Just...somewhere deep inside, know that I do love you, and I wish I didn't have to do this."

Dagovaby at first felt her sadness and her fear. He looked back into her green eyes, and they glowed in the low light. *What is this?* he wondered, and then he felt his own fear, as he sensed his mind shutting down, like doors being slammed one after another. Behind one of those doors were his two tiny boys. And he stared back at her, eyes glazed, and then he felt nothing at all.

37

FATHOMS

A cold world with scrubby vegetation undulated before Galla. She stood with a scarf wrapped around her head and mouth. Prince Hazkinaut stood apart from her, suited against the cold, his face shielded by a light helmet. She could withstand the chill, although she did not enjoy it, but he came from a hotter world.

On this world, in this lonely expanse, the sun rose slowly. It made a halo in the dark smear of clouds above them. Galla saw how the light barely reflected off the *Fithich*, which sat perched over a hundred meters away. She knew the crew all watched her and the Prince, to see what she would do.

And about that...what do I do? How do I make this happen?

She looked off to her left, and saw the still little silver lake that twisted and turned among the low hills. Dark grey and pearl and silver reflected in its surface. But her stone felt quite warm on her chest.

If you are there, she thought, *I hope you'll make yourself known. I could use the help.* And then she felt silly for thinking to a lake. But then again, a lake had taken hold of her, or rather the being in it, back on Perpetua. Would this one do the same?

"I feel ridiculous," she announced to Hazkinaut. "Just so you know. I guess I'll just...hold my arms up and...beam out?"

The Prince said, "I imagine it takes more focus than that. Try focusing on your stone first. See what happens."

So Galla took her necklace off and held the long hexagonal diamethyst above her head. It felt hot now, and threw off rays of purple light. She looked up at it, and it simply shone. Nothing else happened.

"Well," she said, "when we were attacked on Fael'Kar and Beetle's world, I...let out a blast. I'm not being attacked now."

"What about floating?" asked Rob through her earpiece. "Remember when you came out of the Device on that one world... when they were shooting at you?" and his voice went a bit higher at that last statement.

"I'll try," answered Galla. She looked up at her stone again, and it gleamed pleasantly.

Float, she thought. Her feet remained stubbornly fixed to the ground.

She felt hot, and knew her cheeks burned.

"This is embarrassing," she admitted to them all.

"Maybe you need to be threatened," suggested Jana.

"Well," said Galla thoughtfully. "You could shoot at me."

"What the *fuck*!" Rob shouted. "Absolutely not!"

Galla groaned. "Rob, it won't harm me. Not permanently, anyway. But maybe it'll trigger a response. Maybe I can't let go unless there's a reason."

Beetle clicked and wheezed in her comms. "Perhaps I can weave a net for you to fly into, so that you will not hit anything hard."

Galla dipped her head. "You're the sweetest, Beetle. But I think I want to try this with no net."

She turned to the Prince. "I want you to back off." Then she said into her comms, "Jana, on my mark, fire on me."

"I can't watch," Rob announced.

"Then don't, mate," said Guru.

"I can't *not* watch either," replied Rob.

"Didn't think so," Guru said in a gruff voice.

"Guys, come on," Galla said, exasperated. "Let's get this over with. Ready?"

Jana's rich voice came through. "I'm ready. But just so you know: I hate this."

"I'm sorry, Jana," said Galla with a sigh. "Three. Two. One. FIRE!"

And brilliant bursts of light erupted from the *Fithich* and struck Galla, and before she could react, she was flung several meters by the impact of the blast. She tumbled head over heels and skidded to a halt in a patch of shrubs.

The next time, a blast sent her flying high, and she slammed into the ground with a "HUNH!" She lay staring up at the low, slate-hued clouds and blinked. Her comms shrieked at her.

"You okay?" It was Rob, and she could hear the worry in his voice.

She slowly got up, dusted herself off, and walked stiffly back within eyeshot of the Prince and the ship. The Prince looked relieved.

"I am OAKAY!" she shouted, and she waved at the ship. *I'm really not okay*, she thought, rubbing her back and bottom. Hurting annoyed her, and made her a bit angry. Her stone bobbed on her chest and she could feel its warmth increasing.

Panting, she walked back to the original spot. She readied her stone in front of her. "FIRE!" she yelled.

Out came the bursts, but she was ready. She flashed her violet stone in front of her and a brilliant violet light shot all around her, creating a bubble. The blasts bounced off of this bubble, and she stood tall.

Shouts of excitement rose in her comms, and Hazkinaut bowed where he stood.

"Again!" Galla cried, so Jana fired at her again. And she blocked the shots. "Again! I want to try something else!"

This time, as the shots hurled toward her, she raised her stone high and rose up into the air, just before they struck her energy field. She twisted and looked down, and she felt a flush creep up her neck. *I did it. I controlled it.* Wobbling, she lowered her stone, and then she felt her feet on the ground. She caught herself as she fell to one knee.

She stood, and her crew cheered.

Then she turned to Hazkinaut.

"Prince," she said to him, "I want you to focus on my stone, just like you did on the derelict. Let's see what happens. But," and she raised her hands, and looked at him with warm copper eyes, "if at any time you feel unsafe, tell me to stop."

"You needn't worry about *that*, Lady Deia!" exclaimed the Prince, raising his head. She grinned at him.

She said into her comms, "We're going to test telepathic focus on me and my stone."

"Bring on the light show, space babe!" said Rob.

With a smirk, Galla turned to the Prince. "Focus on the stone. I don't know what else to tell you, because I don't know how this really works. But let's find out, shall we?"

Prince Hazkinaut's cranial appendages wavered inside his helmet. They twitched and pulsed, and he stared at the oblong gem around Galla's neck. She held it out in front of her like a tiny shield and watched his eyes glaze a bit.

"Oh!" she cried, for her stone scalded her, and she dropped it in surprise, but picked it up again. She gritted her teeth. "This *really* hurts," she said. "It burns."

"Should I stop?" asked the Prince.

"No-no," gasped Galla, holding on and wincing.

The Prince focused all his thought on the stone, and it seared Galla's skin until she shrieked, so she held it aloft, high above her head, just barely touching it...

And a vivid purple-white swirl of energy flowed from her feet, through her legs, and up her arms, until it all collapsed into the stone, and then emerged again from its tip in a blinding column. It surged into the sky, ripped a hole in the clouds, and shot into space.

The speed with which it shot upward caused a sonic boom. The shock wave sent the Prince reeling, so that he lost his focus. Yet Galla stood still, and the stone went cold, and she brought it down and stared at it, her eyes huge. She went pale, and she slid down onto her side on the ground.

She heard muffled sounds and felt herself being lifted. Rob had run at her until his legs burned, and he held her tenderly, pushing her hair back from her face, loosening her scarf. She opened her eyes at last and saw the blue-green spokes in his eyes, bloodshot, frightened. She batted his cheek with her left hand.

"Fine," she said, and she worked her jaw. It felt hard to speak. "Tired."

So Rob lifted her and carried her back to the *Fithich*. Guru had followed him, and he helped Hazkinaut walk along at first. But the Prince seemed upbeat.

"We did it," he said, satisfied. "Now we need to know how to channel that beam of hers. How do we use it?"

As they sat around the round table and ate dinner, the children flapping and squawking excitedly, Galla was deep in thought. Her bruised body and her singed hands slowly healed.

Ariel and Forster moved a space station by focusing on one of my tiny gems. So how can twenty-one telepaths focus on me, and will that stop the Event? Do we all focus together?

Amidst the raucous sounds of the children, she rose from her seat and slipped away. She walked to the bay and pulled down a sky bike, and powered it up. She shot out of the ship and into the night, broadcasting the bike's lights over the terrain. The lights eventually found their target and reflected off the lake. She parked the bike next to it and walked to its edge.

The clouds above her had broken up, and starlight stole through the breaks and shone softly on the dark surface of the lake. Her stone glowed pale purple. She sighed.

"I know," she said to the lake. "I know you're here. I would like to talk to you. I need your help."

And she watched as the reflected stars blurred, for ripples billowed across the lake, and little splashes met her feet. The lake itself then began to glow. She smiled in satisfaction. And she watched as a long, phosphorescent tentacle emerged and rose into the air, face to face with her. It lunged at her, and wrapped all around her before she could make a sound, and yanked her into that cold lake, down and down.

If she could have screamed, she would have. It covered her face with a sort of sucker, and she could breathe, but she was too frightened to do anything but gasp in the protected air.

The lake stretched deeper than she could have imagined. In fact, it extended far underground into connected pockets for several miles. The creature pulled her through these flooded caverns, until it reached a vast space. She jerked in shock.

Every bit of that immense cave was filled with creatures just like the one that had seized her. And she felt herself go even colder when she realized how similar they looked to the stalks of Paosh Tohon she had faced. The difference was that these beings glowed, whereas Paosh Tohon seemed to absorb light. They were forked and tentacled and mobile, twisting and twirling all around her.

The one creature still held her in its grasp and kept her mouth covered. Another approached it and emitted a bubble, which it stretched over Galla's head and body, and she felt herself released inside it. She sat down on the bottom of the bubble and looked at her captors through it.

She could now breathe properly, so she said, "Why did you bring me here?"

And a resonant voice spoke to her in her mind:

We know of the other beings on other worlds, like us. We know of the bastardization that is Paosh Tohon, a chimera of us and another being bent on torture and expansion. That is not our way.

We know of your stone, and of your task. You need strong minds to help you.

"Yes," said Galla, in awe of these drifting giants lighting up the depths. "So I was told on Perpetua. I found the Devices, and I put my stones in them. We have found telepaths, for when the time comes to act. But *what* do we do?"

There is very little time. The Devices work synchronously only twice in an epoch. That time approaches now, the next in a generation of those humans you represent.

You must channel your force through each stone, and the telepaths must focus on those stones. This will generate enough energy, coiled by the planets' rotation, to send forth a surge to seal the Event. There remains one final piece to this.

"And that's going to be something really easy, right?" said Galla with a sigh. "Just like wrangling all these people in the right place at the right time will be super easy."

The Seltra placed the Devices in such an alignment that they could operate and generate the coil to aim at one fixed point in space. That is where YOU must be.

"Are you going to tell me where that is?" Galla asked, feeling her hair lift as she slid into a temper.

It is hidden. You must travel to the apex of the stars to find it.

"Well," said Galla with a sigh, "we were on the right track, sort of. We knew something had to be there, at the end of the Horseshoe pattern. But when you say hidden...*how* hidden?"

Hidden even from us. And if it were not, Paosh Tohon would already have found it. Know this: if you do not align all the telepaths at the right time, and you miss this opportunity, the Event's repercussions will be fed upon by Paosh Tohon. That will leave it more powerful than it has ever been, and there may be no way of stopping it.

Find the hidden world; that is where you must be ready. Galla-Deia, it could destroy you to do this task.

She stood unsteadily in the bubble, and put her hands on her hips.

"Then let it destroy me," she said firmly. She jutted her chin high. "I'm one person, and my life means nothing compared to the galaxy's."

Your life means everything. Without you, we will be overcome. However, we do not know the limits your body can endure. Know that we will do what we can to help you, but we fear it will not be enough.

"So," she said, "I've got an almost impossible thing to do. I'm probably going to die. And if I don't do it *just right*, the galaxy dies." Her voice began to tremble. "I don't know how I can do this, but dammit, I'm gonna try."

You will not be alone.

"I've always been alone," Galla said with a choke. "In my geode, in space, for who knows how long. Alone. I never fit in with anyone. Always alone."

Not alone. And in the bubble she saw faces: Oni-Odi. Meredith. Sumond, her chef friend from Rikiloi. Aeriod. Ariel. Dagovaby. Rob. Beetle. Jana. Guru. Kein. Hazkinaut. Coniuratus. She hiccupped through tears.

"I'm gonna try," she repeated, "for them. For you."

Begin, the voices told her.

And she sat down in surprise as the bubble was moved at great speed out of the cavern, back through the catacombs, and finally shot up onto the surface and popped, leaving her knee-deep in dark, still water. The beings had gone.

She ran to her sky bike and raced back to the ship as fast as she could. She shoved the bike hastily into its dock, and only then noticed her comms band was not functioning.

"Water damage?" she wondered. But she shivered. "They didn't want me recording anything."

She heard the clang of footsteps running.

She turned to see the faces of Jana and Rob and Guru. Hazkinaut followed, his face sad. Jana's eyes leaked tears. Guru's mouth sat fixed in a grim line. Rob began walking toward her with his arms out.

Galla held her hands up to them and pushed Rob away.

"No," she said.

They have to be all right. Please. Please.

"Galla," was all Jana had to say.

38

ANGUISH

Jana tried.

"Goddammit," she muttered, and she sobbed. "There's only... *Shit*. I can't even say it."

Guru stepped in. "It was destroyed," he said, and he covered his face with his hands. "I'm sorry."

"I don't hear you! I don't hear you!" screamed Galla, covering her ears and pulling her arms onto her head as she curled into a ball on the floor. "They are *alive!*"

Rob tried to hold her, but she snarled at him and threw him off of her, her eyes blazing, her stone hot and sending off little bursts of light as she gasped.

"Don't *touch me!*" she yelled at him. She ran to the cockpit, and they let her go. She ignored the children and Beetle, who gawked at her in silence.

She slammed her fists on the console. "Show me the last coordinates for the Ambrono family. The last comms signal. Anything."

The *Fithich* showed her the last known location of their ship.

Beetle poked its head in cautiously.

"Captain," it said in a soft hoot and with several clicks, "I hope you find the little larvae. I am worried for them."

And Galla bowed her head over the console and wept.

Rob dared to enter and approach her, his eyes haunted by the grief of the woman he loved. She tensed when he placed his hands on her shoulders, but this time she did not push him away.

"They're still alive," she said, her hair coiling tightly. "I don't have proof that they aren't. So they are."

Rob looked at the stubborn crease between her swollen eyes and nodded.

"I know, I know," he said, and Galla for one moment wondered at his calm.

He's matured, she thought, and then selfishly: *I will enjoy him more as he grows older. Not less.*

These thoughts distracted her from the feeling in her midsection, a pain as if someone had drop-kicked her. She forced herself to stand.

"But I know," she said slowly, hating the string of words she felt she must say, "that while they're alive, if Paosh Tohon has them, they'll wish they were dead.

"Rob, I can't let it go. We have to get them."

"You're not focusing," he answered, puffing out a frustrated sigh. *But I couldn't either. Not if it were you*, he admitted to himself.

"I know I'm not!" she shouted. And she clenched her jaw and shook where she stood. He put his arms around her.

"We have to go forward," he told her. "We can't go back. Let's finish the job we're supposed to do. And the sooner it's done, the sooner we can get them."

Galla wailed. "The boys," she said, gasping. "The babies. Oh, this hurts, it hurts!"

"We'll do what we can. But the mission, Galla. It's not just those babies: it's everyone."

"I know that!" she cried. "But you don't understand, there's more to it. I—let me have a few minutes. Call a meeting. I need to tell you what I know. We don't have much time, after all."

39

ASTRAY

"**W**here is he?" shouted Aeriod, his eyes sparking even through the screen.

"I'm telling you, I *don't know*," answered Rez, scarlet with fury. "Don't you think I would know? That he would tell me if he could? He didn't. That means something happened." And his voice broke.

"All I know is, Kein went into the woods, and he didn't come back out on foot. I saw a strange ship rise into the sky, carrying him away. I don't know where it took him."

Rez covered his face with his large hands, and his shoulders shook.

"This is insanity!" Aeriod roared. "The Associates were to send a ship for him, so he could aid Galla. And the ship is gone? With no trace whatsoever?"

"What do you want me to say?" thundered Rez. "Do you think I enjoy this? Not knowing where Kein is, or whether he's alive or dead?" He put his fists against his eyes and hunched over.

"I—I apologize," Aeriod stammered suddenly. "I'll do everything I can to find him, I promise you. As soon as I hear any news, I'll let you know immediately."

Rez leaned his head back and looked at the ceiling and sighed. He turned off the screen.

40

IMPART

Galla's fingers splayed over the shiny black table. She stared out at each face, large or small, and wished she had words of wisdom. She could keep it together only long enough to tell them the most necessary information. Now they all knew what was at stake: time was limited, and they needed more telepaths.

Prince Hazkinaut rose.

"Then here is where we must move forward. Page an Associate, and I will take the children with me. I'll secure my own transport and gather more telepaths. We will make this work."

Galla stared at him as if down a long hallway, dimly lit.

"You've come a long way, Your Highness," she said to him. "Very well. Jana, if you could try to connect us with the Associates."

Just then Jana jerked her head up.

"Someone's trying to get through to us right now."

"Who?" asked Galla. "A hack? Valemog?"

"No," said Jana, and then she took a deep breath and looked at Galla with her inky-dark eyes. "It's a signal like this ship's."

Galla's hair sank all around her shoulders.

"Aeriod."

"Yes."

Galla shook her head and rubbed her temples.

"Fine," she said. "Allow him through."

And she shivered at the sight of the wizard's silver eyes, facing her copper ones, in a hologram above the table. A moment of confusion and consternation flickered between them, and everyone in that room noticed.

"Hi," said Galla lamely.

"Galla," said Aeriod. "I have news."

Galla lowered her head. "So do I. Tell me yours first. I—I can't bear—"

Rob reached over and clasped her hand.

Aeriod glared at her, and his eyebrows lifted.

"Galla," he said. "I recruited Kein at last."

She jerked her head up. "Oh!" she cried. "Oh, thank goodness, we need—"

"Galla," Aeriod stopped her. He closed his eyes for a moment. Then he opened them slowly, and looked at her with sadness. "I—I—it pains me to say it, but Kein disappeared after his ship left Perpetua. Somewhere along the way—quite far by the last signal checks I got. There...there is no trace."

Galla dropped into her seat and stared up at his image.

"Not him too," she whispered.

Aeriod gripped his hands beneath his chin.

"What do you mean? What has happened?"

"Aeriod, I don't know why...but Ariel and Dagovaby took a ship from Mandira. And they...they...something happened, and their ship was destroyed."

She shook as she said this, at the awfulness of making it real just by letting the words leave her mouth.

Aeriod let out a scream of rage and pain. Everyone jumped in horror.

"I must go to Ezeldae," he said finally, his voice deadly level. "We are damned."

41

MIND'S END

Ariel had built her own little towers in her mind. She connected them with scaffolding. In her childhood, she had practiced this over and over as a game. Her parents would never know, because they were not telepaths. She didn't care. There were other mind-snoopers, as she had called them as a child, out there. She would never let them in. Not one of them. Her own little city of towers in her mind stood tall and fortified.

She would have let Galla in, if Galla had been a telepath. She knew that now. She trusted Galla completely, and adored her. She would have given anything to dance with Galla's thoughts, for she knew that would be a lilting paradise, wondrous and beautiful, curious and open, just like the strange lady with her copper-gold-violet hair. She had almost let Dagovaby in, but she stopped short. To let him in meant to risk everything, not just for herself, but for him. So when she pushed into *his* mind and made a fortress for him, she let herself grieve. Because she knew she could not afford to let that emotion come forth later, no matter what happened with Veronica.

Ariel had come close with Veronica too. But something held her back, and she froze. Veronica had sensed it, and been hurt. And Ariel suspected Veronica had her own methods, her own secret defenses...

or attacks. That had proven to be true, but not in a way Ariel could have foreseen. Veronica: the perfect victim, and the perfect criminal.

She and Dagovaby sat shackled in their seats. The small ship carrying them was dank and noisome, hissing steam from various pipes. She had surrendered quickly.

Let's just get this over with.

She did not know the pilot and its assistant. But she could see Valemog insignia on them: one wore it on a tusk, hanging like an ornament. The other wore the emblem on its hulking back, large and deep red, resembling a bloody claw mark from a great beast, or a mouth of red teeth. She did not wish to know if this being was clothed, or had been branded.

She lost count of the junctions. Dagovaby sat slumped next to her, staring vacantly, his gold pupil rings now flat and ochre. She was in control of him, but not for much longer. She had shut down every emotion he was capable of feeling, lest he reveal their children's whereabouts inadvertently. It had felt like a murder, as if she had smothered him. She hoped she was wrong about this, and that somehow he could survive it.

Ariel had fought Forster's prodding when he accidentally came close to her past with Veronica, during their showdown on Mandira. Just as she was now, she was in the mode of shutting people out. She had already felt too exposed when he'd rescued her. And even though she was grateful for his saving her life, she owed him no favors by lifting the veil in her mind. He seemed to sense it, and he had backed off, having been intrigued yet spooked and disturbed on some level. She knew all those things about him. *Still,* she thought, *sure wish I could have had his help for this.*

The communications in the cockpit of the cramped ship became distorted, and as if on cue, both of the captors turned to look at Ariel. The ship went dark then, and floated. Ariel felt her body go weightless. Then she felt a cold, creeping sensation. She fought her fear, for she knew what it was. Paosh Tohon was near. Near, and vast, and staring into her.

The ship jolted, and the pilot rasped something in a language she did not understand. She tried to filter through the sadistic, choppy thoughts it put out, but then it turned to her and pulled forth a long rod, and sent an electric charge at her. She moaned and doubled over. *There will be no more mind reading at this time,* was all she could think.

The ship was being drawn toward something, and the sheer malevolence she sensed appalled her. She glanced at her husband, and thought it best he could not sense this, for it would surely have floored him. She wanted to see where she was, but the ship was windowless. There were many things buried among her little mind towers, and her innermost feelings squirmed there, and she hoped they would not be discovered.

Gravity returned, and Ariel understood the ship had been pulled into some kind of docking bay. It bumped and scraped a bit, then settled. The captors rose, jerked her up from her seat, and pulled her and Dagovaby along. Dagovaby walked as one possessed, as she worked hard to push him mentally. She was exhausted. *Not ideal.*

The smell hit her like a wall: ammonia, and something heinous, some sweet-rot scent like that of preserved flesh. She and Dagovaby were led roughly along a long, ridged, declining corridor that sighed and wheezed, a great throat of a monster. This went on for over an hour, and then the corridor branched. Bays and shrieks occasionally ricocheted through the narrow space. But mostly it was quiet, except for a very faint "ah-ah-ah-ah" that she didn't know the source for. It terrified her. But she fought that down.

At last they entered a tall chamber, and she stopped in her tracks as if bolted to the floor. A strange, roughly anvil-shaped structure stood in this vast space. It was black, with no reflection. And it was huge: easily the size of the tallest building in Circuit Prime on Fael'Kar. And off of it rolled pure malice, and greed, and hunger. She could not see them, but if she had Galla's ability, she would have beheld long tendrils spurting out of this shape, black and branching and snapping. Some of them shot into the air and vanished above; others danced all around her and Dagovaby. She could feel them snapping at her mind. And more loudly, "ah-ah-ah-ah" chattered at the edges of her sanity.

Something moved in front of the huge anvil structure, and the air shimmered. And there stood Veronica: gorgeous, dressed in scarlet, willowy and curvaceous at the same time, her lips blood-red, her eyes bewitching violet, her short, black hair perfect.

Which Veronica are you? Ariel wondered.

And the beautiful lady laughed in rich, sensual peals.

"There's only ever been one of me," said Veronica aloud, smiling. She walked with a marvelous swaying gait to Ariel and stood directly in front of her. Ariel could smell her, and she smelled... human. She smelled like the Veronica of old. This gorgeous creature raised her pale hand and stroked the lank, dark hair away from Ariel's cheeks.

Ariel's shackles fell away. Dagovaby's followed.

"You won't need those," said Veronica.

Next to her, a man stepped forth. His hair was dark and chin-length, and he bore stubble on his chiseled jaw. He wore a visor over his eyes, but Ariel knew instantly who he was.

"Derry," she said, her voice flat despite the vast hall around her. "I thought you were dead."

He laughed at her and shook his head. "Far from it," he said, his voice a sickening murmur.

Derry held in the crook of his arm an enormous gun, and Ariel sneered at it.

"Oh, it's not for you," he said, with a laugh. "I might use it on *him*, though," and he turned and grinned at Dagovaby. "I use it to help people make decisions. It fills them with pellets of acid that drill down into their bodies. So they can decide if they want to live forever in agony, or die."

He cocked his head and looked at Dagovaby's slack face.

"What happened to him?" he asked, but with no real concern at all.

Veronica smirked. "I'll see if I can find out."

Ariel's mind felt the push of this woman, who was no longer human. And while Veronica could not get to her innermost blocks, she was able to penetrate enough to put images in Ariel's mind.

Images of her with Veronica, sweat and lipstick and stolen kisses. Then the breakup.

"Why didn't you help me, Ariel?" asked Veronica, echoing the dream.

"You wouldn't have let me, not really," said Ariel through gritted teeth.

"Guess you'll never know, will you?" said Veronica silkily. "I know why you're here. It won't work. You've reached the end, and you can't go back. But," and she took Ariel's face in her hands, "you've given us the greatest gift: yourself. You were all we wanted."

Ariel tried to pull away from Veronica, but the woman's hands squeezed her face until she cried out. Veronica pulled her head forward until their foreheads touched.

"I will dig through, Little Goose," she hissed. "Every block, every shield you've put up: and oh, they're glorious. Well done, you! But I will not stop digging. You have information. And we need it. And we need you, after we get it: your power is spectacular. The galaxy will realign soon."

Ariel winced in pain, both physical and mental, as Veronica clasped her cheeks with her fingernails and would not release her.

Veronica turned her beautiful head just a bit. "We don't need him, of course. Derry, do as you see fit."

Derry slid his gun off his shoulder and set it on the ground. Ariel could see, then, the bright badge of Valemog over his heart.

He laughed and said to Ariel, "I get to thank you for ruining what was my life, and I do sincerely thank you. MindSynd was a good gig. I'd have stayed in it, had you not moved us without our consent. But again, thank you! You removed me from my limitations." He laughed and laughed.

"I've got a little secret," he said in a singsong voice.

He walked up to Dagovaby and took off his visor. Diamond eyes beamed out. Ariel gasped, and Veronica snickered. Derry reached up to one of his now crystalline eyeballs and pinched at its surface. He pulled forth a long needle of crystal, some six inches long, and held it up for her to see.

"Guess what I can do!" he exclaimed.

And he stabbed the needle deep into Dagovaby's forehead until it had disappeared. Ariel screamed, and Veronica dug her fingernails into her cheeks until they bled. Dagovaby collapsed onto the floor.

Ariel's thoughts whirled in a panic. *I fucked up. I'm sorry. I'm so sorry.*

Veronica laughed and laughed, and Ariel felt fingernails dig into her cheeks, into her teeth, into her skull. They clawed at all her little towers.

42

THE FALL

The last time Aeriod had been at Ezeldae, the Event had begun. That seemed quaint now. The cataclysm continued to wreak havoc on the galaxy, though at a distance, it appeared the Associates had planned well. They ferried refugees to accepting worlds and stations. They kept their fortresses intact.

But Aeriod knew the truth. They had fallen back, away from the Event, avoiding engagement at all. And as the systems affected cried for help, they kept their distance, helping only those who managed to escape Paosh Tohon, which had spread all along the great rent in space and devoured every suffering being it could. Valemog had assisted, seizing escaping ships and taking them as their own. Valemog had therefore amassed huge fleets quickly.

Aeriod swirled around in his quarters until paged. Ushalda herself met him.

"Who else is here?" he demanded of her.

"A fine greeting to you as well, Governor," sniffed Ushalda.

Aeriod glared at her with rage in his silver eyes. "There's no more time for pretty greetings," he hissed, "thanks to your incompetence. Now tell me: *who else is here?*"

Ushalda bristled, and stood straight.

"The Summoners are ready. The Speaker of Bitikk has declined to attend. Vedant is present."

Aeriod felt his cold anger twist at the thought of Bitikk, and the years Galla had spent being tortured there.

"So the sadist refuses to assist," he muttered. "Typical. Never there when you really need it, omnipresent otherwise."

"You would do well to appreciate that we all must act for our own worlds' defenses," clucked Ushalda as they walked toward the meeting hall.

"Oh, I have plenty of my own, need I remind you," snapped Aeriod. "And I'm strained to my limit."

They entered the meeting hall, and Aeriod stood glowing in the blue light from above. The Summoners all whispered and shivered on the fringes of the shadows.

Vedant's whistling voice echoed throughout as it said, "Speak, Governor."

Aeriod spread his cape out with his long arms, and then pulled it all around him, a black monolith with long, silver hair.

"Our plans are sundered to us," he announced. He stood very still.

The whispers and murmurings drifted through the hall.

"Tell us plainly, Governor," said the Summoners, all in one layered voice.

"The two essential telepaths, Kein and Ariel, are gone," said Aeriod. He swallowed. He closed his eyes. *Unbearable.*

Vedant's voice reached a high, irritating pitch. "What do you mean, *gone*? Have they been killed?"

The noise of the hall rose until Ushalda gave a trumpet-like blast to call everyone to order.

Aeriod answered simply, "Unknown. Dead, captured, we don't know."

"Explain!" Vedant shrieked. "You were to deliver them to Galla-Deia!"

"I made the attempt," said Aeriod with a lowered head. "I convinced Kein. Broke his family apart, and much good that did now.

As for Ariel...apparently she and her husband and children surrendered to Paosh Tohon."

The din of horror at this statement pummeled Aeriod's pointed ears, and he reached up to cover them.

Ushalda, vibrating from anxiety, asked what everyone there thought: "Did they know anything about us, our tech, our intelligence?"

Aeriod took a long time in turning to face her.

"Ariel was on board an Associate ship. Some of you Summoners were there. She very likely read your thoughts. And if so, then yes. Assume you are now compromised."

And at that moment a great explosion rocked the building, tearing the roof off the hall. Aeriod stood perfectly still, and watched as ship after ship tore through the pastel skies of Ezeldae. They all bore Valemog's insignia.

The Associates and Summoners scrambled away from the gaping hole above them. Panic and fear swept the counsel, and the air rang with shrieks among the injured.

Dazed, Ushalda cried, "How did they get through our defenses?" And above them a firefight ensued, between Ezeldae ships and Valemog.

Aeriod sighed, and despite the raining shrapnel and fire all around him, he turned and walked slowly away as Ushalda cried out behind him.

He approached the edge of a platform, looked over it at the sky cities below, and raised his arms. His ship materialized, and he swiftly entered it, then it cloaked again. On board, he quickly engaged the engines, shot above all the incoming ships, and sent a volley of blasts at the enemy fighters, before turning and leaving the atmosphere. He approached a junction and opened a channel.

"Galla-Deia," he said, "this message is delayed to you. I apologize. Ezeldae has fallen. If you receive this, it means I have also come under attack. There is something you must do. It is likely our last hope, before it is too late. You must—"

And something struck his ship. And again, and again. Amazed to see his ship lights flicker, he tried to finish the message. The hull hissed from something like acid. His ship defenses were failing.

He turned to see shapes dropping into his ship. Urgently, he whispered into his message, "Map!" and "Innervation!" and he sent it, and destroyed his own console, and wheeled to face whatever fate befell him.

43

ESOTERIC

Galla played the message over and over again. She wanted to see every detail.

The first thing she had said, in her shock and disbelief and even rage, was, "How long ago was this?"

And Jana answered, "At least three days. Maybe more. It's so encrypted, I can't be sure of anything, even with one of his own ships decoding it."

They had seen off the children with Prince Hazkinaut and a bag of Galla's diamethysts three days prior. She had sent communiqués to them, and they had gone unanswered. This haunted Galla. Had she sent them all straight into war?

The only thing she could do was rewatch the recording of her former lover. His eyes when he had said, "Map! Innervation!" were desperate. She had never seen such an expression in them before. He wanted her to decipher what he meant, and she could not.

She paced, and gibbered, and paced again. Beetle joined her, not knowing what else to do. She reached out occasionally and patted Beetle's shell. And she thought.

"You're gonna drive yourself nuts, Galla," said Rob.

She had ignored him completely at first.

"No," she whispered eventually, startling him, for at least an hour had passed.

"Something about this message. I don't understand the last word. But the first. Map. A map. What map? The Horseshoe? We know about that, though. What could he mean?"

Rob sighed. "I don't know," he said, "but you're not going to figure it out without resting. You're going to burn out. Come, let's get some sleep. Guru, can you assist Jana?"

"Of course, mate," said Guru. He turned to Galla, and said, "Rob's right. You're running on fumes; you're grieving. You're under great stress. A good night's sleep can reveal more to you in the morning than you'll ever figure out right now."

Galla stopped, dazed, and looked from Rob to Guru to Beetle. She shook her brilliant hair and blinked.

"You're both right," she said. She tilted her head back and looked at the ceiling, then closed her eyes. "I don't know if I can even sleep at all, but for you, I will try," and she smiled at Rob.

In their bed, Rob curled behind her, pulled her hair away from her face, and kissed her neck. She sat up.

"What about the other telepaths, though? What do we do? Can I get to where I need to be in time? Are we out of time?"

"Please, Galla," he pleaded with her. "Try to sleep. You'll think better in the morning. And it's not like there will be better sleep coming for us than there will be tonight."

She reluctantly agreed, and nestled against him. She kept her eyes open and her thoughts galloping for another hour before complete exhaustion overtook her, and she slept at last.

She jerked awake in the middle of the night and found Rob gone. She checked her command screen. Jana was still piloting. So where was Rob? With a sinking feeling in her stomach, she dressed and slid out of their room to find him.

And there he was, running his hands along a ribbed beam-like structure in the hallway beyond the round room. He did not see her at first. He was muttering to himself, and then he turned and walked along the hallway and touched the door of an escape pod. He walked back toward the room, still not seeing her. She stood perfectly still, watching him with growing alarm. He was walking over to another escape pod, and he touched its door.

Finally she could stand it no longer, and said nervously, "Rob?"

And he turned his head as if he'd heard something in the distance. He stood up straight and swiveled around. She caught sight of his eyes, and that lost, vacant look had returned to them. And she walked up to him. She gave him a nudge.

"Rob!" she said, more loudly and sternly, and he snapped out of the fugue state and looked at her with clear, vibrant eyes.

"Hey!" he said, jovially, leaning down to kiss her. "You should be sleeping!"

"Then that makes two of us. Rob, *what* are you doing? Why are you checking things again?" She wanted to cry.

He put his arm around her. "I'm just doing routine checks. We need to be ready for anything, especially now. Let's go back to bed. My shift starts in two hours." He fell asleep immediately in their bed, but Galla lay awake. Between her concern for him and the tumult of emotions she felt for Aeriod, Ariel, Kein, the Prince, and the children, it took considerable effort for her not to scream in anguish and frustration. But she fought it down.

Map, she thought. *Innervation*.

She breathed. Deeply in, slowly out, as Loreena had taught her on Perpetua. As she continued, she felt the worries slip away. She focused on just her breath, and *map* and *innervation*. That was all she could think of. She felt herself slide between wakefulness and dreaming, and she remembered her return to Rikiloi after decades on Bitikk.

She had walked into the emptiness of the castle, alone. She had peeked in new rooms, and had entered some of them. *Show me the human homeworld*, she had commanded an orrery. But there was something else in that room. In her memory, she walked around, and then she found it: a piece of parchment on a wall, ancient, curled, split at the edges. She had seen a list on one side of it, in an unknown language. She had never thought to ask Aeriod what that list was. She visualized it in her mind. Why was she thinking of it now? What was on the list?

Names, she thought suddenly. *But names of what?* And she could slow her thoughts and look at that list in her mind. There were twenty-one items on that list.

She threw off her blanket.

It's an ephemeris! she thought. *A list of planets! Of all the twenty-one planets with Devices! That has to be it!*

And she remembered turning the paper over to look at the back.

A map!

It was a map of a world she had not recognized. It was not Earth: she knew that, because she had just looked at a model of Earth in the orrery. There were similarities, but the landforms were different, as well as the seas. Something rang in her mind then.

What had the beings in the lake told her?

Find the hidden world; that is where you must be ready.

She stood.

Aeriod must not have known exactly where that world was, but he knew it existed. And he had given her access to its map, without knowing its full significance.

I have to find this planet. Will it matter now, though? If Hazkinaut didn't get telepaths, we're stranded. We have to find out.

She hurried to the cockpit.

"Jana," she said urgently. The woman looked up at her with tired eyes, as if to say, "Please, not now."

"Jana, I'm sorry, I know it's almost time for your shift change," Galla said, wincing. "But I think I'm on the track to figuring everything out. We need to know if Hazkinaut made it back to his palace. Is there a way you could send something encrypted, that only he would know to answer, to see if he made it, and the children are safe? We also need to know if he's recruited enough telepaths for the mission. Can you do that?"

Jana lifted her shoulders and lowered them. She fought a yawn and said, "I think I can, yes. So what's the plan? Is it game time?"

Galla nodded. "It's definitely time to act. We have to get all the telepaths to their worlds as soon as possible. And I need to find the final world, the one where I have to be the focal point."

"Galla," said Jana cautiously, "how are we going to do that, get them safely to the Device worlds? And at the same time, you need to be at this other world...which we have no idea exactly where it is? It's not on any scans, but it's supposed to be in the open part of that horseshoe of stars. It's a lot to ask. How can we be in those places at the same time?"

Rob walked in then, rubbing his eyes.

"Shift change," he told Jana.

"Not yet," she protested. "I'm working on something. You're early."

"Okay, but I'm ready to pilot," said Rob with a shrug. "Keep up your research. And as for being in two places at once, we can do that."

Galla and Jana stared at him as if he had grown antlers.

"I'm sorry, what?" said Jana.

Galla crinkled up her eyebrows at him, and Rob laughed.

"This ship? It can split in two," he said.

44

CLOVEN

Jana smirked at Rob. "Well I'll be damned," she said. "All your late-night antics finally paid off."

Galla raised an eyebrow at that, and wondered how many of Rob's "antics" she'd missed while she had slept. It really didn't matter now, though, because the mission took precedence. She was exhausted, and sick at heart over the Ambrono family.

"This changes things," she said, and she let out a relieved sigh. "This gives us what we need for the final part of the mission. So what I want is for Jana, Guru, and Beetle to assist Hazkinaut in getting telepaths to each world with a Device. It won't be easy, but I know you can do this. The Prince has some of my stones, and they should be enough for everyone who doesn't already have one—"

And she froze.

She put her hands over her mouth, and bowed her head, and cried out.

"What is it?" Rob asked, alarmed.

"The Ambronos. Did they have *their* stones? They should've been safe—"

Guru said quietly, "There's nothing you could have done. They made the choice to leave."

"No," said Galla, a wild look in her eyes. "I need to know. I need to see."

Jana sighed. "Galla, if we were to go to the point they were attacked—or whatever happened—don't you think that's exactly what the enemy would want? It's the ultimate trap. We can't do it."

"*You* can't," said Galla. "You've got to keep going. But I need to do this. I need to find out. I need the exact coordinates of their last known location. Please, Jana. I need…if not closure, I need answers."

Jana hung her head, and pressed her hand onto Galla's right shoulder.

"Of course. I'll do this for you. Just…please, please get out of there as fast as you can."

Galla nodded. "I will."

Jana stepped over to the console in the round room and worked to triangulate the location of the Ambronos' ship.

"And obviously, you'll need a pilot," said Rob, taking her hand.

Galla raised her head and nodded.

"So let's split this thing in two, and go our separate ways," said Galla.

And she looked at all of them, and thought, *Will I ever see all of you again?*

She pushed that thought aside, because now was the time for fighting, and she could weep later.

Rob and Jana worked to find the command codes for the ship's transformation.

"There are mechanical components to activate this too," Rob told them.

Galla, Guru, and Beetle distributed supplies so that both sections had enough food and other items to sustain everyone. Then came the time to say goodbye, and Galla struggled.

They all stood together in the round room, which, if the transformation worked, would be collapsed somehow into a cockpit for the tail section of the *Fithich*. The great geode rested in an escape pod, in what would be Galla and Rob's section.

Like a mother checking her children for school, Galla went to each of them and asked to see their stones. And she kissed each on the cheek, or mandible in Beetle's case.

"Tell me when you and Hazkinaut have secured everyone," she advised them. "Then they'll need to go to their respective Devices, wearing their own protective diamethysts that we've given them. Jana, tell each individual what to expect in each Device, based on what we've seen. Their stones will interact with the one in the Device.

"Beetle, provide any assistance as a go-between for telepaths, Jana, and Guru." Beetle clicked in response.

"Guru, you're a resilient, calming influence. But I know you're up for a fight. So I trust you'll do whatever you need to do."

Guru bowed his head and grinned. "You have my word, Captain. I'll serve you well, near and far."

"I know you will," said Galla, her smile trembling and her eyes stinging. "I know you all will."

Galla and Rob waved to them, and they moved back. Rob found the ribs between the ship's sections and began activating them with switches in intervals a few feet apart on either side of the room. The crew stared at each other as the ribbing stretched and began to slide downward, severing them from each other. It was a slick and rapid process.

Galla watched a panel depicting the split, and the ship shivered as the final transformation took place. She could see the animation of both pieces of the *Fithich*, and marveled at the structure of two new ships.

She called on her comms to Jana, "Welcome, *Fithich 2*, from *Fithich 1*."

"Receiving," called Jana. "This is so damned cool! We have a cockpit now and everything."

"Then fly forth, my friends," said Galla. "And I'll wait to hear from you soon."

"Copy that," said Jana.

And Jana turned *Fithich 2* and approached a junction. The spindles captured the smaller, new ship and hurtled it beyond sight.

Galla stared through the window of her own cockpit, and Rob watched her.

"Hey, cosmic lady," he said gently, "they'll do what they need to do."

"I'm worried about them," she admitted.

"It would be weird if you weren't," he said.

She swiveled around and leaned an elbow on the console.

"Let's see what happened to the Ambronos, if we can."

"Are you really sure about this? What if Jana's right, and it's a trap?" Rob cautioned, his eyebrows high on his forehead.

"I'm giving you an order, Rob Idin," she answered, not unkindly, but with a hint of steel in her voice that he recognized.

"Yes, Captain," he said with resigned wink. "Understood."

45

VESTIGES OF HOPE

Rob flew *Fithich 1* to the coordinates Jana had given. He dreaded it, but Galla's eyes gleamed with a ferocity he had never seen before. Nothing would deter her from finding out the truth of the Brant-Ambrono family. She would go it alone if she had to, and he knew that. So he would help her, because the alternative was unspeakable.

The trip took them away from their goal of the apex of the Horseshoe. But as Hazkinaut and the crew of the *Fithich 2* had to work on their own missions, it gave Galla and Rob time for a thorough sweep. Galla stared at the expanse of nothingness. She wanted to will that family's ship into being; she wanted to reverse time and try to stop them.

"Ariel planned this," she murmured, looking out at distant stars and closer nebulae.

"What?" Rob asked, startled.

"She...she said something to me, back on Mandira," Galla said slowly, "something about putting a stop to it all. I remember it disturbed me, but I wasn't sure I had heard it right. And I think...I think I tried to push that away and not think about it. Because it just seemed too awful and...and preposterous.

"Rob, *why* would she do this? Why would she take her family out here and risk this? I knew her, or thought I did, but she didn't...she wasn't herself," and Galla pulled her knees up to her chest where she sat, and put her head down.

Rob put his feet up on the console, as he was wont to do.

"Well, Galla, she was grieving the death of her mother," Rob said. "And she recently had a baby. I think, and clearly I'm no expert, but it sure seems like there was a lot going on with her. She was in a different mental state. And maybe with telepaths, things are different. Heightened? Again, I don't know. But it makes sense, right? Maybe it was that much harder for her to deal with. And she wasn't able to make the right decisions."

"But why would Dagovaby agree to any of it?" asked Galla. "He's her husband, and the father to those boys"— Galla choked—"and I just can't imagine he would go along with this!"

Rob watched her. He got up, went over to her, knelt on the floor beside her, and rubbed the front of her calves. She raised her red face and looked at him through wet eyes.

"Dagovaby loved her," said Rob quietly. "I could see it going down like this: she made a decision and didn't ask for his input. She probably thought she'd do this by herself. Right? Doesn't that sound like Ariel?"

Galla nodded.

Rob went on, "And so that way she wouldn't put her family in harm's way. But Dagovaby found out, and refused to let her do this alone."

"But the children!" exclaimed Galla.

Rob grimaced. "Yeah, that part I can't figure out. Why not leave them at Mandira? Why put them at risk by bringing them along? No way would they be safer with their parents out here, with Veronica and Derry around."

They could not figure it out.

Galla wiped her eyes, and the two returned to their positions.

"Sweep everything," she commanded. "As far as our sensors can reach, junction to junction. Let's take the ship back and forth, up and down, everywhere, so we don't miss a parsec."

"On it," responded Rob.

All of that day and much of the next, they searched. The ship, despite its diminished size, seemed eerily silent to Galla. She hated it.

"Play some music," she begged Rob. "I can't stand the quiet. My thoughts are too loud."

Rob smirked, and worked his way through his music catalog.

Late the second day, a popping, disjointed message came through.

"It's Hazkinaut," Rob called, and Galla hurried from her quarters to the cockpit.

"Yes?" she asked the fuzzy image.

The Prince said in broken words, "Received...communication... Jana. Broken off."

"What?" cried Galla.

"Missed...rendezvous," said the Prince.

"Fucking *fuck!*" hissed Rob.

Galla covered her face.

"Keep trying," she croaked, almost unable to speak. "I know them. I know they'll do anything for this mission. All I can do is trust their abilities. Just...just let me know when you have all the telepaths in place."

"Yes...Lady..." and that was all they could get before static overtook the message.

Rob looked at Galla with alarm.

She shook her head.

"I can't think about this now. I trust them. It's all I can do right now. Trust them, hope for the best, and that's it."

Rob beamed at her. "That's my brave captain," he said proudly. "I trust them too."

Galla stood up. "Keep searching."

And she paced the length of the truncated ship numerous times, for hours, until Rob paged her.

"Come and look at this," he called.

Galla sighed and walked to the cockpit, deciding not to expect anything.

Rob was examining something on a screen. Strange eddies that had stretched and expanded like ripples.

"What are those?" Galla asked, leaning forward, her hair tickling his cheeks. He slid an arm around her waist.

"Ship tracks," he said. "They've dissipated after several days, but they're still there. Galla, there are three different sets."

Galla stiffened.

"What?"

Rob took a deep breath. "I realize these could be anything. So let me analyze them. See if there's anything that can be traced back to Mandira."

"Yes, do it!" she urged, and she squeezed her fists together. She began pacing the cockpit.

Rob turned to her and said, "Hey, I love the hell out of you, but could you please not do that here? I can't focus."

"Oh," said Galla. "Sure." And she left, to continue her pacing in the remnants of the round room, which was more of a U-shaped, smaller room now.

Galla felt a strange mix of hope, fear, and extreme impatience, and she found that she could not cope with the mixture well. She bounced on her heels, paced forward and backward, and groaned.

Finally, Rob called, "Now," and she almost stomped into the cockpit in her haste.

He turned to face her, his turquoise eyes shining. She did not know how to read his strange expression.

"I've got their signature," he told her.

She felt as if she could not breathe.

"And?" she asked.

"Galla, there is debris."

She felt dizzy and sick, but Rob stood quickly and grabbed her.

"There's more," he said. "Like I said, I found evidence of three ships. I tracked the timing of each as best I could, based on the patterns of their tracks. The Ambrono ship got here first.

"A second ship arrived later. It approached the Ambrono ship; it could have docked with it. As best I can tell, that ship then moved away and left. At that point, I think the Ambrono ship was still fully intact, because of the signatures it left behind.

"Look here." He gestured to the simulation on his screen. "This is another signature. A third ship arrived, and moved very close to the Ambrono ship as well. Then this third ship moved away toward a different junction, and disappeared. After that, the Ambrono ship exploded."

"I don't understand," said Galla.

"Two different ships rendezvoused with their ship," said Rob. "I don't really understand it either. But something happened, something strange."

Galla bit her lower lip. She did not want to admit the destruction of their ship, but it was plain to be seen. So she had to accept that.

"So they met someone," she said quietly. "Got really close. But that ship did not harm theirs. And why would the third ship move so close to theirs, only to destroy it?"

She and Rob stared at the simulations over and over again.

They looked at each other.

"Prisoners," they said at the same time, and Galla felt her innards churn.

"But that first ship—" Galla began.

"Galla," said Rob, his eyes gleaming. "Someone met them first. I think they meant for that to happen."

They grabbed each other's hands.

"The babies," said Galla in a whisper. "They met someone to take the babies."

"It makes sense!" exclaimed Rob.

"But who *was* it, and where did they go?" asked Galla.

"I don't know. I only know the junction that ship used. The ship's signature isn't like anything else I've ever seen."

"Paosh Tohon has Ariel and Dagovaby," said Galla grimly, "but not the children. Or so we hope. This is the *only* hope I have right now. So I'm going to cling to it. Let's follow that ship's tracks."

"But Galla," protested Rob, "if we do, we might put *that* ship at risk. And if, in fact, that was the escape plan for those kids...we'd have blown it for Ariel and Dagovaby. And for the kids."

"Oh, dammit," said Galla with a moan. "You're right. Well, let's do the next best thing, then. Let's track the area and see if there are any other clues. Without making it obvious what we are doing, if that's possible."

She felt her diamethyst grow warm, and she looked down. It was glowing.

"Wait," she said.

Rob looked up at her and saw the stone.

"Sweep this area around us," she said.

"What are we looking for?" he asked.

But he soon found out. In one neat little arc, expanded outward from where they were initially dropped, they found four little stones suspended in space. Rob siphoned them onto the ship, and Galla ran to find them. She came back with them, and they glowed in response to her own larger stone. Two were on long loops of web that Beetle had spun, and the other two were on much smaller loops...just the size for tiny ankles.

Galla fell to her knees in front of Rob and wailed.

"Their stones! They have no protection!"

Rob slid down beside her and took her distraught face in his hands.

"I know, Galla," he said, smoothing back her wild hair. "But all we can do is hope now. You've got to go forward. Let's find that hidden world, and stop anything from getting worse. Can you do that? For them, no matter what's happened to them?"

Galla wanted to scream. She wanted to curl up, and she wanted to explode, simultaneously.

Help me, she thought.

But as she lay on the floor, with Rob holding onto her with anguish in his eyes, she swallowed, and finally pushed herself up.

"I'll keep going," she said. "I don't know if anything I can do will help. But doing nothing is the worst thing there is. So let's go."

Rob aimed *Fithich 1* toward the junction that would take them closer to the apex of the Horseshoe. It opened up and pulled the ship in.

And in the vacuum left behind, among the ship track eddies and debris, a little claw-like object came to life, scanned the area, and shot off into another junction, full of secrets and recordings and ill promises to its master.

46

CORNERED

Jana put her head in her hands. She had worked for hours to filter through chaotic communications between the Associates and other worlds. She finally teased out that Ezeldae, the seat of galactic government, had been sacked. And she knew Aeriod had been attacked, but did not know his status. She had nothing new to report back to Galla, and she grew unsettled.

"I don't like it," she muttered.

Guru cleared his throat. "I am wondering if we should head back to Mandira at this point. How much time is left, do you think, before the window closes on this mission?"

Jana shook her head. "God knows. I think it's getting close. Which is damned unfortunate for everyone. But once Galla gets where she needs to be, hopefully we're good." She twisted one of her emerald earrings nervously.

Beetle shuffled into the snug cockpit and declared with pops and whistles, "We have word from Prince Hazkinaut that all the telepaths will be in place in time. There should be a good chance to assist him, to make absolutely sure."

Jana nodded. "I know. But his communications are going in and out. I've tried fine-tuning everything...and if *I* can't do it, nobody can. This is *my* wheelhouse.

"And look at this. I put all the data and parameters in I could think of, based on the info Galla got from those lake beings. Here's the simulation." She showed Guru and Beetle an animation of the twenty-one Device worlds being activated.

"Given the time delay for junctions and things like that, there seems to be a workaround for instantaneous action here," Jana said, pointing to an enhanced image. "Keep in mind, this is all speculation on my part for how this would actually *look*."

The image showed a planet rotating, and a coil of energy emerging from it and joining that of another world in the Horseshoe, and so on. They converged at the apex of the Horseshoe, where Jana had placed a theoretical planet, since she did not know what else could be there.

"I mapped all of this in relation to the Event, and it's uncanny— planned, I'm guessing, so that anything emerging from the apex would aim right at the terminus of the Event. What that force does, I don't know. Seal it up?"

"And Galla has to be the one who all that energy goes through?" asked Guru, in an awed voice. "Can she survive that?"

Jana lowered her head. "We have no way of knowing. But if she doesn't do this, we're screwed."

An alarm sounded, and the two humans jumped. Beetle turned its head.

"What is happening?" the great insect asked.

"Something's out there," whispered Jana, and she held her breath. "Can they see us, or do our defenses still work?"

Guru leaned back from the window, as if whatever it was could see him. Shapes in the darkness of space, hard to discern, surrounded them. Their presence sent chills through him. *The sea at night can bring good or ill, starlight or not*, he thought.

"Did they come out of the junction?" he asked.

"Some junction," said Jana. "Not the one closest to us. I don't like it."

"So let's turn everything off," Guru suggested.

"Already lowered the power to the point it's like background noise," Jana replied. "They shouldn't be able to see anything. No heat, no power, nothing...Aeriod set us up pretty well."

"What are they?" Guru asked.

"No clue," said Jana. "They're disguised themselves. I don't like it."

"So now what?" Guru fidgeted, and clenched his fists. "I don't like waiting. Give me something to swing at them: that's what I'd prefer."

"Nope," retorted Jana. "Silent running."

Beetle stared at the window, and swiveled its head back and forth. Its antennae stretched.

"Something is reaching out," said Beetle.

Jana shuddered despite herself. "What the hell does that mean, *reaching out*?"

"Something is reaching out with its mind, from these shapes," Beetle replied.

"Oh shit," hissed Jana. "We didn't think about that, did we? Shielding from *minds*."

"Fuck!" said Guru.

Jana seized her purple stone, and Guru and Beetle reached for theirs.

"Please let these be working," she said, "please let these be working, please—"

Something crackled, and Jana slapped her hand over her mouth.

"No, not right now!" she wheezed.

It was Prince Hazkinaut, trying to message her. The interference was considerable, but he seemed urgent. Jana switched her controls so as not to receive the full message yet. The Prince would see it as bouncing back. As for whether he would understand what was happening, Jana could only hope.

"Goddammit," she said, "whoever's out there probably saw the message in some form."

Guru paced. "They've not attacked us yet. Could they be friendlies?"

Jana shook her head. "I don't think so. I think they're waiting for us to reveal ourselves. Or they already know everything. Hell if I know."

"Shit," whispered Guru.

Beetle looked back and forth between them.

"There is only one thing to do," it said suddenly.

Jana turned her head to look up at the large insect, and crinkled her forehead.

"And what's that?"

"This is a swarm surrounding us," said Beetle. "And there are only two options within a swarm."

"Which would be?" asked Guru, but he dreaded the answer.

"Surrender or run," said Beetle.

"If we run, they definitely know we're here," said Jana.

"And if you do not, they will take you anyway," reasoned Beetle.

Jana swore a long thread of vivid words until they almost sounded like a song.

Guru sighed in frustration. "Damned if we do, damned if we don't."

"Then we may as well be damned," Jana replied, gritting her teeth. "Strap in, you two. We're running."

Beetle crawled into the ductwork, and Guru strapped into his seat. Jana thrust the ship to full power, and the *Fithich 2* pummeled ahead, glancing two of the shapes. Instantly, their veils dropped, and each ship bore a red insignia.

"Valemog," whispered Jana.

The ship shuddered as blasts rocked it. Aeriod's protections were working. But they could not know for how much longer.

"Where's the junction?" yelled Guru, gripping his seat as the ship trembled from constant attack. Blades of light and grappling beams reached for them, claws in the dark, teeth at the helm.

Jana closed her eyes.

"Please work," she muttered. "Guys, you're not gonna like what I do, but I have to try and stop them from following."

The junction splintered the darkness with its brilliant rays, which Jana shielded from view quickly. She turned the ship around, then sprayed fire in all directions at the ships before her. Many shots made their mark, and explosions bloomed in the attacking fleet. But her own ship strained and whined, and she quickly flipped it, sending a final volley, and the junction seized her.

It shut behind them, but Jana knew it would not be for long.

Where to go? she wondered, her heart hammering, her logic straining. She had seconds to push ahead as fast as the ship would go, when the ship's alarms sounded again.

"Fuck me," she said, "they're behind us," and sure enough, something stabbed through the nether-space of the junction and struck the ship. This time it flew spinning.

"So they can definitely see us," said Guru, his voice cracking.

"They can sense us," Jana corrected him, "which is bad enough. We must have sustained enough damage to show our signature back there. Guru, Beetle, I don't know what to do."

Beetle crackled and snapped, and said, "We can leave this junction, and find a place to hide."

"That they can't find?" Jana asked, in disbelief.

She looked at the giant insect, and it was trembling all over, through its wings.

"You okay, Beetle?" she asked in alarm.

"Find a place to hide," said Beetle, shivering. Guru put his hand on Beetle's wings.

"It's okay, we'll figure something out," he said.

"Find a place to hide," repeated Beetle.

Guru and Jana stared at each other and swallowed.

Jana wasted no time, and scanned each junction's destinations on the ship's controls. She leaned back and put her hands on her temples. "I don't know which one."

Guru watched the approach of ships behind them. "Anything," he urged.

"Fuck it!" Jana yelled. She opened a junction and shot through. It closed behind her, and she did not dare to see if anything else would emerge.

The system they entered contained three gas giants and numerous smaller, rockier worlds, and countless asteroids, lit by its red star.

"Only one place with a decent atmosphere," she announced. "Underground water supply maybe, by the signature. Not sure anyone's there. We don't have much choice."

She hastened to get the ship down onto one of the small worlds, and it listed badly on its final descent.

"Gonna be a rough one," she told her crew. "Hang on."

And the ship slammed into a silicate dune, sending a spray of grey sand high.

Shaking, Guru asked, "How well hidden are we?"

"Well," said Jana, wiping sweat from her brow, "we're definitely not giving off much now. Unless they come after us with a telepath."

She started. Beetle shook all over.

"Beetle, what is it? What's wrong?"

Beetle let out a high-pitched sound, and she and Guru covered their ears.

"Someone has followed us," Beetle said, making many frenetic pops.

"No!" gasped Jana.

"They are landing," said Beetle, jolting violently now. "Go to the back of the ship."

Jana looked through her screen, and sure enough, the long, spindly legs of a Valemog craft hovered above them. She looked at Guru.

"Do we blow up the ship?" he asked her. "I don't want to be taken by them."

"Back of the ship," repeated Beetle, and not knowing what else to do, Jana and Guru ran to the back of the ship.

"What are you going to do, Beetle?" asked Jana, and just then the hull screeched. Something was ripping into it.

Beetle scurried up to Jana and Guru, and stood on its hind legs.

"I am sorry, Jana and Guru," said Beetle. And out of a flap on its chest, something shone, and dripped. Beetle grabbed both Jana and Guru, and turned them around before they could react.

And Beetle pierced the backs of their necks with its stinger, and they collapsed.

47

INERT

Only silence. The Prince's appendages flickered and stretched and curled back in on themselves. He would not give up. He looked at the children. Silderay blinked with great dark eyes.

They communicated telepathically, out of earshot of the others.

"*They do not respond,*" said the Prince. "*Something has happened. The message bounces. I fear they were attacked.*"

"*Probably,*" said Silderay. "*That's what they do. They attack, and they take people.*"

"*I am sorry, Silderay, that you should see this happen. Let us hope it is not what happened, though. Let us hope we are all ready. We have everyone we need,*" said Hazkinaut. "*But Lady Galla is not responding either.*"

"*She would want us to make sure everyone is where they are supposed to go,*" said Silderay. "*We have to hope for the best. That's what I do.*"

The Prince felt a surge of affection for the young creature.

"*You are wiser than your years,*" said he, "*or perhaps you are most foolish. But I choose to side with you on this. We hope for the best. And we hold to our promise. We guard the Devices, until the time is right.*"

"*We will hide,*" said Silderay. "*That is what I do too. We can hide a bit longer.*"

I wonder how long that will be? thought the Prince to himself, shielding that final thought from the child.

He felt chilled, and his feathery head appendages coiled in toward his scalp.

He could feel the time escaping, and he had never felt so power-less. *I have been a prince for many years. I did not walk outside of my home in full view. Only as the Cogniz. All I ever knew was safety, deca-dence, subterfuge. I feel the time falling all around us, and I have no power. All of that was a fantasy. I have no power.*

But then he stopped himself. *No. Galla-Deia believes in me. I believe in her. We will stand, even if everything else falls. She taught me that much.*

48

FOUNDERED

"Almost there," announced Rob. "We've got no communications. Are you sure you want to go ahead?"

Galla stood with her hands on her hips, her gold-copper-auburn-purple hair swirling all around her shoulders. "I'm standing by my promise. Let's find out what's at the apex of the Horseshoe. I want to be ready. There can't be much time left. We can only hope everyone is where they need to be."

Her copper eyes gleamed, in apprehension, in fear, in a feeling of destiny...it was the only way she could think about it. She felt that everything was lining up where it needed to be, despite the tragedies of the Ambrono family. And she thought to herself, *We will find the children.*

Exhilaration and determination coursed through her. She took a breath and looked at Rob.

"We have time for a kiss," she told him, her russet-amber eyes smoldering, her eyebrows arched. Her hair curled this way and that, like a cat's tail. "Make it count."

Rob did not hesitate. He took her face gently in his hands, and smoothed the wild strands of hair away from her cheeks, and looked at her with his eyes broad and open. He ran his fingers along her nose, over her cheekbones, across her lips. Every bit of her felt electric.

And his hands lifted her hair and he brushed his lips and tongue just under her ear, then down her neck. She felt fiery tingles all through her, in her breasts, between her thighs. She cried out, and he met her cry with his lips. Tender and fierce, they drank each other in, breathing only when needed. She pulled her necklace off and set it down. Shaking, they explored each other. Their clothes fell aside so their skin met. Galla breathed in the scent of Rob as she gasped in his ear.

And then the alarm sounded.

They pulled apart at last. Galla sighed.

"Damn," said Rob, but he was radiant. "Guess we should..."

"Yeah...we should," answered Galla as they quickly dressed, and with stolen glances and sneaky grasps at each other, they made their way to the cockpit.

She heard a staccato sound before she could register what happened. Rob groaned, and she turned to see him double over, and she broke her concentration and ran to him.

"Rob!" she cried, and he winced, and looked at his chest to see little coils burrowing through his clothes, each with wisps of smoke escaping. He began yelling.

Galla whipped around and looked behind her, and found Derry staring at her, surrounded by steam.

How did he get in? she wondered, stunned.

Derry lifted his head and laughed.

"You can enter now, my Lady," he said, and he opened his hand to reveal a black and red sphere, about the size of an apple, which he set on the floor.

Rob shrieked in agony, and Galla could see blossoms of red spreading across his abdomen. The bullets had drilled into his flesh, and they were releasing acid into his body in every direction.

"Don't—let—them—take—me," he choked out. "Escape—pod. Hurry!" and Galla picked him up in her arms and ran.

She felt a volley of bullets hit her back, and she clenched her jaw from the pain of their impact, but they could not make purchase in her skin. She made it to the escape pod with her geode, and opened it and set Rob inside. His face contorted in pain. She could see he had not put his own stone back around his neck after their moment of passion earlier. Panicking, Galla thrust her stone at him. When the diamethyst touched his skin, he went slack-jawed from temporary relief. She hated to pull it away from him.

"I'm facing them," she whispered. "I'll be right back."

And fighting every instinct to stay with him in his anguish, she closed the door and turned back to the hall. The black and red sphere had opened up with a hiss, and little tendrils reached out and up: the tendrils of Paosh Tohon. She watched them grow, and could see the tentacles whipping around and coalescing into a form. Feet, then legs, then a body, arms, and a head, and she knew before it had finished who it was.

"Veronica," she said in a terrible voice, "you cannot kill me."

And the beautiful being before Galla, taller than she and dark-haired, with violet eyes, raised her chin and laughed. Derry joined her. For sport, he fired another volley from the acidavyper, and Galla moaned from the impact, her clothes hissing from the acid, but she stood straight again.

"We can destroy you," hissed Veronica, marching forward, and out of her sprang slimy, rope-like cables that flew all around Galla and squeezed her.

Galla stood immobile, staring defiantly back at Veronica. Then she took a breath, closed her eyes, held her blazing purple stone, and burst the cables, which went flying everywhere and letting out little screams as they fizzled on the floor.

"Not today, you can't," said Galla through gritted teeth.

She marched forward, grabbed the acidavyper, tore it in half with her hands, and threw it aside. Derry wavered then.

He shouted, "Stop her!" but Galla caught him by the throat and lifted him up.

"You could've been a good and decent man," she told him, "but you killed and you maimed while you played the victim every time.

Not anymore," and she hurled him against a wall, where he slumped down.

She turned to Veronica.

Veronica stared at her now through diamond eyes that blazed. But Galla had no time to think about that.

"You took my friends, but you can't take me!" she shouted.

Veronica simpered. "But Lady Deia, that's why we took your friends! So we can make them feel pain forever. If you surrender, we'll set them free. You can make their pain go away, just like that. Why would you want to extend their suffering?"

"Bitch!" screamed Galla. "You'll never let them go! I'm going to go and find them and bring them back. But not before I'm done with you!"

And she seized Veronica, and clenched her arms around the woman-thing, and squeezed her so she could not move.

Veronica wheezed, "You can't be rid of me, without killing your friends!"

Galla tossed her hair.

She squeezed and focused and felt the slime of the creature in her arms as it tried to slither away. But Veronica could not escape her steadfast grip.

Galla said with quiet focus, "Stop talking. I will eliminate you, and then I will save my friends."

And with all her hair extended and her muscles flexed, Galla squeezed again and again, and Veronica let out a shrill scream, her skin burning and the smoke rising from it violet. With one long, horrific howl, Veronica turned into a being of cinder, and Galla crushed her into powder. The powder flew in a whirlwind around her, but Galla stood strong, and then it dissipated.

Doubled over and gasping for breath, Galla looked to where she had thrown Derry. He was unconscious. Then she turned and sprinted back to the escape pod.

She opened the door. Rob sagged where he sat, leaning against her geode, his eyes closed. Galla covered her mouth. The door of the pod whooshed shut behind her.

She knelt beside him. She felt his neck. He was fading.

He said in a rasping voice, "Dead man's switch. I set it to blow. Launch us."

No, she thought. *That's what he was working on, all that time. No!*

"What?" she asked, trembling all over.

What can I do? How can I help him? she begged the Universe. She leaned her ear to his chest.

A heartbeat. Weaker, erratic. She pressed her face into his, her tears and his blood and saliva mixed on her lips.

His lagoon-blue eyes flickered open.

"One. More," he sputtered.

"Anything," gasped Galla.

"One more," he repeated, and Rob's mouth slid over hers. Her lips caught his and he lingered there. A freezing kiss. Seconds, minutes, hours: all frozen.

He shuddered. He slumped down. His heart stopped.

And a silver diamond appeared on his arm and fell off.

She screamed.

Then everything jolted. A sickening, warping buckle shook the escape pod. The *Fithich* shattered in all directions behind it, sending the pod spinning.

Gagging over her own swallowed tears, Galla wrestled away from Rob's body. They were weightless now but bumping into each other, the geode and Rob and Galla. She did not see her large stone anywhere, as it had floated off of her neck. The silver diamond spun in the air now, but she had no time to register it. Galla stretched her fingers to the control panel. Only flashes of the controls remained, as its functions wound down.

Strobes of light winked all around her. They were spinning in a junction. Until they weren't.

The pod burst out of a junction. *Too close, too close to something*, was all that Galla could think. Gravity snatched the pod and ripped it from space, and she grew heavy. She and Rob and the geode pressed against the ceiling of the pod as the gravitational force of something pulled them forth.

And they entered an atmosphere. The pod could stand no more. It splintered all around Galla in a burst of fire and metal and shrapnel. Her stone was gone. Her geode was gone. Rob, gone.

Her hair vanished in fire. All she could see were flames.

THE END

PRONUNCIATION GUIDE

Aeriod (AIR-ee-od)
Auna (AWN-a)
Bitikk (bit-ik)
Cogniz (COG-niz)
Coniuratus (con-yur-AH-tus)
Dagovaby Ambrono (da-GOV-a-bee am-BRO-no)
Demetraan (DEM-eh-tron)
diamethyst (di-amethyst)
Ezeldae (ez-el-DIE)
Fael'Kar (fail car)
Fithich (fith-itch)
Galla-Deia (GAL-a DAY-a)
Ika Nui (IK-a NOO-ee)
Ixinerro (ix-ee-NAIR-oh)
Kein (cane, rhymes with skein)
Mandira (man-DEER-a)
Mehelkian (me-HEL-kee-an)
MindSynd (mind send)
Oni-Odi (oh-nee oh-dee)
Paosh Tohon (pay-OSH to-HON)

Questri (QUEST-ree)
Rez (rez)
Rikiloi (RIK-i-loy)
Seltra (SEL-tra)
Seyvelk (SAY-velk)
Shorudan (shore-OO-dan)
Silderay (SIL-de-ray)
Sumond (soo-MOND)
Tartiph (tar-tiff)
Udramoth Dur-Mithtoth (OO-dra-moth dur MITH-toth)
Ushalda (oo-SHAL-da)
Valemog (vale-mog)
Vedant (vee-DANT)
Veeldt-Ka (veelt-KA)
Yaddifor (YAD-i-for)

ABOUT THE AUTHOR

Dianne dreamed up other worlds and their characters as a child in the 1980s. She formed her own neighborhood astronomy club before age ten, to educate her friends about the Universe. In addition to writing stories, she drew and painted her characters, gave them outrageous space fashions, and created travel guides and glossaries for the worlds she invented. As an adult, Dianne earned a Bachelor of Science and spent several years working in research. She published *Heliopause: The Questrison Saga®: Book One* in 2018 and *Ephemeris: The Questrison Saga®: Book Two* in 2019. Dianne has written several short stories across genres. Dianne is also a science and content writer and watercolorist. She lives in Southern California with her family. The fourth and final book of *The Questrison Saga®* arrives in 2021.

jdiannedotson.com

facebook.com/jdiannedotsonwriter

twitter.com/jdiannedotson

instagram.com/jdiannedotson

CPSIA information can be obtained
at www.ICGtesting.com
Printed in the USA
FSHW011304190520
70389FS

9 780999 408261